4/22

Love, Decoded

ALSO BY JENNIFER YEN

A Taste for Love

Love, Decoded

JENNIFER YEN

RAZORBILL

RAZORBILL

An imprint of Penguin Random House LLC, New York

First published in the United States of America by Razorbill,
an imprint of Penguin Random House LLC, 2022

Visit us online at penguinrandomhouse.com.

LIBRARY OF CONGRESS CATALOGING-IN-PUBLICATION DATA
Names: Yen, Jennifer, author.
Title: Love, decoded / Jennifer Yen.
Description: New York : Razorbill, 2022. | Audience: Ages 12 and up
Summary: High school junior Gigi Wong is determined to be picked for a contest
that could lead to an exclusive tech internship, but when her matchmaking app goes viral
Gigi must deal with the unexpected consequences of helping her friends find love.
Identifiers: LCCN 2021042814 | ISBN 9780593117552 (hardcover)
ISBN 9780593117576 (trade paperback) | ISBN 9780593117569 (ebook)
Subjects: CYAC: Love—Fiction. | Friendship—Fiction. | Application software—Fiction.
High schools—Fiction. | Schools—Fiction. | LCGFT: Novels.
Classification: LCC PZ7.1.Y48 Lo 2022 | DDC [Fic]—dc23
LC record available at https://lccn.loc.gov/2021042814

Book manufactured in Canada

ISBN 9780593117552 (HARDCOVER)
1 3 5 7 9 10 8 6 4 2

ISBN 9780593524145 (INTERNATIONAL EDITION)
1 3 5 7 9 10 8 6 4 2

FRI

Design by Rebecca Aidlin
Text set in Minister Std Light

A reminder to those who fear they are not enough.

Your imperfect story is someone's favorite read.

Chapter 1

If love is one of life's greatest mysteries, then you want the best detective on the case.

Okay, so maybe I'm not the Sherlock Holmes of relationships yet, but it's only a matter of time. After all, there's something I know that most people don't:

Love is amazing, frustrating, and often complicated, but what it isn't . . . is magic.

It's science.

Love is facial symmetry, body proportions, and hormones. It's sizing up the person in front of us in seconds, looking for the right combination of physical features and personality traits we want to pass on to our future children. Love is nothing more than our brains doing math, and unsurprisingly, some people need more help than others.

That's what my great-aunt Rose tells me, anyway, and she's one of the best—or, if you ask her, *the* best—matchmakers you'll find outside of Asia. For her, love comes down to the numbers. Height. Weight. Sun and lunar signs. Your family's lineage. How much money you make. What zip code you live in. Even how many exes you have. All of those things matter when you're looking for your soul mate, the one person who is supposed to be your better half and complete your world.

(I'm not so sure about the last part, but that's a discussion for another day.)

I admit I'm still new to this whole love thing. The closest I've come was watching my brother James fall for his girlfriend, Liza, last summer. Auntie Rose said she knew it was a good match because he went through her "Four Stages of Love"—confusion, denial, fear, and concession. Considering James hasn't stopped smiling since they met, I suggested happiness be added as the fifth, but Auntie Rose dismissed it, saying I still have a lot to learn. Nonetheless, I do come from a distinguished line of skilled "mathematicians," and there's no doubt I've inherited the matchmaking talent. Several of my friends would still be dating Netflix if it wasn't for me.

Last year, Auntie Rose decided it was time I start training to take my place as the next generation of matchmakers in the family. In fact, she loves recounting that at just six years old, I pointed to a groomsman and a bridesmaid at a wedding and predicted they would get married. How much of this is true is up for debate, but she's certain it was a sign of things to come. According to her, all I need is a little time to nurture my matchmaking talent. That's why I've been spending my Saturdays at Rose and Jade, the Asian import and souvenir shop Auntie Rose owns in Chinatown.

This weekend, however, I'm at the Metropolitan Museum of Art. I need to choose a painting to critique for my art history project. It counts for 40 percent of the final grade, and I need an A if I want to stay in the top 1 percent of our class. I walk into the first room of the old European masters' wing. Cream-colored walls are lined with oil paintings of all sizes, framed in gold and lit by soft light overhead.

Despite the beauty around me, I'm immediately drawn to the well-dressed pair of visitors standing in front of a painting of a foxhunt. The two must have come together. They're standing shoulder to shoulder, though there's always distance between their bodies. The woman stares up at the piece of art, pointing at one of the figures on horseback as she says something to the man. He leans toward her, closing the gap ever so slightly. The woman continues talking, completely oblivious to the fact that the only thing he's admiring is her.

I wonder if I should say something . . .

Nope. Bad idea. Only Auntie Rose can pull off walking up to random strangers to offer her services so easily. I would say she's charismatic, but I suspect it's also the shock of being stared down by a five-foot-one elderly Asian woman wielding a designer bag in one hand and her business card in the other.

"You're doing it again, G."

I drag my gaze over to my best friend, Kyle. "Doing what?"

"You know what," he answers, cocking his brow. "That squinty thing you do with your eyes when you're playing matchmaker."

He proceeds to imitate the supposed gesture, pursing his lips while narrowing his eyes like he's forgotten his glasses. That is, if he needed them. Unlike me, who inherited my family's tendency to go nearsighted in high school, Kyle sees perfectly well, especially from his six-foot vantage point.

"First of all, I don't 'play matchmaker.' I take it very seriously. Second of all, I do not *squint* at people. That's rude," I retort.

He laughs, his light brown eyes forming crescents. Though he's half Chinese, many times people assume otherwise. While Kyle shares his mom's apple cheeks, button nose, and dark hair, he's also got the angular jaw, prominent eyebrows, and deep-set eyes from the European side of his family tree.

I jab him in the side with my elbow, and he lets out a startled yelp. That gets the attention of the nearby attendant, who shoots a disapproving look our way. Kyle nods slightly in apology before ushering me over to another Rubens painting. When the monitor moves to the other side of the room, he leans down to whisper at me.

"Then what do you call it when you don't *squint* at them?"

"I'm paying attention to the details." I tuck an errant strand of hair behind my ear. "Small gestures add up to a grand love, you know."

"Is that another Rose rule?" he quips, grinning.

I shrug. "Laugh all you want, but I wouldn't question her methods. We're barely a week into January and she's already booked her matchmaking clients for the next three months."

"You've got to be kidding me. Do that many people need her help?" he answers, incredulous. "We live in New York City. There're 1.6 million people in Manhattan alone. It should be easy to find a date."

"They're not looking for a hookup, Kyle. Her clients want to find their soul mate."

Kyle shakes his head but concedes. Meanwhile, having decided I have no desire to spend hours expounding the virtues of any of the paintings in this room, I gesture for us to check out the next one. We make our way past multiple displays, but it isn't until we reach the impressionist painters that I make a beeline for the other end of the gallery.

Without a word, Kyle sits down on the bench in front of a Renoir portrait entitled *Madame Georges Charpentier and Her Children*. He pats the spot next to him.

"Why are you sitting?" I frown but plop down anyway. "We just got here."

"Because you're going to pick this painting," he answers, the corners of his mouth twitching.

"How could you possibly know that?"

"What? You don't think I can read minds?"

I scoff. "Not according to your ex-girlfriends."

"At least I have exes," he counters, waggling his eyebrows.

"And I have standards."

"Ouch."

He clutches his chest, but I roll my eyes. Kyle heaves a sigh and smiles.

"Okay, okay. I know because it's one of your favorite paintings. Every time we come to the Met, you insist we stop by to look at it."

"That doesn't necessarily mean it's the one I'm going to pick."

"So you're telling me you *don't* care if people know that the painting actually depicts a boy and a girl, not two girls?"

Kyle grins with the smugness that only comes with ten years of friendship. I cross my arms over my chest and huff.

"I hate you."

"No, you don't," he replies. He nudges me with his shoulder. "You love me. Admit it."

"Whatever."

He keeps bumping against me until I crack a smile. I poke him in the arm.

"You're lucky that I *do* love you, because no one else would put up with someone so annoying."

Kyle blinks for several seconds before shrugging. "It's not my fault you're so predictable."

"Says the guy who likes watching the same zombie movies over and over again."

"Hey! That's not true," he protests. "The only thing those movies have in common *is* the zombies. Besides, it's not like you don't watch every single one of them with me."

He's got a point. One of the reasons we became such good friends is our shared love of science fiction and fantasy. I still remember his shock when I answered a Star Wars question correctly during Trivial Pursuit. It's been years since our families have gotten together to play board games, but Kyle and I turned movie night into one of our traditions.

Before I can offer a response, an announcement is made overhead. The museum will be closing in fifteen minutes. Kyle stands and offers me his hand. I take it and pull myself up off the bench. We leave the gallery and head toward the museum's grand entry hall. Our shoes keep a steady rhythm on the stone floor as we pass under giant archways and between Roman columns on our way out the door. As we near the entrance, we pause to zip up our coats.

"Speaking of which, I'm thinking of rewatching *The Witcher* soon." Kyle glances over at me. "Want in?"

"Depends. Are you planning to provide more running commentary?"

He halts. "Wait . . . you don't like it when I do that?"

Do I mind pausing the show every fifteen minutes so he can go off on a tangent about some obscure mythology from the books? I start to tell the truth, but change my mind at the slightly pained look on Kyle's face.

"You know I'm kidding. I like it when you tell me about everyone's backstories."

Kyle's shoulders relax as he reaches over to tug the collar of my coat into place.

"Great! How about next weekend? I'll let you pick the restaurant we order from this time."

I shake my head. "Sorry. I'm still waiting to find out when our first round of tests will be. I need to have enough time to study for everything."

"Sure, okay, but you really don't have to worry, G," he answers as we walk down to the sidewalk to hail a cab. "You have a lot of the same teachers I had last year. Their tests aren't that bad."

"To you, maybe, but you remember everything you read. The rest of us peasants have to work for those A's."

"You forget I've seen you memorize an entire Shakespeare soliloquy in fifteen minutes before getting a hundred percent on the project."

I wave my hand dismissively. "It was only ten lines, and it took me thirty minutes, not fifteen."

His reply is put on pause as a cab pulls up to the curb. Kyle opens the door so I can climb into the car. After he confirms the address, our driver pulls out onto the street.

"My point is, I can't make any plans to hang out until I know what my schedule's going to look like," I say. "Plus, my dad's still out of the country. I need to stay home in case my mom needs my help."

As if on cue, my phone pings with a notification that someone's sent a message in my family's group chat. I check it in case it's something important, but I groan when it turns out to be Dad's "Meme-of-the-Day." He's always going on about how we should start our days with a laugh. Of course, since he's in Asia right now, his morning is our afternoon, so he hasn't been sending as many memes. I kind of miss them, but there's no way I'd admit to it.

"Everything okay?"

Rather than answering, I show Kyle the meme. It's a Twitter post of two cats, each looking out of a different window. The caption reads "romeow and mewliet." He chuckles.

"That one's not bad, actually."

"I'm going to pretend you didn't say that."

Kyle's face turns serious. "Seriously, though, how's your mom been doing?"

"She's been better. You know how it is. She agrees to too many events and then ends up getting sick." I shift my gaze out the window, pushing aside the heaviness that blankets me. "A few days of rest and she'll be fine."

"And you? Will you be fine?"

I glance back at him. "Yeah, why?"

He inhales. "Because James has always been there to help, and now that he's in college . . ."

It's only been a semester, but the house feels so empty without him. James was supposed to spend Christmas with us, but Dad asked him to stay in Houston to help out at his firm's satellite branch.

Kyle must sense the shift in my mood, because he slides his hand across the seat and gives mine a squeeze.

"Didn't James say he was thinking of coming for spring break instead?"

I force a smile. "You're right. It's only a couple more months. He'll be back before I know it."

Kyle's grip tightens. "Gigi—"

Whatever he's about to say is cut off as a car veers into our lane. While our driver honks and swerves to avoid him, Kyle shifts his hand to steady me by the shoulder. I flash him a smile, and he lets go. The rest of our ride back is silent. Once we get out of the car, he walks me to the front stoop of my house.

"Thanks for coming with me today," I say, looking up at him.

"Well, it was the only way you could squeeze me into your busy schedule." He winks. "Besides, you know I never turn down a chance to go to the Met."

"And you know my schedule is never too busy for you."

"Then say yes to *The Witcher* next weekend."

I sigh as I unlock my door. "Kyle."

"Say yes," he repeats. "Say yes or I'll . . ."

"*No*," I answer emphatically when it dawns on me what he's threatening to do. "Don't you dare."

He takes a deep breath. "'O Valley of Plenty! Toss a coin'—"

I clap a hand over his mouth. "Fine! I'll come, I'll come. Just stop singing before you embarrass us both."

The truth is, while there're half a dozen people walking down our street, no one is paying us any attention. Nonetheless, I wait for Kyle to nod before removing my hand. After unlocking my door, I step inside, turning to look at him.

"Good night, Kyle."

He grins wickedly. "'Toss a coin to your'—"

I shut the door in his face.

Chapter 2

"There are no guarantees in love, but I can promise you the next best thing—marriage."

It's Great-Aunt Rose's favorite saying, the first thing she tells every client who walks through the door seeking a matchmaker. What usually follows is either nervous laughter or stony silence, which she insists tells her a great deal about how easy they will be to match.

"A good sense of humor is a necessity," she insists. "Laughter is one of the foundations of a lasting relationship."

Personally, I think patience is the key. After all, I've watched countless prospective clients attempt—and fail—to complete her lengthy compatibility questionnaire. At fifteen pages long, it rivals the most complicated personality tests my Intro to Psychology class has to offer. Still, if they want a chance to be matched by Auntie Rose, they must answer every question.

Luckily for clients like her three-o'clock, Miss Wu, they no longer have to suffer through the eye-watering task of reading Times New Roman size-ten font. Their matchmaker has recently joined the twenty-first century and gone digital. Technically, the credit should go to me, since I'm the one who turned the Godzilla of questionnaires into an online form.

That's not even considering the nearly six months it took to convince Great-Aunt Rose to switch over, or the summer days I gave up transferring her handwritten notes into a database. She had decades of information on her clients in there, and she insisted every single bit—including her successes—be included.

"I like to refer to them when I have new clients," she explained. "It's the best way to predict what type of match will be the best fit."

On this point, she and I agree, though not for the same reasons. She sees those successes as a confirmation that her method works. To me, it proves her supposedly unique matchmaking process can be replicated by a computer . . . not that I'm going to tell her that. I enjoy living too much.

After taking last Saturday off to get started on my art project, I'm back at Rose and Jade today to continue training. I glance up as Great-Aunt Rose pokes her head through the beaded curtain that separates the back room from the front of the shop.

"There you are, xiǎojī! Is everything set for Miss Wu?"

I've never liked that nickname, a play off Gigi and the fact I was born in the year of the chicken. Since Auntie Rose only calls me xiǎojī when we're alone, I suspect she knows, though it doesn't keep her from using it. I carefully arrange the last individually packaged pineapple cake on the snack tray before answering.

"Yep. I just have to heat up water for the tea and we'll be ready to get started."

"Yes," she corrects automatically. "Yes, not 'yep.' Proper ladies don't use such impolite language. And last I checked, I was still your auntie."

I bite my tongue. It's also improper to talk back to your elders . . . especially one as senior as Great-Aunt Rose. You don't get served first at family dinner unless you're pretty up there. Of course, between the Asian genes, an extensive (and expensive) skin-care regimen, and weekly Pilates and spin classes, her real age is anyone's guess. Even her hair remains shiny and black, though I'm positive there's a well-paid colorist out there keeping her secret.

To be honest, I'm not sure how we're actually related. I gave up trying to figure that out when my middle school family-tree project turned into a mess of overlapping branches. What I do know is that she is by far the most stylish woman in my life. Even Mom, glammed up for a formal gala, doesn't quite carry herself with the same sophisticated air. Every time we meet, Great-Aunt Rose's hair is swept up into an elegant chignon, her makeup is flawless, and she's dressed in something tailored to accentuate her trim frame. While she's not a fan of flashy labels, even those who don't know anything about fashion will tell you Great-Aunt Rose looks expensive.

She narrows her eyes at me. "Well?"

"*Yes*, Auntie."

"Good." She scowls. "I'm going to see if Amy has finished unboxing the shipment of paper fans we got this morning."

I bite my tongue. Amy only started last week, but that doesn't keep Auntie Rose from expecting perfection. It's why none of her employees tend to last more than a few weeks, and the reason I still help out in the front on occasion while she's seeing clients. Though she spends most of her time matchmaking, Great-Aunt Rose insists on keeping the shop open.

"It's what kept a roof over my head and food on the table when I first started," she told me when I asked her why.

Like most souvenir stores, Rose and Jade has shelves lined with tourist-trap items like beaded boxes, ceramic dragon figurines, and cheap qipao and Tang suits. Suspended above us are a variety of paper lanterns and open umbrellas, along with strands of origami cranes that flutter every time the air conditioning kicks on.

At the moment, I'm standing in the ten-foot-by-ten-foot back room that serves as the office, break room, and kitchen. It's also where she holds her matchmaking sessions. Always one to make the most of any space she's in, Great-Aunt Rose hung fishing wire across the ceiling, draping swaths of soft gold satin to cover the panels above our heads. Strings of tea lights envelop the room in romantic mood lighting, and fake potted plants and an aromatherapy diffuser complete the room. To be honest, it looks more fortune-teller than matchmaker, but the clients seem to like it.

The matchmaking area is separated from the rest of the room by an ornate lacquered wood screen, though I suspect it's less about privacy and more about hiding the dirty dishes in the sink. The star of the show, however, is the circular mahogany table. It's one of Great-Aunt Rose's prized possessions, shipped directly from China and put into place when she first opened for business. It has stood in silent witness to the hundreds of successful matches she's made over the years.

For now, though, it serves as a place to put the tray of food I'm carrying.

I fill the electric kettle with water and plug it in. I'm just preparing the tea set when the front door chimes. I steal over to the curtain and peer through. With the aisles blocking my way, I can't see who's stepped into the shop. I can only make out the faint murmurs of conversation. It doesn't take much to guess what's being said, at least when it comes to Auntie Rose. I've heard her opening speech enough times over the last two years that I could recite it in my sleep.

The kettle whistles loudly, and I head back over to tend to it. Pouring the boiling water into the teapot, I wait a few minutes for the leaves to steep. From the other side of the screen, the rhythmic clacking of the beaded curtain announces Miss Wu and Great-Aunt Rose's arrival. I stay out of sight, waiting for the signal to appear.

"Please come in, Miss Wu," Great-Aunt Rose says in Mandarin. "Feel free to have a snack. In fact, I think some tea is in order."

I slap a practiced smile onto my face and step around the screen, placing the tea set down as Great-Aunt Rose gestures toward me.

"Miss Wu, this is my assistant, Gigi. Gigi, this is Miss Wu."

"Welcome to Rose and Jade," I say, also in Mandarin. "Let me know if there's anything you need."

At five feet tall and with dark-rimmed glasses hiding her features, Miss Wu looks barely older than me. However, from what I remember when I spoke with her mother initially on the phone, she's in her midtwenties. It was hard for me to understand some of what Mrs. Wu relayed on the phone because of her heavy Beijing accent, but that much I got. Kyle would never let me live it down, since he's fluent enough to watch C-dramas without the subtitles. I did catch the fact that Miss Wu's mother thinks she's hit some sort of invisible expiration date for finding a husband. I can't say I understand.

"Xièxiè," she mumbles after sitting down.

I pour her a cup of tea. "Bié kèqì."

I gesture at the snack tray, which Miss Wu politely refuses. With nothing more to do, I smile and excuse myself. After I'm back around the screen, I sit at the folding table we use to eat and grab the tablet. With Auntie Rose waiting for me to signal that she can start the session, I tap on the Spotify app and select the usual playlist. A second later, instrumental music begins to play on the Bluetooth speakers nearby.

With that done, I quietly pull my chair next to the screen, pen and pad in hand. It's the one rule I promised to follow when Great-Aunt Rose started my training.

"You have to stay out of sight," she told me. "The questions I ask are very personal, so clients won't open up if they know you're listening."

As I strain to hear what is being said, I swallow a groan. Though it's the first time I've sat here today, my back remembers the pain from last weekend.

"Now, Miss Wu, tell me what you'd like to find in your perfect match," Auntie Rose begins.

"Well," Miss Wu replies in Mandarin after a pause. "He should be tall, preferably six feet or taller. He needs to have a full head of hair. Double eyelids. College educated, making at least 75K a year. No more than five years older than me. And definitely no accent."

I cock an eyebrow. That's a lot to ask from someone who walked out of the house wearing no makeup and her hair pulled up in a messy bun. If I've learned anything working here, it's that the kind of guy she wants expects someone who looks more polished. I sneak another peek at her through the crack between the panels of the screen.

A tour tee, boyfriend jeans, and a pair of flip-flops? Really?

Thankfully for Miss Wu, Great-Aunt Rose is diplomatic. She leans back in her chair.

"I can help you, Miss Wu, but you're going to have to make some changes."

Her client stiffens in her chair. "Changes?"

"Even bees make their honey from the prettiest flowers. A fresh haircut, some lipstick, and a nice dress can make all the difference. You do want to find a quality man, don't you?"

Miss Wu fiddles with her earlobe. "Of course. I'll do whatever you ask."

"Good, good." Great-Aunt Rose smiles blithely. "Now, let's go over your questionnaire."

She flips to the first page of the printout I made for her earlier. It's one of the compromises we made when she agreed to go electronic—the clients get to use an online form, but she gets to see their answers on paper.

Knowing the rest of their session won't teach me anything new, I decide this is as good of a time as any to read through the *Worldly* article submissions. The theme for next month's issue is—as expected for February—love. I move over to the foldout table and pull my laptop out of my bag. I boot it up before clicking on the folder containing the articles I downloaded earlier from my email. The first one belongs to Summer, and as I read, something nags at me. On a hunch, I pull up our school's website and search *Worldly*'s online archive. A few minutes later, I find what I'm looking for.

"Romantic Traditions around the World."

I lean back against my chair and shake my head. Summer really submitted an article we printed last February? The only thing preventing me from accusing her of plagiarism is the fact that she wrote the original one. I can hear her now.

Why would I change something that's already perfect?

Shaking off my irritation at Summer's non-effort, I move on to the next submission. The article is written by the one person whose accomplishments always exceed my own—Anna Tam. As expected, by the end of the first page, I've dragged it into the "pending" folder in *Worldly*'s shared drive. The interview with her grandparents about being in an interracial relationship back when it was illegal is both powerful and poignant.

It's also right up Kyle's alley. He's always looking for thought-provoking pieces, and as senior coeditor, he has final say.

This is the kind of stuff we should be publishing, Gigi, I can hear him insisting. *As journalists, it's our responsibility to educate our readers.*

For the next thirty minutes, I run through the rest of the submissions, adding to the pile for Kyle to review when I'm done. I have one more article to go when I hear Auntie Rose scoot back her chair.

"Give me a week or so to look over my list. I'll email you some potential matches, and we can talk about who you like at our next session."

I stay where I am as they head through the beaded curtain. A moment later, I hear the front doorbell chime as Miss Wu leaves the shop.

"Xiǎojī, are you ready?" Great-Aunt Rose calls out as she returns to the back room.

I hesitate, staring at the last file. It's from Melody, one of our senior writers. Her article will be a quick read, but . . .

"Gigi?"

Melody can wait. I close my laptop.

"I'm coming, Auntie!"

After putting everything back in my bag, I join Great-Aunt Rose at the matchmaking table. She hands me the page of notes she made during her session with Miss Wu. While I glance over it, she opens her notebook containing the precious handwritten biodata for all of her past and current clients. Tucked inside is the clear yellow ruler she uses to help her read the minuscule print within the seemingly endless columns and rows of information. It took me weeks to learn the code Great-Aunt Rose uses to keep track of everything, especially since a lot of it is in shorthand Chinese.

"Pen, please," she tells me.

I jump up and walk back to the table, plucking a red pen out of the cracked coffee mug that holds all her writing utensils. It's her preferred color when she begins matching. I walk it back to her and hold it out.

"Auntie, why are you still doing this by hand? I transferred everything onto the computer for you for a reason," I remind her. "Matching will go much faster if you use it. If you don't remember how to do the criteria search, I can show you."

She scowls. "The last time I tried to do that, I ended up deleting half the database."

"You didn't delete it. You only moved it off-screen. It took five seconds to fix it."

"I'd still rather do things this way," she answers stubbornly. "It's always worked for me. Not to mention I can't add the face or palm reading results to my client profiles."

"You know there's no science behind those readings, right?" I can't help but say. "It's educated guessing, like psychics."

Auntie Rose narrows her eyes at me. "I'm going to pretend I didn't hear you say that. I have always taught you that a . . ."

"Successful matchmaker marries science and art," I finish.

She arches an eyebrow, but nods. "Exactly. I spent years studying my craft, learning the tricks of the trade from your great-grandmother. She used face and palm readings as well as the biodata, and it gave her a ninety-five percent success rate."

I highly doubt those readings contributed much to that percentage, but I keep it to myself. Getting her to use the database is only the first step. If I want to convince her to go completely electronic before I head off to college, I'm going to have to play this smart.

"If you want to add the reading results, I can teach you how to do that too."

"No, thank you," she replies firmly.

I pout. I put in so many hours creating that database, sacrificing my own eyesight trying to decipher her scribbles, but she won't even use it. Great-Aunt Rose puts the pen down and closes her notebook with a sigh.

"All right, xiǎojī. Go ahead and show me how to do this again."

I hop up from the table and retrieve the tablet. Then I open a browser and click on the bookmarked link for the database. Once it loads, I turn to Great-Aunt Rose.

"Okay, so the first thing you need to do is . . ."

Chapter 3

"I don't see why I had to fill out that ridiculous form if you were going to ask me all the same questions today."

Great-Aunt Rose's right eye is twitching, and her mouth is set in a tight line. It's been a long day, and we're both ready to head home. Mr. Lawson is not her typical client for many reasons, not the least of which is how his dark tan, blinding veneers, and power suit all scream flashy playboy, not a lonely bachelor looking for Mrs. Right.

How he even ended up here is a mystery. While she used to post advertisements in Asian newspapers, Great-Aunt Rose's reputation has grown over the years to the point where she only accepts referrals from previous clients. Which brings me back to the Wall Street broker slouched unceremoniously in his chair.

"As I stated in our initial phone call, the form provides valuable information that I use to select your ideal matches," Auntie Rose practically hisses at him while I set up the tea set. "And if you had completed the questionnaire before arriving, you would know that the questions I'm asking now were not included."

His mouth falls open; clearly, he was not expecting such a direct reply. Mr. Lawson straightens and props one elbow on the table, resting his chin on his knuckles in a move I've seen Dad use during business meetings.

"If done correctly, it imparts dominance and authority," I remember him telling James. "Remember that if you're ever in negotiations."

That, however, is not what Mr. Lawson conveys. Now that he's moved closer, it's easy to notice the dark streaks of self-tanner along his jaw that weren't properly rubbed in. The sleeve of his suit jacket is too short, revealing a Rolex that was likely bought from a stall down the street. The only authentic thing about him is the annoyance in his hazel eyes as he pulls a pen out of his breast pocket.

"Why do you need to ask me so any questions, anyway? It's not like the girls will be picky. I'm good-looking, live in a nice apartment in the city, and I make plenty of money."

"Mr. Lawson, all the male clients I work with can claim the same," Great-Aunt Rose informs him. "You must be able to offer more than that. That's why the questionnaire is important."

He makes a frustrated sound. "Oh, come on. Those girls just want a green card."

"*Excuse me?*"

Auntie Rose's jaw drops. I'm so shocked by his words I over-pour the tea, spilling it onto the table. I quickly soak it up with paper napkins before sneaking a peek at Great-Aunt Rose. Judging by the laser beams she's shooting out of her eyes, she's debating whether to slap Mr. Lawson into another dimension.

"Exactly what kind of service do you think I offer here?"

He looks genuinely confused. "Don't you handle mail-order brides?"

"Who told you that?"

"The guy I work with. He referred me to you."

"Is that so? What's his name?"

Mr. Lawson is thrown off by her question, but stammers out a name that she scribbles down. Then Great-Aunt Rose gets up and walks out to the front of the shop. I hear the distant sound of the cash register opening, and a moment later, she walks back and waves a handful of bills at Mr. Lawson.

"Here's your money back. Please leave now."

He stares at her in shock. "What? That's it? You're not going to help me?"

"Mr. Lawson, I am *not* in the business of selling brides," she states firmly. "I cannot help you."

He sputters for several seconds before snatching the money from her and stomping out the door. Great-Aunt Rose closes her eyes and rubs her temples. I transfer the teapot and full cups onto a tray and am about to take them to the sink when she stops me.

"No sense in wasting a perfectly good pot of tea." She reaches into her pocket and places some money into my free hand. "We need something sweet to save the day. How about you run over to Kam Hing and bring back some sponge cake?"

"Sure, Auntie."

"Coconut for me like usual," she reminds me. "And whatever flavor you like."

I grab my coat off the rack behind the screen and put it on, zipping it all the way closed. With the money tucked into the cardholder on the back of my phone case, I head out of the shop and make a right. I weave through the crowd of Saturday-morning shoppers and tourists for two blocks until I cross Baxter Street. I turn right and walk past the blue and white facade of the Chase bank to the unassuming glass doors of the building that houses the coffee shop.

I get on line behind the other customers waiting to buy Kam Hing's famed sponge cakes. The aromas of sweet cakes and savory cafeteria food mix with the strong scent of coffee. Novelty signs hung along the counter keep us entertained with funny sayings, as do the cute animated drawings of a sponge cake family on the wall to our left.

Once it's my turn, I place our order, pay, and then head toward the door.

"Gigi!"

I look around the room for the owner of the vaguely familiar voice. My eyes land on a girl waving at me from about halfway down the line, though it would be impossible to miss her. Dressed in a bright orange puffy jacket that's almost swallowed her whole, she could put a traffic cone out of a job.

"Hi," I say slowly.

Oh no. Why can't I remember who she is? Think, Gigi, think.

I've definitely seen her somewhere. A mass of thick black curls surround her heart-shaped face. Her doe eyes, wide button nose, and round cheeks make it hard to tell how old she is.

"What are you doing here?" she asks with a toothy grin. "I mean, I know what you're doing here, obviously, but, you know . . . this doesn't seem like the kind of place you would come to, considering . . ."

She rambles on as I try to ignore the way my stomach starts to knot. I feel the eyes of the woman she's with boring into me as I try desperately to recall her name.

Does it start with a G? Gina? No . . . that doesn't sound right. Maybe Brenda?

Her—relative?—pokes her in the arm. "Etta, pay attention! You're holding up the line."

Etta! Of course. Relief washes over me. I've seen her around SYC—the Suzuki Youth Center—where I volunteer as a mentor to students from low-income backgrounds. Now that I remember who she is, I'm surprised I didn't figure it out sooner. For as long as I've been a volunteer there, Etta's never missed a weekend. She's the only mentee with perfect attendance. Then again, she's usually surrounded by a trio of rowdy brothers, all of whom are usually one second away from burning the place down. I swear she has the patience of a saint.

Etta smiles apologetically at her companion. "Sorry, Lola."

They both take several steps forward to close the line, while my stomach growls. Before I can make a hasty exit, Etta turns back to me.

"So what did you get? The sponge cake?"

"Oh, um . . ." I glance down at the bag of rapidly cooling pastry in my hand. "Yes."

"That's why we're here too. Someone brought a box of them to church last weekend and they were *so* good! I think I'm going to get the chocolate, but maybe I'll try the green tea instead . . ."

As she talks, I edge my way toward the door, hoping Etta will get the hint. She doesn't, but her lola nudges her and looks at me pointedly.

"Oh, I'm so sorry! Gigi, this is my grandma. I call her Lola. It means 'grandma' in Tagalog," Etta says quickly, oblivious to what her grandmother actually meant. "Lola, this is Gigi, one of the girls I told you about from the Suzuki Youth Center."

Her grandmother manages a small smile, and I bow slightly in return.

"It's very nice to meet you, ma'am." I glance at Etta. "I'm sorry, but I should go. I need to get back to my auntie's shop."

"Really? What kind of shop is it?" she asks. "Where is it? Maybe I can visit after we finish."

"Your friend needs to go, Apo," her grandmother chides. "Her tiya is waiting."

Etta gasps. "Of course. I'm so sorry, Gigi! Maybe we can catch up tomorrow at SYC? You'll be there, right?"

"Yeah, definitely," I agree right away. "I'll see you tomorrow."

I throw a parting wave at the two of them and rush out the door.

♡

I never made it to SYC. A little after I walked back into Rose and Jade with the sponge cakes, our cell phones blared a winter storm advisory. Since the dreadful Mr. Lawson was her last client for the day, Auntie Rose decided to close the shop early. The next morning, I woke up to three extra inches of snow from the storm we had overnight. Dad refused to let me leave for my volunteer shift.

"It's too cold for you to be out there, Gigi."

It'd only been two days since he'd been back, but Dad was already being overprotective.

"Fernando can drive me," I protested. "I wouldn't be walking."

Dad shook his head. "I gave Fernando the day off. His daughter's been sick the last few days and he wanted to spend time with her."

"I'll take a taxi or an Uber, then."

"You know how I feel about those. I don't trust the drivers to be safe," Dad replied. "Besides, don't you want to spend time with Mom and me? We haven't been together like this for weeks."

That gave me pause. He had been gone for a long time, traveling overseas to Asia while coordinating an expansion of his consulting firm there. It was only a matter of time before he'd have to leave again.

"Of course I do, Dad. Just let me text Mallory."

After I messaged our volunteer coordinator to let her know I wouldn't make it, Mom, Dad, and I hung out at home and binge-watched *The Witcher*. We had started watching the first episodes of the most recent season, but Dad made us promise to wait until he got back to finish. I didn't have the heart to tell them I'd already watched it all with Kyle. It's not like I caught most of it over the random tidbits he kept interjecting anyway.

Afterward, Dad and I made dinner while Mom took her usual afternoon nap. Then I headed up to my room to finish my homework. That's when I received an email from Mrs. Brown, our Peer Squad faculty advisor, asking me to stop by her office before class. Though it's not unusual for her to do so, I wasn't the next in line to be assigned a mentee. Maybe one of the other mentors had to back out.

When my alarm goes off on Monday morning, I rub my eyes with a groan. It's been over a week since winter break ended, but the adjustment's been worse than when we came back after COVID. After taking a few minutes to stretch, I plod my way into the bathroom and get started with my morning routine.

I do my best to shake off the tendrils of sleep as I walk into my closet. Tapping on the floor-length smart mirror on the back wall, I check the weather before deciding on a burgundy Armani jacquard sweater, dark-wash Paige skinny jeans, and my favorite pair of black Chanel booties. The outfit is more casual than usual, but I'd rather be comfortable than be a fashionable Popsicle.

I head back into the bathroom to do my makeup and add loose curls to my hair. Then I slide my laptop into my book bag and head downstairs for breakfast. Since Mom isn't up yet, and Dad's already left for the office, I grab a cashew shake from the fridge and head out the door. There're less than ten blocks between Superbia and our house, but Fernando is driving me to school so Dad doesn't worry himself into a heart attack.

I spot the car about half a block down the sidewalk and make my way over to it.

"Hi, Fernando," I greet before tugging my seat belt into place.

"Good morning, Miss Gigi."

Though his unnaturally black curly hair has thinned and his face is now etched with lines, the grin from our family's driver has remained the same over the years.

"How's Maria?" I ask. "Dad said she wasn't feeling well."

"She is much better. Thank you for asking."

Fernando merges into traffic and heads downtown on Park Avenue, the orange glow of the rising sun flickering into the car between the buildings we pass along the way. Fifteen minutes later, he pulls the car in front of the school.

"Thank you for the ride."

He waves from the driver's seat. "Have a good day, Miss Gigi."

I walk up the stone front steps and pull open the heavy wooden door, careful to track in as little snow as possible with me. As I enter Superbia, I'm greeted by the faint sounds of footsteps and people talking. Climbing the stairs to the third floor, I make a right and head all the way down the hall, stopping at the door with Mrs. Brown's name etched into a gold placard. I raise my fist and knock.

"Come in."

I step inside the cluttered office, pausing when I notice Mrs. Brown isn't alone. Seated across the desk from her is someone wearing a familiar bright orange coat.

"Ah, Gigi, we've been waiting for you." Mrs. Brown gestures toward the empty chair. "Have a seat."

"Hi, Gigi," Etta says as I sit down next to her. "I bet you're surprised to see me here."

That's an understatement, but I manage to keep my surprise to a small nod.

"Etta is one of our merit scholarship recipients," Mrs. Brown explains. "She was supposed to start at the beginning of the school year with the others, but there was a mix-up with her paperwork. We finally got it straightened out last week."

I turn to Etta. "Oh, that's great! Congratulations."

She grins happily. "Thank you."

"I suppose you're wondering what this has to do with you," Mrs. Brown continues. "I asked you to come because I was hoping you would help Etta get settled. She mentioned you two were already acquainted."

"Oh, please say yes, Gigi," Etta begs, her brown eyes imploring. "It would mean so much to me."

I would have agreed since Mrs. Brown asked personally, but her puppy eyes seal my fate.

"Of course, Etta. I'd be happy to show you around."

Mrs. Brown beams. "Gigi is a wonderful peer mentor. Now, why don't you show her your schedule so she can help you find your first class?"

Etta hands me the sheet of paper she's been clutching. A quick check reveals her class is just down the hall from mine. Mrs. Brown stands, and we do the same. After shaking her hand, Etta follows me out into the corridor.

"Thanks again for doing this," she says with a nervous grin. "I had no idea Superbia was so big. I'd be lost by now without you."

I tip my head toward her. "No problem at all. And I'm sorry I wasn't at SYC yesterday. I had something come up with my family."

"Oh, it's okay. I wouldn't have gone either, except it was nice to get out for a bit. My brothers were tearing up the house," Etta tells me. "Do you have any siblings?"

I nod. "I have an older brother. His name is James."

"Oh, does he go to this school too?"

"He did, but he graduated last year."

The pang returns, but I pretend not to notice.

"That's awesome. I'm the oldest, and I want to attend college too, but it's a lot of money and my parents can't really afford it. I might have to get a job and go to school at the same time. Honestly, I can't believe I got this scholarship. I know it's going to be harder here than at my old school, but I think it'll be worth it because—"

"We're here," I interject. "This is your class."

Etta freezes, wisps of sound seeping between her lips before she presses them closed. I immediately regret being so abrupt.

"Sorry I cut you off. I didn't want you to be late," I explain gently. "We can keep talking when I come get you after class, okay?"

She brightens. "Sounds great! I'll see you then."

Etta strolls into the classroom, heading straight for the teacher and handing him her schedule. He glances at it and then points at a desk. She turns and waves at me before taking her seat. Now that she's in the right place, I rush to my own class, making it inside with a few seconds to spare.

"Good morning, Mrs. Chow," I say to my AP Chemistry teacher. She smiles. "Good morning, Gigi."

"I'm sorry I'm late today," I feel compelled to explain. "I was helping a new student to class."

Mrs. Chow chuckles. "There's no need to apologize. You're not actually late."

As if proving her point, the bell rings as I sink into my chair. A few of my classmates slip in at the last second, and Mrs. Chow frowns at them before taking her place at the front of the room.

"All right, class. Let's get started."

Chapter 4

"Settle down, everyone."

I'm counting down the minutes until I can answer the siren call of my bed. Okay, so maybe it wasn't the best idea to show up to school on a Wednesday with only four hours of sleep, but Prince Chang and Seo-bi were in the middle of trying to save Korea from a zombie apocalypse. It's not like I could have fallen asleep without finishing the season.

I stifle a yawn as Ms. Harris refers to the syllabus she's handed out for computer science class.

"We still have a lot to cover before the end of the year. As a reminder, in addition to preparing for the AP exam, you will need to complete the last two stages of your app project."

I'm still reading through the syllabus when I hear a loud groan.

"You're making quality assurance due in three weeks?" Tyler whines. "But that's not fair! We've only been back since last week. Why can't you make it due later?"

Normally he'd be in trouble for talking back like that, but as the youngest teacher at Superbia, Ms. Harris has always kept things casual. It's not uncommon for her to be mistaken for a student during parent-teacher conferences because of her baby face, ever-changing hair color, and love of flashy shoes. In fact, Ms. Harris offered to give extra credit to the student who found her next pair. So far, no one has been able to claim that dubious honor.

She crosses her arms over her chest. "If you're really upset about it, I can push it back to right before spring break . . ."

Groans fill the room, and several students throw Tyler dirty looks. Ms. Harris raises her hand for silence, though it takes a few minutes before the room quiets down.

"That's what I figured, which is why I didn't do that." She smiles encouragingly. "There's no reason to worry. All of you have written the majority of the source code for your apps, which means you've made it past the toughest part of the development process. Besides, isn't this the reason a lot of you took this class? So you can become the next Steve Jobs?"

"Fu—" Tyler stops himself. "I mean, forget Steve Jobs. I want to be the next Elon Musk."

"Elon is a genius," Summer retorts. "Something you aren't . . . among other things."

She drops her gaze purposefully, sending a wave of snickers through the room. Tyler sits up straight in his chair and glares at her.

"Well, you never complained when we were—"

"All right, that's enough," Ms. Harris interrupts. "Save that conversation for biology class. It's time for us to get started on today's lesson. Everyone, please open up your textbooks."

She moves over to her desk and picks up the remote for her laptop. With the press of a button, the PowerPoint presentation projected on the screen at the front of the classroom changes slides.

"Now, before we turned off our brains for winter vacation, we were reviewing the different programming languages used for iOS applications. Who can tell me which ones are most common?"

I should know the answer, but my brain currently feels like swiss cheese. Thankfully, there's always someone ready to flex their knowledge. Another yawn takes hold of me as Tyler blurts out an answer. As expected, it's the wrong one. Anna raises her hand and quietly offers the correct one, which earns her a smile from Ms. Harris. As much as I want the same approval, every blink of my eyes is longer than the last, until I start at the sound of chair legs scratching across the floor.

Oh no. Did I really fall asleep in class?

I glance at Ms. Harris, sighing with relief when her gaze is pinned to her laptop screen. As she closes out her presentation, students start packing up. She holds up a hand.

"I know everyone's tired, but class isn't over yet. I have a couple of announcements to make before you're dismissed. First, I'll be doing a random check on Git tonight, so I hope you've been compiling your work. If your program isn't updated, I'll have to deduct points from your final grade."

Considering I finished Quizlr, my app, before we went on break, I'm not really concerned. However, more than a few of my classmates look like they've been told the world is ending.

"Second, I've found a really exciting opportunity for everyone. How many of you have heard of SJW Tech?"

A handful of students raise their hands, with Anna's shooting up faster than all the others.

"Yes, Anna."

"SJW Tech is one of the premiere private computer engineering firms in the country. They've made it onto the *Fortune* 100 Best Companies to Work For list three years in a row."

Ms. Harris smiles at her before opening a browser window and clicking on a bookmarked site. SJW Tech's homepage pops up, and she clicks on a menu link that directs her to a second page. I lean in with the rest of the class to read what's on it.

Good news! SJW Tech is hosting its first Junior Coding Contest this year to find the next generation of talented programmers! Open to high school students aged fourteen to eighteen in the state of New York, the inaugural theme for this year is "With a Twist." Each contestant must draw inspiration from existing apps and create an original program. Faculty mentoring is allowed, but the code must be written entirely by the student. Entries must be nominated by faculty, and one entry is allowed per school. Initial submission deadline is February 21st, and semifinalists will be notified on March 15th. Our panel of esteemed industry judges will select the top three apps to post on our website for public voting. The winner will be announced at a special dinner hosted by SJW Tech on April 1st. The prize is a summer internship with our head programmer, Austin Jang.

Anna gasps. "Austin Jang is one of the top computer programmers in the country right now! One of his programs even won an Apple Design Award."

We all turn to her in surprise. Anna's usually so quiet that most people forget she's there. In fact, there was a week last year when she was sick with the flu, and it took three days before someone noticed she wasn't in class. For her to speak up three times in one class period is practically unheard of.

Though her parents are second-generation Chinese American, Anna Tam reminds me of the fobby graduate students that Auntie Rose sometimes matches. She's thin in a fragile kind of way, and she rarely wears makeup beyond a layer of tinted moisturizer. She even dresses like she wants to disappear, typically in clothes that are oversized and neutral in color.

Today she has on a gray Rag & Bone knit sweater, pairing it with white corduroy pants and brown leather boots. Anna's straight black hair has fallen out of her low ponytail, and the oversize glasses perched precariously on her nose distort her features.

Luckily for her—but unluckily for me—what she lacks in style, she makes up for in substance. As of last semester, Anna is standing between me and valedictorian status.

"That's right," Ms. Harris confirms. "And a letter of recommendation from him would make any college application stand out from the rest. That's why I'd like to nominate one of you to represent Superbia."

Murmurs circle the room. Ms. Harris waits for the talking to die down before continuing.

"If you would like to be considered for nomination, you'll need to turn in your app before the deadline."

Tyler raises his arm. "Will there be a cash prize if you win?"

"Unfortunately, there isn't a cash prize, Tyler," she answers with a patient smile. "But you'll get bragging rights if you win."

"I'd rather have money," he moans. "Maybe I'll ask my mom instead."

"Good idea," Summer snipes. "You'll never win the contest anyway. You can't even spell success."

"This coming from someone who pays for hers," Tyler shoots back.

The room explodes into hoots and hollers. Fortunately for Ms. Harris, the last bell rings, ending the fight and sending many of her students rushing out the door. Anna weaves around the desks toward Ms. Harris, while I stuff my textbook and laptop into my bag. As I walk to the front of the room, I catch the tail end of their conversation.

"Of course. I'll mentor you for the contest, though I don't think you'll need much help. You're already working ahead of what I'm teaching in class."

"Thank you, Ms. Harris," Anna tells her with a grin. "I won't let you down."

She throws her backpack over her shoulder and races out the door, nearly crashing into me in the process.

"Oh! Sorry, Gigi," she tosses over her shoulder.

I watch her disappear down the hall before turning to wave at our teacher.

"See you tomorrow, Ms. Harris."

I've nearly made it out the door when she calls my name.

"Gigi, can I talk to you for a minute?"

I curse silently.

Please don't let it be about me falling asleep in class.

I spin on my heels and press a smile to my face. "Sure, Ms. Harris. What's up?"

She returns the smile, but something in her hazel eyes makes my heart bang against my rib cage.

"Is everything okay with you?"

"Yes, everything's fine," I answer quickly.

"Are you sure? It's not like you to doze off in the middle of class." She pauses. "If there's anything I need to know about . . ."

"No, there's nothing! I . . . I just messed up my sleep schedule during break, that's all." Heat spreads through me in a wave, and I bow my head. "I'm so sorry. It won't happen again."

Ms. Harris walks over to me, placing a hand on my shoulder.

"Don't stress, Gigi. I'm not upset with you. I only wanted to check how you were doing."

"I'm okay," I answer automatically. "In fact, I'm great."

She chuckles. "In that case, I do have one other question. It's about your app."

"My . . . my app?"

A million questions fly through my mind. Does she not like my idea? Did I miss a line of code? Could I have forgotten a deadline? I can't afford to get a B in this class. It'll ruin my GPA.

She perches herself on the edge of her desk, crossing her legs in front of her. I briefly admire the high-tops covered in fuchsia glitter on her feet.

"How are things coming along with Quizlr?"

I came up with the idea for my app while removing malware from a friend's phone for the third time. They downloaded it accidentally after clicking through to a pop culture quiz site from someone's tweet. Quizlr stores the tests on a secure server and allows users to post their test results to their social media accounts.

"I'm pretty much done with all the coding," I reply after a breath. "I got a head start on it at the beginning of the year."

"Ah, I see."

An unnerving couple seconds pass before she tips her head to the side. "Are you thinking of submitting Quizlr for consideration?"

I relax. So that's what this is about. Ms. Harris wants me to enter too.

"Maybe? I'm not sure yet. Do you think I should?"

"You're a very talented programmer, Gigi. There's definitely a chance you could win. But I'm not sure if Quizlr will be a competitive submission."

I stiffen. "What do you mean? What's wrong with it?"

"There's nothing wrong with your app," Ms. Harris assures me. "The code's been well written, and it functions the way it's meant to. But you'll be going up against some pretty sophisticated programs. If you want to win, you'll need to make some improvements."

I know Quizlr isn't the fanciest program I've ever written, but . . . too basic? Needs improvement? My heart sinks lower with every word. A thought flashes through my traitorous mind.

Anna's program is probably perfect already.

I realize I've spoken the words out loud when Ms. Harris's eyebrows shoot toward the sky.

I grimace. "I didn't mean to—"

"Both of you have work to do on your apps," she says, cutting me off gently. "You have the skill to win. Remember, you got Quizlr up and running in less than a semester. That normally takes students the whole year—*if* they manage it at all. Don't count yourself out yet."

She stands and walks over, tugging me into a side hug. "You're going to do great. And if you get stuck and need someone to bounce ideas off, I'm here, okay?"

"I will, Ms. Harris. Thank you."

I leave her packing up her things as I rush into the hallway and toward my locker. Quickly transferring everything I need to complete my homework into my bag, I slip my arms into my winter coat and zip it up all the way. I take one last glance down the hall before heading toward the front of the school.

Despite her reassurance, my stomach churns at the thought of handing in a subpar app. I've been writing code for two years—though mostly for fun—and could have produced something far better. Suddenly, getting an A in the class doesn't feel like enough anymore.

I have to enter the contest. Not only that, I have to win.

And I know just how to do it.

Chapter 5

"Took you long enough."

I skid to a stop outside Superbia's large wooden front doors, spinning toward the voice that called my name. Kyle's leaning against the stone archway of the front alcove. Despite wearing only a leather jacket, his dark brown hair tousled by the wind, he looks warm in the midst of a flurry. I roll my eyes at him.

"You could have left without me."

"And risk you being accosted?" Kyle's breath comes out in a white puff. "What kind of a guy do you think I am?"

"Accosted? By who? Some dangerous criminal out to rob me of my precious textbooks? They can have them as long as they turn my homework in on time."

He throws his head back and laughs. "I was going to say some shady car service looking for a victim to overcharge, but I guess that works too."

"You do realize I can call Fernando, right?"

"And drag him all the way from Queens when he's off to drive you a few blocks during rush hour?" He scoffs loudly. "I had no idea you were so heartless."

As he says this, Kyle reaches for my book bag. I hand it to him.

He throws it over his left shoulder before offering me his right arm. I loop mine through his elbow, and we start making our way uptown on Park Avenue.

"First of all, he gets twice his usual rate for working on short notice," I say after a few minutes. "Second of all, I'd only do that if I had no one to walk me home."

Kyle smirks down at me. "Then you're lucky I waited for you."

"You say that as if I wouldn't have other offers to do so."

"Ah, but we both know I'm the only one you wouldn't be tempted to shove into oncoming traffic after three blocks."

I poke him in the ribs. Kyle clutches his side like he's been stabbed.

"What was that for?"

I shrug. "Just practicing."

"For what? Murder?"

He dodges me this time and jogs ahead, though I catch him at the next intersection. He offers me his arm again, which I accept. Once we've crossed to the other side, Kyle tilts his head in my direction.

"Why were you late, anyway?"

"Ms. Harris asked me to stay behind. She wanted to talk about a couple of things."

"Things like . . ."

I quickly relay what happened with Ms. Harris. When I'm done, Kyle nudges me with his shoulder.

"Sorry, G. I know that was upsetting to hear."

"I'm disappointed in myself," I admit. "I know she wasn't expecting the next TikTok or *Candy Crush*, but I could have done better."

"I thought she said your app was fine for class. She complimented you on how fast you got it done."

"Yeah, but she also told me it wasn't strong enough for the contest."

"So . . . make it better."

I stop in my tracks. "That's not the point. I should have known better. If I had programmed Quizlr to do more from the very beginning, Ms. Harris wouldn't say it needs improving now."

"You're being too hard on yourself, G," Kyle chides. "No one's perfect. We all make mistakes."

"Well, I don't." My voice drops to a whisper. "I *can't*."

"Gigi—"

He's interrupted as an elderly woman ahead of us gets her purse knocked to the ground by a businessman rushing to get past. Kyle leans down to help her collect her things. I spot a couple of items rolling toward me and hand them back to the woman.

"Thank you so much," she says once her belongings are back in her handbag.

"You're welcome, ma'am," Kyle tells her. "Have a good day."

We continue on our way. Whatever he was planning to say gets lost in the fog of our individual thoughts. At the next intersection, I turn to Kyle.

"It doesn't matter anyway. I'm going to prove that I *am* good enough. I'm going to win that contest."

Kyle stares at me. "Uh, not that I don't support you, but why do you have to prove anything?"

"I just . . . do."

"No, you don't," he insists. "You're already the best programmer I know."

"I'm the *only* programmer you know," I retort. "Actually, that's not true. You know Anna. She's planning on entering the contest too, by the way."

Kyle lets out an exasperated sigh, but ultimately says nothing. A few seconds later, I turn back to him with a frown.

"I do have a problem, though. If I win the contest, I won't have time for the internship. I told Auntie Rose I'd continue apprenticing with her this summer."

"Are you really serious about doing that? Becoming a matchmaker?" he asks. "It seems like a hobby, not an actual job."

"You think my great-aunt pays for all her designer bags by selling souvenirs? Please. She gets her money from matchmaking." I pause to weave my way through a small crowd. "Besides, it's not about the money. It's about a legacy."

"But does your family actually expect you to carry on a career that isn't going to exist much longer? There're tons of dating apps, and more popping up every day."

I balk at him. "Are you kidding me? Those dating apps are like searching abandoned storage units for treasure. Most of the time all you're going to find is trash. If you want quality, you go to a matchmaker."

"Another Rose saying, I'm guessing," he observes.

"But you do have a point," I reply, ignoring his comment. "Which is why I'm working on a computer program based on her matchmaking methods. It'll be way more accurate than what's available. It might even bring the whole matchmaking business into the twenty-first century."

Not to mention help me win that contest.

"What are you going to call it? Matchmaker 2.0?" Kyle jokes.

I smirk. "More like Matchmaker 3000."

"Supercharged. I like it."

We take a right once we reach my street. Halfway down the block, we reach the black wrought iron gate in front of my house. Kyle touches me on the arm, and I look up at him.

"Don't let what Ms. Harris said get to you. I've seen what you can do with a computer," he tells me softly. "You're seriously amazing."

I say nothing. Kyle stares down at me for an extra second before shrugging my bag off his shoulder. I grab it in one hand and open the gate with the other. I glance back at him.

"Thanks for waiting for me."

He winks. "Sure, but if you're late again, you'll have to pay me twice my usual rate."

"Two times nothing is still nothing, Kyle."

"So what you're saying is I should charge you more."

"What I'm saying"—I aim my gaze at the dark redbrick building two doors down—"is that my dad knows where you live."

Kyle shudders. "Since I'd like to live to see graduation, I guess I'll keep walking you home for free."

"That's what I thought."

He sticks his tongue out at me before making his way to his own house. We unlock our doors at the same time.

"Good night," he shouts.

"See you tomorrow!"

I step into the house and shut the front door behind me. I'm grateful for the heat that surrounds me, and the soundproofing Dad had installed. The city noise is replaced by blissful silence. Inside the foyer, I shrug off my coat and hang it in the closet. Then I toe off my shoes and nudge them into their rightful cubby. Walking past the spiral staircase and into the kitchen, I'm momentarily surprised to find myself alone.

Oh, right. James isn't here.

Ignoring the pang in my chest, I check the refrigerator and find my favorite Fuji apples sliced and waiting on a shelf. I grab some caramel sauce and add it to the plate before heading up three flights of stairs to my room. I drop my bag on my bed, but bring the plate with me as I climb two more levels to the master bedroom.

I hesitate and glance at my watch. Mom's usually done napping by now. I raise my hand and knock on the door.

"Come in."

I open it and step into the suite. I peer down the narrow corridor to the right, but the bedroom looks empty.

"Mom?"

"I'm in here, bǎobǎo," she calls out.

I turn to my left and head into the dressing room. Mom is standing in the doorway to her walk-in closet, one finger pressed against her lips.

"What's the occasion?" I ask as I place my snack on the island in the center of the room.

She turns and opens her arms. I walk into her embrace, inhaling the scent of her favorite rose perfume.

"A fundraiser for the Wang Society for Animal Rights."

I pull back and watch as she flips through a few hangers in search of the perfect gown for the evening.

"I hope there won't be any dogs this time."

The last fundraiser Mom attended was for the Humane Society, and none of the organizers mentioned they would be bringing some of the animals to the event. Within minutes of her arrival, Mom had to be wheeled out on a stretcher after having a severe allergic reaction. It was all anyone could talk about for a week. I'm just glad

I didn't find out until she had been stabilized at the hospital.

She shakes her head. "No, thank heavens."

"You should still pack your EpiPen," I reply automatically.

"Already in my clutch."

"Are you sure you should be going to another event so soon?" I ask after a pause. "You just started feeling better."

She bops me on the nose. "I'm fine, bǎobǎo. There's no need to worry about me. Besides, I'm on the board of directors. They'll be expecting me."

The doorbell rings, and Mom gestures toward the stairs.

"That's probably Celia. Can you go let her in while I change?"

Celia is Mom's favorite stylist, and she has done her makeup and hair for years. They met when Mom saw an advertisement recruiting people to sit for practice sessions at the local cosmetology school. Apparently, Celia did a terrible job at first, but they clicked and became fast friends.

"Sure."

I leave her and head down to the front door. It's hard to see who it is through the frosted glass, but I recognize Celia's neon pink tracksuit.

"Hey, babe," she greets as I open the door. "Your mom home?"

In addition to loving colors that can be seen from space, Celia has had half of her makeup tattooed on. It's a wonder Mom never comes out looking like Pennywise.

I nod. "She's waiting for you upstairs."

Celia rolls her makeup luggage to the elevator and presses the button to call it. Once the circular car arrives, we step in and slide the door closed. A few moments later, we get off and I lead Celia to the dressing room. While I plop onto the nearby settee and finally dig into my apples, Mom sits down on the chair in front

46

of her vanity. Celia unpacks her case and spreads out the various drawers, pulling out the colors that will suit Mom's navy sequined dress the best.

While Celia begins prepping her skin and adding foundation, Mom's brown eyes shift over to me.

"So how was school today, bǎobǎo?"

"It was fine," I answer before popping another slice of caramel-covered apple into my mouth.

"Did anything exciting happen?"

I start to offer my usual reply, but change my mind.

"Actually, yeah. Ms. Harris told us about this app contest run by a top computer engineering firm. The prize is an internship with their head programmer."

"Close your eyes for me, babe," Celia interjects, an eye shadow brush hovering over Mom's face. "Unless you want more Plum Ecstasy in your eye than on your lid."

Our conversation is put on hold for several minutes while Celia carefully lays down the eyeliner and mascara for Mom's eye makeup.

"So this contest is for a summer internship?" Mom asks when she can move around again. "I thought you were spending this summer with your great-aunt."

"I am," I affirm. "But winning would look great on my college applications."

She shifts her gaze toward me. I know what she's going to say before she even opens her mouth.

"I thought you had decided to go to Columbia."

That isn't entirely true. Columbia is one of the colleges I've been considering, but after seeing how happy James was going out of state, I wanted to do the same. When I told Dad, he tried convincing me to stick with Columbia instead.

"It's an Ivy League school," he said. "You can live at home while receiving a quality education."

"I've lived here my whole life, Dad. I want to see more of the world, and going out of state would give me that chance."

He scowled. "You don't have to go anywhere to learn about the world. That's what the internet is for. Besides, once you graduate you'll be able to travel anywhere you want. In the meantime, why not enjoy the comforts of home?"

That was the last time we talked about it since he started traveling for work again. To be honest, I'm relieved, because I haven't come up with a reason that he wouldn't immediately shoot down.

"It never hurts to apply to more than one school," I reply. "It's always possible that I won't get into Columbia."

"Nonsense. You're an excellent student," Mom insists.

I dip another piece of apple into the caramel. "You can't get into college with only good grades. Almost everyone has that."

"I suppose that's true," she concedes. "But you also have a list of extracurriculars a mile long. They'd be foolish not to accept you."

I pout. "I'd feel better if I knew that for sure."

"There are no certainties in life, bǎobǎo, except your family. Dad and I will always support you, no matter what. In fact, even if you didn't go to college, we'd be fine with that. I didn't go, and I think I did pretty well."

Mom pauses so Celia can apply her lipstick. "Besides, you're already a winner. You're a Wong."

She says that with the conviction of someone who's experienced the power of the Wong name firsthand. Her own family was very influential back in China, but after a jealous rival spread rumors about their business dealings, many of their clients cut ties. That's when they decided to get a fresh start and immigrated to the United States. With what was left of their fortune, my grandparents bought a bakery in Chinatown. Mom was in middle school then, but after a couple of years, her parents saved up enough money to enroll her in Superbia. She would take shifts at the bakery to help pay for her tuition.

Mom continued working at the bakery after graduating high school. That's where she met Dad. She says it was love at first sight. He swears she put something in the cake. Auntie Rose called it divine intervention, since she's the only one who would have seen it coming. No matter the reason, they fell in love. They've been married twenty years, and are still nauseatingly cute when they're together. Theirs is the kind of love I'd want . . . assuming I had the time to look for it.

When Mom took over her family's bakery, Dad convinced his parents to invest. He even had plans to help her expand it to more locations. Mom loved owning Sweet Dreams, offering a mix of Chinese and European pastries, all made fresh and in-house every single day. She kept working even after she became pregnant with James. Then one night, Dad found her unconscious on the kitchen floor of the bakery. That's when doctors at the hospital found out she had an irregular heartbeat.

After that, Dad refused to let her keep working, and they sold the bakery. Now her biggest worries are which party invitations to accept and how many nonprofit boards to sit on.

"Did you hear what I said?" Mom asks.

I make a noncommittal sound, dipping my finger into the caramel sauce and licking it off. Mom stares at me before sighing.

"When do you have to turn something in?"

I make a face. "Three weeks?"

"That's not a lot of time, bǎobǎo. You have other responsibilities, like your other classes and your volunteer work."

"Okay, but I already have the perfect idea, and I've got some of the code written too."

The last part slips out before I can stop myself. I meant to keep the recently named Matchmaker 3000 a secret until it was done, but I need Mom on my side.

"Oh?" She cocks her head. "What is it?"

"I've been working on a computer program that uses Auntie Rose's techniques to match clients," I say slowly.

She narrows her eyes at me. "Does your great-aunt know about this?"

"Kind of?" I try laughing, but it comes out as a squeak. "We've talked about . . . something like it."

"And what did she say?"

My silence is answer enough. Mom sighs again.

"Don't say I didn't warn you."

"What's important is that I have part of the app written," I push on. "So three weeks is totally doable."

"Are you the only person entering from Superbia?"

I pop a slice of apple into my mouth before answering. "There is one other person that I know of for sure."

"Who?"

"Anna Tam."

She waves her hand in my direction. "Why don't you let Anna enter instead? Ms. Harris will be happy when she wins, and you won't have all that extra stress. Problem solved."

The apple lodges halfway to my stomach. At least, that's what I call the tightness in my chest when Mom predicts Anna's win with such certainty. Even my own mother considers me second best. Sometimes I wonder if she wishes Anna were her daughter. Back when she attended Superbia with Mrs. Tam, Mom was the one who was the best at everything, the one who came in first each time.

"But I really want to win," I tell her.

"Gigi, you don't need to win a silly contest. You're young, beautiful, and everyone loves you. And it's not like you don't have other things going on at school, right? You've got the newspaper—"

"Magazine," I correct.

"Right, magazine," she repeats. "And that student mentoring group, the . . . uh, what's it called?"

"Peer Squad."

"Yes, the Peer Squad. Didn't you mention something about that?"

I sigh. I need to stop talking to Mom when she's getting ready for an event. It's like she has the attention span of a goldfish.

"Sort of," I reply. "There's a new girl at school who I know from SYC—Etta. I've been helping her get settled."

"Exactly! You've already got so much on your plate."

"I don't know. What if I disappoint Ms. Harris? She asked me to enter."

That's not entirely true, but there's no reason to tell Mom that.

"Bǎobǎo, I highly doubt that Ms. Harris will mind if you prioritize your health. Remember, you have a heart condition too. You shouldn't put so much pressure on yourself."

I bite my tongue. Because of Mom's arrhythmia, both James and I were checked regularly to see if we inherited the same condition. Neither of us did, but when I started second grade, Dr. Samuels found a heart murmur that wasn't there when I was born.

Though all the extensive testing Dad asked for came back normal, from that point on, my parents decided I was as fragile as Mom, if not more so. This hasn't changed despite Dr. Samuels reminding them every annual checkup that it's nothing to worry about. I've never had any fainting spells or had to take medication, but they're still convinced something bad could happen to me.

"You know what? We can talk more when you're not so busy," I end up saying.

Mom peers at me. "Are you sure? I'm not leaving for another hour."

"No, it's okay. Celia still has to do your hair. Plus, I need to do some homework."

I pop the last slice of apple in my mouth after coating it generously with caramel. Standing up with the empty plate in one hand, I walk over to Mom and give her a quick squeeze.

"Have a good time at the fundraiser."

"Thank you, bǎobǎo," she answers. "Oh, don't forget to—"

"Make sure Dad eats dinner when he gets home," I finish for her. "I won't."

She blows me an air kiss, and I leave her in Celia's capable hands. After dropping the plate into the kitchen sink, I make my way back to my room. Pulling my laptop out of my book bag, I turn it on and open the file for Matchmaker 3000. Cracking my knuckles, I let my eyes drift down the lines of code.

"Now . . . where were we?"

Chapter 6

I continue walking Etta to her classes for the rest of the week. In truth, it didn't really take her more than a day to figure out her schedule, but she begged me to keep walking her.

"I feel so out of place here," Etta explained. "I've tried talking to people in class, but most of them ignore me."

Sadly, that's not surprising. Even without her loud voice traveling down the corridors, Etta sticks out. Each time I pick her up, she fills the time with loud, nonstop chatter, drawing the eyes of those around us as we pass people in the hall. All the extra attention sets me on edge. One wrong move can turn you from popular to outcast in a flash. As sweet as she is, I'm more than a little eager to leave Etta behind each period.

There's also her choice of wardrobe. When I initially convinced her to drop off her coat at her locker, I didn't expect her to be wearing a faded rock band sweatshirt, turtleneck, and boyfriend jeans combo underneath. That sort of outfit might pass for fashion at her old school, but at Superbia, it makes Etta an easy target for climbers.

Like Summer Benson.

As captain of the Starlets, Superbia's junior dance team, Summer moves with the grace of a swan but stings like a viper. While her five-foot-five frame might have robbed her of a chance to be a famous supermodel, she's decided to be the next best thing— a social media influencer. With burgundy-brown hair and deep blue eyes, Summer spends more time taking pics of her outfit of the day than studying. There isn't a girl in the school who doesn't want to be her, or a guy who doesn't want to date her.

At least, that's what she'll tell you if you make the mistake of asking her.

Summer walks up to us as I meet Etta by her locker. She's flanked by her that-can't-really-be-their-names frenemies, May and September. While they might not coordinate outfits like the mean girls on TV, they're definitely as vicious. It's too bad May doesn't realize she's the latest in the carousel of token Asian girls Summer likes to keep around. I know because I used to be one of them. I was one of her "besties" in middle school, until I grew three inches taller than her and got scouted to walk a show for an up-and-coming fashion designer.

"What do we have here?" Summer asks, baring her teeth in a poor imitation of a smile. "Another one of your . . . volunteer projects?"

If Etta notices the insult, she doesn't acknowledge it. Instead, she shoves her hand toward Summer before I have a chance to make introductions.

"Hi! I'm Etta. I'm new here."

Summer accepts her hand, but holds it the way most people touch food they've just picked up off the floor.

"I'm Summer."

Etta's smile dims, but she quickly recovers. "It's really nice to meet one of Gigi's friends."

"I wouldn't call us that," Summer answers as the other girls smirk. "Friends are on the same level."

I take a step forward and look down my nose at her.

"Yes, and we both know who's coming up short."

May claps a hand over her mouth as a giggle escapes her, but not before she finds herself on the receiving end of Summer's furious glare. Etta glances between us, unsure of what to make of our odd conversation. Before anyone can throw another insult, Tyler appears at Summer's side.

"Good afternoon, ladies."

If Summer is the self-professed queen of Superbia, then Tyler is—well, *was*—her king. They broke up again over winter break. The star of Superbia's junior varsity rugby team, he loves the attention he gets for his blond-haired, blue-eyed, California-surfer vibe. Though I'm positive he gets the tan from a bed and at least half of those sun-kissed highlights come out of a bottle. He, nonetheless, is at the top of many dream-boyfriend lists here at school.

"If you're here to ask me to go to lunch with you, Tyler," Summer snaps, "save your breath. I'm busy."

Tyler lets out a terse chuckle. "Not everything is about you, Summer. I'm having lunch with someone else."

That sounds like a total lie. Anyone with half a brain would stay far away from anything—or anyone—belonging to Summer.

As if proving my point, she spins and glares at him. "What? With who—"

"Hi, Tyler!" Etta interrupts with a broad smile. "Thanks for the recommendation the other day. I think I'm really going to like *Bleach*."

For a split second, Tyler's eyes light up. Then, as if remembering he has an audience, he looks her up and down with a bored expression.

"I'm sorry. What are you talking about?"

"*Bleach*. You know, the anime series you said I had to watch?" Etta explains.

Tyler scoffs. "You must be confusing me with someone else. I don't watch *cartoons*."

"But it's not a cartoon! It's anime." Her voice rises slightly. "You know that. You said . . . I thought . . ."

I'm not entirely sure what's going on, but I know it's not going to end well. Every time Etta opens her mouth, the red in Summer's cheeks grows darker. Tyler may not be her boyfriend anymore, but it doesn't mean she tolerates other girls talking to him right in front of her.

"Etta, we should go if we want to make it to lunch," I quickly interject.

Despite the significant look I send her, her brows still knit together as she turns to me.

"What? Lunch?"

"*Yes*, lunch. As in we're supposed to have it together. Today."

Etta blinks at me before her eyes widen.

"Oh, oh yeah! Lunch. Right. We're having it. Lunch. Together."

That was anything but subtle, but there's not much I can do about it now. With a bright smile, I loop my arm through hers. Etta glances at Tyler one last time, but he avoids her gaze.

"It was nice to meet you," she squeaks to no one in particular.

I practically drag her down the hall with me. Neither of us say a word until we've left the school behind and are walking down Park Avenue to one of my favorite lunch spots.

"Are we really going out to eat?" Etta asks, frowning. "I didn't bring any money. I packed my lunch."

I glance toward her. "Don't worry about it. It's my treat. Now, what's going on with Tyler?"

"I don't know." Etta shakes her head, her thick black hair flying around her face. "I . . . I thought maybe we were starting to be friends, but now . . ."

"Friends? I don't understand. How do you know Tyler Edwards?"

"From class," she explains. "We sit next to each other in English, and he's behind me in biology."

"And you guys have been talking?" I ask.

She nods. "Remember how I said most of the other students ignored me when I tried to be friendly? Well, he's one of the few who didn't. It was just hi and bye at first, but a couple of days ago, I had my phone out before class and he asked about my lock screen."

Etta pulls her phone out of her back pocket and shows me a digital painting. "I drew it myself."

"That's a really gorgeous Eren Jaeger," I say, remembering the five hours I endured of the show after Kyle demanded I give it a chance.

"Gigi! You like *Attack on Titan*?"

I shake my head. "No, but I recognize the character."

"Oh." She deflates a bit. "Well, anyway, Tyler knew it was Eren too. It turns out he's a huge anime fan and gamer. We talked for an hour after school that day about which series were our favorites."

That comes as a complete surprise to me. The only things I know about Tyler are his skill on the rugby field and his unerring belief he knows all the right answers—despite being proven wrong time and time again in class. Of course, it wouldn't surprise me if he started talking to Etta because she's the only one at Superbia who wouldn't run away from him to avoid being Summer's next target.

"I don't understand why he acted like that back there," Etta murmurs. "He's the one who told *me* about *Bleach*. He even pointed out some episodes to watch if I wanted to check it out."

"My guess is that he didn't want to upset Summer."

She frowns. "Why?"

"I know you're new, so you haven't figured this out yet," I say, tugging on her sleeve so she'll speed up while crossing the street. "But they don't call her Queen B because she's sweet like honey."

"Okay, but what does that have to do with Tyler?"

"He's her ex. They broke up over winter break."

No one at school is sure who ended things this time and why. The rumors range from Tyler forgetting to get her a Christmas gift to Summer cheating on him with a ski instructor she met in Banff. All anyone knows is that they didn't end on good terms.

"If they're broken up, then why does it matter if I talk to him?"

I answer as we pause at the next intersection. "Because they've broken up three times in the last six months, Etta. And they always end up back together."

Her shoulders droop. "Oh."

"I'm not saying that you shouldn't talk to him," I say softly. "But you should be careful. There're lots of people at Superbia who love stirring up drama."

"I never considered that," she admits. "It was just nice meeting someone who likes the same things I do."

My heart aches at her downcast eyes. Impulsively, I grab her gloved hand and give it a squeeze.

"Look, I know things got off to a rough start, but I promise it'll get better. You'll meet other students who are way more fun to hang out with."

"I wish there were an easier way to meet friends. I know not everyone's going to like me, but people could at least give me a chance."

Her words tickle the back of my mind, but I forget about it as we turn left and follow the crosswalk to the other side of Seventy-Eighth Street. By the time we reach Lexington and take another left, something else occurs to me.

Even bees make their honey from the prettiest flowers.

If there's one thing I've learned from matchmaking, it's that first impressions are everything. Etta might not be searching for love, but a different look might help her be accepted at Superbia, even if she's already off to a rough start.

I nudge her with my shoulder. "You need a breakup makeover."

"What? What do you mean?" she asks with a giggle. "I didn't break up with anyone."

"I don't mean with *someone*. I mean with *something*. You broke up with your old school to come to Superbia."

"Okay . . ."

"So maybe it's not the best analogy," I reply, "but the point stands. Everyone loves reinventing themselves. You get to be anyone you want."

Etta's breath catches, but she shakes her head. "I like myself. I don't want to be anyone else."

"Then let's make your outside match your inside," I suggest. "So people can see the real you."

She looks down at her clothes. "This doesn't show the real me?"

"It . . . is you, but not the version of you that makes people want to get to know you better," I hedge. "That's what you want, right?"

"I would really like that," she confirms.

"Then let's do it. In fact, why don't we go shopping this weekend? I can take you to some of my favorite shops."

She grins. "That would be amazing, thank you! I'm so glad we're friends. I don't think I could have survived this week without you."

"I'm glad too," I tell her, nudging her shoulder with a smile. "And I'll do my best to help you meet new people. I love Superbia, and I want you to too."

We finally arrive at Mighty Bowl, where we join the rest of the lunch rush. Because the line is long, I pull out my phone and place our order in advance. By the time we reach the counter, it's ready to be picked up. With our lunch hour rapidly disappearing, we rush back to school and find a table in the cafeteria to eat. Then I walk Etta to her first afternoon class.

"I'll see you next period," she says with a wave.

Once she heads through the door, I turn and make my way down the corridor. By the time I slip into my seat, I know exactly which stores we'll be visiting for Etta's makeover.

The weekend can't come soon enough.

♡

"That date was a complete disaster," Miss Wu announces as she walks in for her follow-up session Saturday morning. "I can't believe you matched me with that pompous a—"

"Language, please," Great-Aunt Rose warns, throwing a glance as I approach with the tea. "Have some tea and almond cookies, and we can talk about what happened."

I fill the cups with oolong tea and carry the tray back to the kitchen. Though I give them their privacy as usual, I stay close enough to hear the conversation as I clear the breakfast Auntie Rose and I had off the folding table.

"Miss Wu, I sent you three matches based on what you told me you wanted during our last session. You chose Mr. Chen based on his profile," Auntie Rose states.

"Yes, but he wasn't at all what I expected."

"In what sense?"

Miss Wu is silent for a second. "I don't know. I mean, Aaron fit all the criteria I gave you, but he was just . . . wrong. Not only did he show up ten minutes late for our date, but he kept checking his phone during the entire dinner. He actually told me he was expecting someone more put together, whatever that means."

It's probably good Miss Wu can't see me right now, because my cheeks are bulging from holding in my laughter. James teases me about my lack of a poker face. Meanwhile, the harrumph Great-Aunt Rose makes is one I instantly recognize, so I'm not surprised when I hear her reply.

"This is why we talked about the difference between a check-list and real compatibility, Miss Wu. Just because someone looks good on paper doesn't mean he's a good fit. I gave you what you wanted, but as you see, it's not what you need."

"But what about chemistry?" Miss Wu challenges. "I don't want a loveless marriage like my parents."

Auntie Rose tsks. "Chemistry isn't only about physical attraction. It's also how someone makes you feel, how their personality complements yours. Haven't you ever seen a woman or man with someone who was not equal to their beauty?"

"Yeah, but that's because they're with them for the money."

This time, I let out a snort. Of course, it's my luck they both go silent at that moment. While I cover with a cough, I can imagine the scowl on Great-Aunt Rose's face.

"Perhaps some of them are," she acknowledges, "but I know from firsthand experience that chemistry is more than skin deep.

Many of the couples I have matched wouldn't describe their partners as their ideal physical type, but they are nonetheless very happy together."

I can't resist sneaking a peek at Miss Wu's reaction, so I creep to the wooden screen and peer through the crack. I must make a noise, though, because her head suddenly turns toward me. I hold my breath until she turns back, but Miss Wu's voice drops to a near whisper from that point on. After ten minutes of straining to hear the conversation, I give up and go back to snacking on the extra almond cookies. The sweet flavor and buttery texture distract me long enough for Miss Wu to say goodbye and leave the shop.

"You can come out now, Gigi."

I tense at the use of my actual name. Auntie Rose only uses it when she's mad at me. I pop the last bite of cookie into my mouth before crossing the room to her. Auntie Rose gestures at the seat across from her, and I slide into it.

"I'm sorry," I say before she launches into a lecture. "I didn't mean for her to find out I was listening. I'll be more careful next time. I promise."

She regards me for a long moment before leaning back against her chair. I relax and turn my attention to the words she scribbled on the notepad in front of her.

"So what's next for Miss Wu? Is she going to go on a date with one of the other matches you sent her?"

"No. I will assemble a new set of matches for Miss Wu since she wants to start fresh. She did, however, wisely agree to let me recommend who I think will be the most compatible," Auntie Rose tells me. "She'll come back in another week or two to discuss the matches. I already have one man in mind, but I need to look for two more."

"I can do a database search if you want," I offer.

"Believe it or not, xiǎojī, I've figured out how to use your database thingy. I admit it does save me time now that I've got the hang of it." She picks up her cup of oolong tea and takes a sip. "But that's not the hard part. The trick will be finding someone with the right combination of traits for Miss Wu."

I lean my elbow on the table and prop my cheek against my palm.

"What do you mean?"

"Well, for example, I have to decide what I think is most important in her potential matches. Do I want someone who is introspective, someone who is kind, or someone who knows how to take charge of situations? Should he be a good cook, enjoy being active, or be someone who likes a simple life?"

"Wouldn't it be easier to find men who have the most traits in common with her?" I ask. "You're always saying it's best to choose similarities over differences."

"In most cases, it is. 'Opposites attract' is an exception, not the rule. The more two people share with one another, the better," she agrees.

I swipe another almond cookie off the table. "Then why don't the dating apps that say they match based on compatibility work?"

"Because personality tests are based on how we see ourselves, and most of us are terrible judges of our own character," Auntie Rose explains. "We have an idea in our head of who we are, but it's not always how we actually come across to other people. If you want the best results, you have to be objective. That's why my questionnaire focuses on the facts."

I opt not to point out that those *facts* include Eastern and Western astrology along with face and palm readings. Besides, this could be my chance to bring up Matchmaker 3000. Trashing her methods will get me nowhere.

"But people still prefer doing things online nowadays. Think of how many clients used to complain about how long your questionnaire was," I settle for saying. "Now all they have to do is click some buttons, and boom, they're done."

"Maybe, but a computer won't ever be able to replicate what I do for my clients." Great-Aunt Rose crosses her arms over her chest. "Each client is different, which means the criteria you choose to focus on are different. That's why matchmakers are still in high demand. Mr. Chen is the perfect example. He's like an avocado."

Though her tendency to make weird analogies isn't new, this one throws me for a loop.

"He's a what?"

"An avocado. They can look perfect on the outside but be rotten on the inside," she explains. "When people focus only on the superficial, love never goes well. A matchmaker sees beyond that, but sometimes our clients need to come to that decision themselves."

"Which is why you gave Miss Wu Mr. Chen's profile and let her go on that date."

"Yes, exactly."

Auntie Rose takes another sip from her cup, peering at me from over the edge of it. "In fact, I think this is a perfect time to take the next step in your training."

My heart starts pounding. "What do you mean?"

"I want you to go through your database and come up with three men you think would make good matches for Miss Wu. Let's see how close you get."

"Really? You're going to let me match Miss Wu?"

"It's only a practice match. I will make the final decision about who gets presented to her," she clarifies, "but this is a good way for me to see what you've learned so far."

This is exactly the opportunity I need. If she agrees with the picks I get from Matchmaker 3000, she'll have to admit the app works. Even better, it'll prove the program works in time for the contest.

The doorbell to the shop chimes, and Auntie Rose looks at her watch.

"Hopefully that's my art scroll delivery. I've been waiting on it for two days." She pushes her chair back and stands. "Ms. Chiang will be here in about half an hour. Can you clean up before she gets here?"

"Yep. I meant yes. No problem," I reply.

"All right, then. Let's get back to work."

I smile to myself. That's exactly what I intend to do.

Chapter 7

"I'm not sure this is really . . . me."

I glance up from my seat. After Auntie Rose gave me permission to leave early, I had Fernando swing by to pick up Etta before dropping us off in the East Village. I've brought her to one of my favorite shops off East Ninth to try on some new clothes. She's stepped out of the dressing room in the latest of the outfits I picked out for her, a black-and-white cowl-necked sweater paired with black jeggings. I point to the pedestal in front of the three-way mirror, and she steps onto it obligingly. After making her turn this way and that, I purse my lips and frown.

"What don't you like about it?"

"The jeans are too tight," she answers, rubbing her hands over her thighs. "I feel fat in them. Plus, they're too long. They bunch at the bottom."

I walk over to her, squatting down to roll the cuffs until the material smooths out.

"There. Much better. You just need to get them tailored. They have a seamstress here who can do it."

"Oh."

The single syllable passes through her lips as a sigh, and I raise my eyes to meet hers.

"What? What's wrong?"

Etta tugs at the hem of the sweater. "Isn't this too short? It doesn't cover my butt."

"There's no rule that says a sweater has to do that," I tell her, though I take a more critical look. "It does hit you in the wrong spot, though. Maybe a longer one would be more flattering."

"I do like the material," Etta concedes, brushing her fingers over one sleeve. "It's so soft, and warm too."

"That's because it's a hundred percent merino wool," I explain.

"How much is it?"

I carefully pull out the price tag to look. "It's only four hundred dollars."

"Four hundred—" Her mouth falls open. "That's too much, Gigi!"

Her exclamation draws the attention of the shop clerk. I shoot her an apologetic look before pushing Etta into the dressing room and following her inside. I pull the curtain and turn to her.

"It's okay. Merino wool isn't for everyone. We can find something else." I pick up the pile of items still waiting on the stool. "What's your budget? Three hundred dollars? Two hundred?"

It takes me a second to notice Etta's gone completely silent. She's wringing her hands and doesn't quite meet my eyes when I stop sorting through the clothes in my arms.

"Etta? What is it?"

"Oh, um . . . I really appreciate you inviting me to go shopping with you today, Gigi."

I frown. "But?"

"But I can't afford anything in this store . . . or any of the stores in this neighborhood. I'm sorry."

I cringe inwardly. Why didn't that occur to me? I first met Etta because she's a SYC mentee, not to mention she's attending

Superbia on a merit scholarship. She's probably never stepped foot in a real boutique until today.

"I should be the one apologizing," I immediately reply. "I should have been more considerate. I hope you'll forgive me."

Etta shakes her head. "No, no! I don't want you to feel bad. I should have said something from the beginning. I guess I was too excited about coming today."

An awkward silence falls between us. Since all the shops I wanted to take her to out are of her price range, my grand plans for an afternoon of shopping have gone out of the window. Etta toes the floor with her shoe.

"I guess I should go home."

She practically shrinks into herself. No, this isn't acceptable. I promised Etta a new wardrobe, and I'm going to find a way to make it happen. Pulling out my phone, I open a browser window. Staring at the search bar, an idea pops into my head, and I type it out. Two results pop up. Tucking my phone back into my purse, I clear my throat.

"Now that I think about it, I've been in a retro mood lately. There're a couple of really amazing thrift stores nearby. How about we check them out instead?"

Etta's eyes light up. "Are you sure?"

I shrug. "Yeah, why not? I've found some amazing outfits there."

"Really?"

I nod. "Yeah, totally."

It's not a complete lie. I've won multiple Halloween contests with the costumes I've found in thrift stores. While that's obviously not the look Etta's going for, I'm sure we can do better than what's hanging in her closet.

"Why don't you get changed?" I suggest. "I'll wait for you outside."

"Sounds good!"

I step out from behind the curtain and nearly careen into the salesclerk. She backs up and bows slightly.

"Oh, I'm so sorry, miss. I . . . I wanted to check in and see if either of you needed anything."

I highly doubt that, given the way she was sneaking around. The clerk must be new, since the rest of the staff here knows me. It's part of why I come to the boutique. They make a point of knowing each and every one of their customers by name.

"No, we don't need anything," I answer firmly. "Thank you."

Etta pushes open the curtain, stepping out with her jacket on and zipped. I notice the clerk eyeing the satchel bag Etta's carrying.

"Let's go!"

Etta starts toward the front of the shop, but the salesgirl quickly blocks her path.

"Excuse me, miss—"

I step in and draw myself up to my full height. "Hi, I'm Gigi. What's your name?"

"Uh, Victoria," she stammers.

"Nice to meet you, Victoria. Is Ellen in the back? I'd like to say hi."

She swallows hard at my mention of the shop owner's name.

"She . . . she's not here right now, but I'll let her know you stopped in."

I pretend to examine a lock of my hair. "That's okay. I have her number. I'll text her."

Victoria visibly pales. I give her a few more seconds to question her life decisions before putting her out of her misery.

"Thank you for all your help today, Victoria. I'll be back soon."

"Yes, please do," she quickly replies. "And if there's anything you need, or your friend—"

"Etta," I fill in for her.

"Yes, Etta. If there is anything either of you need, please let me know."

"I'll be sure to remember that."

I brush past her and loop my arm through Etta's. She tips her head to the side like a confused puppy.

"I missed something, didn't I?"

"I'll explain once we leave," I say under my breath. "Come on."

Throwing a final smile at poor shaken Victoria, I drag Etta out the door.

♡

Three hours later, I'm nursing swollen feet as we browse through the fourth—and hopefully the last—thrift store of the day.

"I should have worn more comfortable shoes."

Etta turns from the rack she's flipping through to meet my eye. "Did you say something?"

"Oh, I was thinking about what we still need for your new wardrobe," I fib. "We've got shirts, sweaters, pants, dresses . . . What else are we missing?"

I purse my lips, ticking off the staple pieces in my head. It's then that my eyes land on the glow-in-the-dark jacket slung over her shoulder.

"I can't believe I almost forgot! We should get you a new coat."

Etta's hand comes up and tightens around said coat. "Do we really need to?"

"Is it too much to get today?" I ask, thinking of the bags we're holding up at the register. "I know we bought a lot at the other stores. Maybe we can come back another time."

I'm personally a fan of calling it quits, because the growl my stomach lets out is downright menacing. I was so focused on writing code for Matchmaker 3000 between clients at Rose and Jade earlier that I skipped lunch.

"It's not that," Etta answers, fidgeting with one of her unruly curls. "It's . . . I know this jacket is old, but I love it. It fits me perfectly, and it's warm too."

"But the color . . ."

"It's not something I would pick for myself," she acknowledges, "but my lola gave it to me as a gift for my birthday. She was with me at Kam Hing, remember?"

I nod. Though our meeting was brief, Etta's grandmother reminded me a lot of my āmà—small but fierce. My paternal grandparents moved to California five years ago because Āgōng said he needed more sun. We usually video chat once a week, but recently Āgōng and Āmà decided to take all the cruises they had to postpone due to COVID. They've been out of the country for almost as many weeks as Dad's been traveling for work. I talk to them more often than my grandparents on Mom's side because they've been living in Taiwan since I was twelve. I only see them when we visit.

"She put aside money from her pension for weeks to buy it for me," Etta continues, unaware of my thoughts. "That's why I wear it all the time. I want her to see me using it."

Her words remind me of all the things my grandparents have bought me over the years. I have no idea where most of it is anymore. In fact, now that I'm thinking about it, Mom might have donated some of it to the charity auctions her organizations were holding. I've never even worn the locket from Tiffany's Āmà bought me for my sixteenth birthday last year, the one with a picture of the two of us in it. It's tucked into the jewelry case in my room.

Maybe Etta doesn't need a new coat.

"You know what, Etta? That jacket goes great with the other stuff we picked today. We don't have to get anything else."

I glance at my watch. With Dad on another business trip and Mom at a board meeting, I'm free for the night.

"Why don't we grab something to eat instead?"

Etta lets out a yelp. "Oh no! I didn't notice it's almost dinner time. I'm so sorry I kept you this long."

"It's not a big deal," I assure her. "I had a lot of fun shopping with you today. But I am pretty hungry."

"Come to think of it, I am too. Let me just call my mom and see if it's okay with her."

Etta pulls out her phone and dials her house. When her mom picks up, she starts talking.

"Ma, pwede ba kami lumabas ni Gigi? Magdidinner lang kami so malalate ako konti ng uwi."

What follows is a slew of questions, all of which she answers without batting an eye. Eventually, the conversation lulls, and she hangs up with a grin.

"She said it's okay! Let's go!"

With our plans set, I gesture for her to follow me to the register. I ask the cashier for her bags before turning back to Etta.

"So what are you in the mood for? There're some great places around here we can try."

"Oh, I know another great place—Kusina Pinoy Bistro! They have the most amazing Filipino food." Etta's face falls. "It's out by where I live, though. Is that okay?"

Dad would be furious if he found out I strayed that far from home, but he's not here and I'm not telling.

"It sounds great. Let me call Fernando and we can go."

"Oh, you don't need to do that. We can take the train. It won't take that long."

My stomach clenches. "It's not a problem, Etta. Fernando has to take you home anyway, so it'll be on the way."

"But it's almost dinnertime, and his family always eats together. I don't want to make him leave," she answers as we walk to the door. "Especially since he'd be coming from Queens to pick us up and then turning around to go home."

I cock my head toward her. "How did you know Fernando lives in Queens?"

"We were chatting on the way here. It turns out our families live ten minutes apart. We're basically neighbors."

While I knew where Fernando lives, I didn't know about his family dinners. There've been plenty of times when he's driven Mom to a party or dropped Dad off at the airport past the end of his shift. I always assumed his family, like mine, ate at different times.

"I've never taken a train anywhere," I admit as we step out onto the sidewalk.

"What? Never?"

I shake my head, and Etta laughs. "I'm revoking your New Yorker card. But don't worry, it's easy. I'll show you."

She leads me to the nearest subway entrance, and we descend a set of steps to the underground station. Etta helps me purchase a MetroCard. When I swipe it at the turnstile, nothing happens. It takes two more tries while people walk through on either side of me to finally get the card to register. By the time we make it down to the platform, I'm practically shaking.

Etta smiles at me. "See? That wasn't so bad."

"Yeah, it was okay," I answer, though I'm clearly not.

Fifteen minutes later, we're on the R train toward Queens. Etta manages to find us a couple seats near the middle of the car, and I watch as people enter and exit the train at each stop. After what seems like an eternity—though in reality forty stomach-grumbling minutes—she gestures for us to stand.

"Our stop is next," she informs me.

I force a smile, resisting the urge to point out we could be halfway through appetizers by now. When the doors open, we exit and walk up the steps into the station. From there, Etta guides us through a couple hallways before we climb another staircase and pop out onto the street. Just as I'm convinced I'll pass out from hunger, we arrive in front of Kusina Pinoy Bistro's large picture window. We walk into the busy restaurant, and I'm surprised to find a spacious dining room with walls of alternating stone and wood panels. The central walkway is flanked by tables and chairs along each wall, with steam and chaos coming from the kitchen at the back.

The hostess smiles brightly as we approach her stand. "Welcome to Kusina Pinoy Bistro. Do you have a reservation?"

Before either of us can answer, a middle-aged Filipino man with bushy brows and thick, curly black hair appears and envelops Etta in a hug.

"What are you doing here, Etta?"

"I brought my friend Gigi for dinner," she replies with a smile. "I didn't know you were working tonight, Tiyo."

"I picked up an extra shift since one of the managers called in sick." He turns to me with an easy grin. "Hi, Gigi. I'm Etta's uncle Ernesto."

"It's nice to meet you, Mister . . . Ernesto," I finish, realizing he never gave me a last name.

He chuckles. "There's no reason to be so polite. Any friend of my Etta is family. You can just call me Tito."

"Um . . . thank you, Tito."

"You two need a table?" he asks Etta.

She nods. After consulting with the hostess, Ernesto walks us a few steps to a table right behind the hostess stand.

"I'm sorry, but this is all we have right now," he says. "Saturday nights are always busy."

Etta smiles as she slides into the chair against the wall. "It's perfect, Tiyo. Thank you."

I take the seat opposite hers, and Ernesto drops two menus on the table before heading deeper into the restaurant to check on the other tables. I read through the dishes but realize I'm in over my head and put down the menu.

"What do you like here, Etta?"

"Everything's amazing," she answers. "It depends on what you're in the mood for, I guess."

"What are they known for?"

"Definitely the calamare gigantes, for starters. And the oxtail kare-kare is a must-try. But if you like adobo, I would recommend the chicken version."

"That all sounds great. Why don't you order for us?" I suggest.

Our waitress stops by to introduce herself and take our drink orders. When she returns, Etta orders a selection of her favorite dishes.

Once our server walks off, I take a sip of my iced tea. "I'm glad we—"

Etta interrupts me. "Anna? Is that you?"

I spin around in my chair. Sure enough, Anna is standing in the doorway, staring at Etta with owlish eyes.

"Um, hi, Etta . . . Gigi."

Etta's gaze shifts to me. "Wait, you know each other?"

I was about to ask her the same thing. The only way they would have met is if Mrs. Brown assigned Anna as her Peer Squad mentor, but Etta asked for me instead. Before either Anna or I can reply, Etta smacks herself on the head.

"Of course you do. You're both SYC mentors from Superbia."

Ah, that answers my question as well. They must have met through the center too. Anna and I are assigned different days, so we rarely bump into each other there. Since it would be rude not to at this point, I gesture for Anna to come closer. After a moment's hesitation, she walks over to our table.

"Are you meeting someone here for dinner?" I ask politely.

She shakes her head. "No. I was going to order something to go on my way home."

"You live in the area?" I ask.

If Anna notices my surprise, she doesn't let on as she shakes her head.

"I don't, but I was meeting one of the SYC mentees at a café nearby. She hasn't been able to visit the center because her grandmother's been sick, so Mallory asked if I was willing to meet her here instead."

"That's really nice of you," I say.

I mean it, but part of me wonders why Mallory didn't ask me. Then again, I did cancel on her the last week because of Dad, and it's not the first time I've had to. Hopefully she isn't mad at me.

"Do you eat here often?" Etta asks.

Anna nods. "I love Filipino food, and this is my favorite place. I probably stop by at least once a month."

"In that case, you should join us! We'll ask them to bring another chair," Etta offers.

"Oh, no, I don't . . ."

Anna's protests go unheard, and a few minutes later, she's sitting to my left. An awkward silence falls between us, and I scramble to find something to talk about.

"Ms. Harris told me you're submitting your app for the contest," I blurt out.

Anna adjusts the glasses perched precariously on the bridge of her nose. "I . . . yes, I am. I assume you are too?"

"Maybe. I haven't decided."

That's half true, since I haven't talked to Ms. Harris about switching my app from Quizlr to Matchmaker. She'll need to approve the change for me to submit it as my contest entry since it's not the one I wrote for class.

"You should! You're a great programmer," Anna says without hesitation.

"So are you. In fact, you're better," I begrudgingly answer. "I'm sure you'll be adding to Superbia's trophy case soon."

"That's sweet of you to say, Gigi, but we both have the same chance of being nominated."

Our little game of No, You're Better ends when the waitress plunks what looks like a fried alien on a skewer onto our table.

Anna's mouth falls open. "You ordered the squid."

"How could I not?" Etta grins. "It's Gigi's first time here, so I wanted to make sure she tried all the best dishes!"

She points at the menu she had the waitress leave at the table. "You're welcome to get more food if you'd like, but I think I ordered too much already."

Anna shakes her head. "I'm sure it'll be more than enough. I usually get that and some of the lumpiang labong and I'm full."

"I can see why," I interrupt, pointing to the giant sea monster in front of us. "This is intense."

"Don't worry. That's what the scissors are for," Etta tells me. "We're going to dissect it."

"Ugh, if you want me to eat this it's best not to compare dinner to a biology project," I tell her, pretending to gag.

She giggles so hard she lets out a snort, and that gets all of us laughing. Once she catches her breath, Etta does the honors and cuts the ginormous appetizer into smaller pieces on the plate. After watching the others dip their sections into the orange sauce that came with it, I do the same before gingerly taking a bite. Any reservations I might have had evaporate as the first bits of crunchy outer breading meet my tongue, giving way to the slightly chewy texture of the squid. I can't quite put my finger on all the different spices, but I love how they come together in my mouth.

"So? What do you think?" Etta asks when I finish chewing.

"Mind. Blown. It's easily one of the best things I've ever eaten," I exclaim. "I can't believe I didn't know this place existed until now."

"Well, now you do, and we can come here as much as you want," she insists happily. "Tiyo Ernesto can get us in anytime."

Our main courses follow shortly after. Etta ordered all the dishes she recommended to me earlier, along with something called sinigang na baboy, a soup-based pork dish. Each bite I put in my mouth is more delicious than the last, to the point I almost miss the question Anna poses to Etta.

"Were you two meeting up for dinner?"

"We went shopping earlier," Etta informs her. "Gigi offered to help me pick out some new clothes."

Anna smiles. "Is it for a special occasion?"

"Not exactly. Gigi thought they might help me meet some new friends at Superbia."

My breath catches. Hearing her say those words aloud sounds wrong somehow.

"Gigi is definitely the expert in that," Anna replies, her gaze flitting to me briefly. "She's one of the most popular girls in school."

There's nothing in her tone that rings of insincerity, but something about it nonetheless stings. I find myself repeating what I said earlier.

"Etta is such a nice person, and I wanted people to see that about her instead of . . ." I pause, my mind going blank. "Well, I only meant they might not give her a chance because . . ."

Anna turns to me, a strained smile perched on her lips. "I get it. I know what it's like when you're different. I'm glad Etta has you to help her."

I don't know what to say to that. Anna and I were pretty close after we met in fourth grade, but all that changed during freshman year. We went from texting all the time about what book series we were reading and what our favorite shows were to her leaving me on read for hours. I knew she was having a hard time, but I could never get her to tell me why. Eventually I gave up, and we stopped talking altogether.

Maybe I should have tried harder.

She would have.

"Gigi? Are you okay?"

I drag myself out of my reverie to find Etta and Anna both staring at me. Hoping the dim lighting will hide the heat surging into my cheeks, I nod.

"I . . . got distracted thinking about whether I'd have room for dessert."

"You have to make room for the mais con hielo," Etta insists, missing the tension that's threaded between her two dinner companions. "I know it sounds weird, shaved ice with corn and evaporated milk, but it's so yummy."

As expected, Anna tries to lighten the mood.

"I can tell you it's worth the calories . . . unless you eat the whole thing by yourself like I do."

I force a smile I don't quite feel to avoid dragging everyone else down. By the end of the night, though, the sweet dessert and Etta's endlessly cheerful chatter help me forget the few uncomfortable moments with Anna. We part ways after paying the check—Anna and I agreed secretly to pay Etta's share—and head out into the night. I pull out my phone to call Fernando, but think better of it. Instead, I call an Uber.

"Thank you for recommending this place, Etta. I haven't felt this full in a long time, but I couldn't stop eating."

She grins broadly. "I'm happy to hear that! I know you probably eat at some really fancy restaurants, so thank you for giving it a shot."

"Thank *you*, Etta, for convincing me to try something different." I reach out to give her a quick hug. "I don't think I would have if you weren't here."

Later, when I've made it safely back home, I reflect on the day. As I lie on my bed, staring out my window at the night sky, one last thought crosses my mind.

Maybe different isn't so bad after all.

Chapter 8

The next morning, I'm rudely awakened by the sound of my phone. I stayed up far too late trying to fix a bug in Matchmaker 3000's code, but after three hours, I finally gave up. I grab the phone off the nightstand, intending to send whoever it is to voicemail, but the name on the caller ID pulls me from the sleep still wrapped around my mind. I push myself up against the headboard, dragging a hand through my bedhead before answering the video call.

"James!"

"Good morn—" He moves closer to the screen and squints. "Did I wake you up?"

I shake my head. "No. I was just . . . relaxing in bed."

"Glad some things never change," he says with a dimpled grin. "Still a night owl, I see."

"And you're still annoying."

He laughs, the sound making my heart ache. I've missed it.

"I'm sorry I didn't call you sooner. I thought I would have time to get back into the routine after the holidays, but my professors jumped right in with work," he laments, jostling the camera as he sits down.

"I understand," I reply. "Mine did the same. It's been horrible."

"I'm sure it's nothing you can't handle."

"I don't know, James. There's a lot going on this year."

He listens patiently as I rehash everything that's happened so far this semester. When I finally take a breath, James leans forward and cups his chin in his hand.

"So are you going to enter the contest?"

"I might as well, right? I need to show Ms. Harris that I can do better than Quizlr. Plus I already wrote half the code for Matchmaker." I heave a sigh. "But as usual, Mom and Dad think I'm putting too much pressure on myself."

"What do *you* think?" he asks.

I groan, covering my face with my hands. "I don't know. Maybe a little? Everything is due in two weeks, and I have quizzes and tests coming up in other classes. Not to mention I have my art critique to do. Oh, and Anna's going to submit her app, so it's possible I'll do all this work and not get nominated."

James regards me quietly. If it were anyone else, the silence would be unbearable, but I know he prefers to think before speaking.

"But you still want to enter the contest," he states.

"Yes." I press my lips together tightly. "Am I being stupid?"

"Not if you're doing it for the right reasons."

"You mean beating Anna and rubbing it in her face isn't a good reason?" I ask with a grin.

He rolls his eyes. "Come on, Gigi. I know you better than that."

"You're right," I reply. "I'm the 'make myself so perfect you give up trying to compete' type."

"Wow. That sounds . . . perfectly exhausting."

I let out a groan. "You did not just say that."

"I did, and I'm not taking it back." James winks. "Now give me the real reason you want to enter the contest, or else I'm telling Mom you gave Mrs. Kwan her secret lemon Christmas cookie recipe."

"You wouldn't!"

"Wanna bet?"

"*Fine*. Let me think for a minute."

I adjust the pillow at my back, chewing a nail on my right hand. It's a habit Great-Aunt Rose would definitely tsk over, but what she doesn't know won't hurt her—or, more aptly, me.

"I guess . . . maybe I want to have something to fall back on? You know, in case matchmaking doesn't work out."

He frowns. "Are things not going well with Auntie Rose?"

"Actually, it's going great. She's letting me make a match for the first time."

"Then what is it?"

I rub my face. "Sometimes I wonder . . ."

"You wonder if you're doing all this for you or someone else?"

I stare at James through the screen. "How did you—"

"Because I've been there, remember?" he answers softly. "That fight I had with Dad right before I started college?"

I do remember, though it wasn't so much a fight as a cold-shoulder marathon. If anyone understands what it's like not to live up to someone's expectations, it's my brother. When he told Dad over the summer he was planning on staying undeclared for now instead of majoring in biotech, Dad didn't talk to him for three days.

"I've never seen Dad that upset before."

"It was tough," James admits, "but it's my life, and I have to live with my decisions. The same goes for you."

"It's not the same, though. I've wanted to be a matchmaker

since I was old enough to know what one was."

"That's not true," he tells me. "You used to say you wanted to be an animal trainer. Then it was a scuba instructor, a teacher . . . even a firefighter at one point. It wasn't until Mom talked to Auntie Rose about how you matched the groomsman and the bridesmaid at Uncle Charlie's wedding that the whole match-making thing came up."

Now that he's mentioned it, I do remember wanting to work with animals. Ultimately, I shrug it off.

"It doesn't matter anyway. I'm really good at matchmaking. Even Auntie Rose said so."

"And I can shove eight dumplings in my mouth at one time, but that doesn't mean I should be a competitive eater," he replies.

"Oh, for the love of—"

An arm appears on the screen, shoving James out of the way before his girlfriend, Liza, appears.

"Please ignore him. Also, hi."

I wave. "Hey, Liza."

Her straight black hair is pulled back into her usual ponytail, and she's wearing a navy-blue long-sleeve shirt with a white apron over it.

I squint at the silver panel behind her. "Are you guys baking?"

"Of course. It's Sunday," she answers. "Otherwise known as the second-busiest day at Yin and Yang."

Yin and Yang is her family's joint restaurant and bakery. They host a junior baking contest every summer, and that's where she and my brother met. Apparently, Liza was not very impressed with him at first, but James won't let her tell me the whole story. She must be special, though, because we Wongs are more known for chasing a ten-year plan than looking for love. I've already told James they're not allowed to break up, because she and I have invested too much time trading K-pop recommendations— Seventeen, The Boyz, and Enhypen from me and GOT7, Monsta X, and EXO from her.

Liza pans the phone to show me the pastries she just pulled out of the oven. Each is a beautiful golden-brown color, with black sesame seeds sprinkled on top.

"We're making red bean buns now."

"Oh, I can smell them from here," I say, my mouth watering. "I wish Mom still made them."

"Well, when I come up and visit Jeannie next time, I'll be sure to bake you some," Liza promises.

Jeannie is her older sister. She's a part-time model and psychology student at NYU. I haven't had a chance to meet her yet, but if she's anything like Liza, I'm sure to love her.

"Anyway," she says, pulling my attention back to her. "What your brother is trying *very poorly* to say is that even if you're good at something, it doesn't mean you have to make it your career. You should choose something you feel passionate about. Something that makes you excited, that gives you a purpose in life."

"But I have a purpose," I tell her slowly. "If I become a matchmaker, I'm helping to carry on my family's legacy. Besides, my dad needs my help taking care of my mom, so having a flexible schedule will be really important."

James reappears on the screen, tugging Liza against him and tucking his chin onto her shoulder.

"First of all, Mom is more than capable of taking care of herself. She was doing it long before you were born. And second, none of that sounded like *you* talking."

"Except it was me!"

James falls silent. I immediately regret raising my voice to him. Before I can apologize, Liza pipes up.

"If you really feel that way, then that's great. Why stress yourself out by entering the contest when you're so busy already?"

I open my mouth, but close it when no answer comes out. She offers a gentle smile.

"Look, I get that family legacies are a thing. My parents want me to take over the bakery one day, but being a good baker—"

"You mean the *best* baker," James interjects, nuzzling her hair.

Liza shoves him away half-heartedly. "Go bag those red bean buns while I talk to Gigi."

I suppress a laugh as James does something I never thought I'd see him do—pout. She points at the tray.

"They're not going to pack themselves."

She waits until he picks up a cellophane bag before turning back to me.

"Where were we? Oh, right. If I take over Yin and Yang in the future, it's going to be because I really want to, not because I feel obligated to."

I wish I could tell her that I'm not free to choose like her or James. No matter what he thinks, Mom does need someone to look after her. So does Dad, really.

Thankfully, I'm saved from replying when both of them turn toward someone who just walked into the kitchen. I can't make out what's being said, but Liza nods several times before turning back to me.

"Time for me to go before my mom kills me," she jokes. "It was really nice talking to you."

She hands the phone back to James, who walks the camera to a quieter corner of the room.

"I'm sorry. I didn't mean to lecture you."

I shake my head. "It's okay. I know you want the best for me."

"Well, I won't tell you what to do. You have enough people doing that already." He takes a deep breath and exhales. "All I'm asking is that you take time to listen to the voice inside of *you*. Do you really want all of this, or are you trying to make someone else happy?"

For hours after we hang up, I think about what he said. He's right, of course. There are so many voices in my head—Dad's, Mom's, Auntie Rose's, even Ms. Harris's. Every one is telling me how I should think, what I should do, talking over one another until I can't hear anything at all.

Maybe it is time to turn down the volume.

Maybe it's time for me to start talking.

Chapter 9

It's Monday, and I'm sitting in computer science, staring at the clock as Ms. Harris shows us the basic principles of quality assurance. Her mouth is moving, but all I hear is the roar of blood in my ears. My call with James and Liza made it clear to me that I want to enter the contest, but then cold, hard reality hit. What if Ms. Harris doesn't like Matchmaker 3000 any more than Quizlr? I don't have another idea, and I certainly don't have time to write another app.

"Okay, everyone," she concludes, tugging me out of my reverie. "Your homework is to come up with the questions you want your testers to answer when they perform quality assurance on your apps in two weeks. Have a good night."

I hang back and wait for the rest of the class to leave before approaching Ms. Harris. She's busy shutting off the projector and retracting the screen, so it isn't until she turns around that she notices me.

"Oh, Gigi!" she exclaims. "You scared me. I didn't realize you were standing there."

"Sorry, Ms. Harris. I thought you saw me."

She moves over to her desk, powering down her laptop. "What's up?"

"Um, well, I thought about what you said, and I have an idea for the contest."

"Wonderful. I'm excited to hear what you're going to do with Quizlr."

"Th-that's the thing," I stammer. "I decided not to use Quizlr. I have another app I think would be better to submit."

Ms. Harris sits down and crosses her legs. The motion draws my eyes to the rainbow-colored wedges she's wearing today. She smiles and turns her ankle to give me a better look at them.

"I found these on the clearance rack at Barneys. Don't you just love them?"

Personally, I would have left them on the rack, but I keep this to myself. What matters is Ms. Harris loves them.

"They look great on you."

She admires them for a second more. "Anyway, I'm excited to hear about this new app idea! Tell me more."

I give her a quick rundown on Matchmaker 3000, including how it works and the fact I've written the first half of the code. As I'm explaining everything, Ms. Harris's brows grow furrowed. By the time I stop talking, they are practically touching. I wait for what feels like an eternity before she speaks.

"What you've come up with is really clever, Gigi. It *is* a fresh take on a dating app."

Despite hearing this, my heart sinks. "There's a but, isn't there?"

"I'm afraid so," Ms. Harris replies. "Remember, your app should be working flawlessly when you enter the contest. Have you considered how to troubleshoot any issues before the deadline?"

I swallow a groan. No, I hadn't thought of that. Even if I can get the program finished in time, Auntie Rose will never let me test it out on her clients. Without user trials, there will be no way to know if Matchmaker 3000 works properly.

"Normally, I'd say you could test it during the quality assurance phase, but there're obvious problems with that," she continues gently.

Considering today's lecture on ethical testing in technology, it's not hard to guess what she's referring to. Using my classmates to troubleshoot a dating app for the purpose of winning a contest is all sorts of wrong.

"I'm sorry, Gigi. I truly love this idea," she tells me. "And under other circumstances, I would tell you to run with it. This time, though, I think you'd be better off revamping Quizlr."

The thought gives me a pounding headache. Not only am I back to square one, I don't have the slightest clue as to how to make Quizlr contest-worthy. Ms. Harris stands and walks over to me.

"There's still plenty of time, Gigi. I know you'll come up with something brilliant. In fact, knowing you, it'll be . . ."

Please don't say it. Please.

". . . perfect."

She smiles brightly, but it's not enough to lighten my mood. My frustration must be written on my face, because she puts a firm hand on my shoulder.

"Sometimes the best ideas come when you're not trying so hard to find them. Take a night or two off and relax. Clear your mind, and I'm sure you'll work it out."

"Thanks, Ms. Harris."

"Anytime. That's what I'm here for."

She turns to finish packing up her bag, while I drag myself out of the classroom and up the stairs to the second floor, where the *Worldly* crew is finalizing February's issue. I follow the voices to the room that serves as the magazine's office. As I walk in, Kyle is holding court at the circular table near the back of the room like an Arthur among authors.

He cocks an eyebrow at me. "About time you showed up. I thought you forgot about our meeting."

"Like you'd let me," I throw back. "But sorry I'm late."

Kyle pulls out the chair next to him, and I sink down into it. He gestures to the bags of chips and cookies on the table. I shake my head.

"Can we get started now?" Summer whines. "I have plans."

Melody rolls her eyes. "We all have things to do, Summer. You're not special."

"Don't compare your PJs-and-pizza night with my exclusive invitation to the soft opening of the hottest new restaurant in town," Summer snipes back.

That gets my attention. "Wait. Are you talking about Shibui?"

Everyone in the city has been talking about Shibui for months. Their cuisine is supposed to be a marriage between the latest trends in haute gastronomie. At least, that's how the press releases have described it. Outside of that, no one knows anything about the restaurant. They haven't even released the name of their head chef. The soft opening is next Saturday night. I would know, because Mom happens to be friends with Amelia, one of the co-owners. She's the one who got us on the guest list.

"That's exactly what I'm talking about," Summer confirms. "And unlike some people, I want to look my best. Which is why we need to stop chatting and start working so I can make my spa appointment."

"You're the one doing all the talking," Melody grumbles.

Summer scowls.

"Since our last meeting, I've put together the articles that will be going into the February issue," Kyle says, interrupting them both. "But we need to vote on which article will be the feature."

He pulls up the list in his email and projects it onto the wall. As I skim through the titles, most are articles I placed in Kyle's folder after reading them. One, however, takes me completely by surprise. I lean over to whisper in his ear.

"Why did you include Summer's article? It's the same one she wrote last year."

He keeps his eyes straight ahead. "We both know what would have happened if hers wasn't on the list. That's why I talked to her first."

"And she convinced you to reprint her article?"

"No," Kyle stresses. "I agreed to let her resubmit it with new material, and that's what she did."

I suspect there's more to the story than that. However, judging by the tightness in his jaw, I'll have to wait to get to the bottom of it.

"You know the other writers are going to be pissed if they find out you did that," I tell him in a low voice.

"They're not going to know unless *someone* tells them," he whispers back before addressing the room. "All right, everyone should've had enough time to review, so let's take a quick vote."

Kyle posts a numbered list of the same articles, and we text our top five choices in anonymously. He waits until everyone has submitted their answers before revealing the results on the screen. As I predicted, Anna's interview with her grandparents and Melody's article on the history of love potions are the most popular, so much so they are tied for first place.

"That can't be right. We should take another vote," Summer insists.

Kyle nods. "Agreed. I'm going to repost the poll for Melody's and Anna's articles. Everyone please send in your pick."

"I was talking about my—" Summer shuts her mouth when she's met with dirty looks. "Fine. Let's vote."

This time when we text, Anna's article comes out ahead by one vote.

"We have a winner," Kyle announces. "Congratulations, Anna. It's a fantastic article. I think our readers will love it."

He starts clapping. One by one, others join in, until the entire room is applauding.

"Thanks," Anna answers, looking slightly dazed.

"That's all we needed to discuss today, so unless someone has something they want to bring up . . ." Kyle glances around the room, but no one speaks up. "Okay, we're done. Have a good weekend, guys."

Summer is out the door before he finishes his sentence. The rest of the group trails out a few minutes later.

Anna stops Melody by the door. "I just wanted to say that I thought your article deserved to win."

"That's really nice of you," Melody replies. "But what you wrote? It made me cry. Hearing about how your grandparents risked their lives to . . ."

I'm not able to hear the rest of what's said as they walk out together, so I turn my attention to Kyle as he tosses the snacks into a plastic bag and packs his laptop into his backpack.

"Why are you looking at me like that?" he asks without turning his head.

I cross my arms over my chest. "Why did you really keep Summer's article?"

"I told you. She rewrote it like I asked."

"Yeah, but you've never made an exception like that before. So why her? Why now?"

His light brown eyes meet mine, and something awful occurs to me. I groan.

"No, Kyle. Please tell me that's not why."

"What are you talking about?"

"Don't tell me you have a crush on Summer."

"No!" he practically shouts. "That's not the reason."

"Then what is it?"

He heads toward the door without responding. Pressing my lips together, I follow him into the hallway.

"Kyle, talk to me."

He pretends not to hear me, walking down the corridor and out of the school in complete silence. As I'm getting ready to call him out, he spins to face me.

"I'll tell you, but this stays between me and you, okay?"

"I swear."

"I didn't make an exception for her. At least, not at first." He drags a hand through his wavy hair. "I told Summer we wouldn't reprint her piece. But the next morning, I got called in to Principal Gee's office. Summer and her parents were there."

"What? You're kidding me!"

Kyle shrugs. "Apparently, Mr. and Mrs. Benson are major donors to the school, and they threatened to pull their support if Summer's article wasn't printed. They even demanded it be made the feature, but thankfully Principal Gee put her foot down. In fact, she's the one who made Summer rewrite the article so it would be fair to the other students."

I nearly step onto the crosswalk while the signal is red. He catches me just in time.

"Watch out."

I smile gratefully, but my mind is racing. I knew Summer was competitive, but flexing her parents' money to get what she wants? That's low even for her. As usual, Kyle guesses exactly what I'm thinking, and he shakes his head.

"Let it go, G."

"How can I? That's cheating!" I scowl. "The other writers work hard to get their articles included, and she just shoves her way in."

"At least she didn't get the feature," he answers. "Anna deserves it. Her article was very well written."

There's a slight hush to his voice that irks me. With how busy I've been, it's been a couple months since I submitted an article. Even so, Kyle has never talked about my writing with that kind of admiration.

"Yes, I'm aware she's a super-talented writer. Probably the best."

"Why do you have to say it like that?" he asks with a chuckle.

I turn to look at him. "Like what?"

"Like it's killing you to admit it."

This time, I'm the quiet one. We're halfway home before Kyle bumps his shoulder against mine.

"You know, Anna may be a better writer, but that doesn't mean you're not a good one."

I give him major side-eye. "Thank you for pointing that out. I really needed that."

"I'm serious, G."

"So am I."

He sighs. "Gigi . . ."

"Can we please talk about something else?" I ask, barely managing to keep the edge out of my voice.

"Like what?"

"I don't know . . . like how we're going to set the February issue?"

We turn onto our street. Kyle looks at me. "It's pretty much set, and you know it. The only thing I have to do is pull Anna's article into feature position."

"Fine, then something else." I chew on the inside of my cheek. "Oh! Are you going to Shibui next weekend? Amelia must have sent your parents an invitation too."

He shakes his head. "I promised my mom I'd go with her to see *Hadestown*."

"I guess that's a reasonable excuse. I bet the food's going to be amazing, though."

"Then you'll have to go back with me," he suggests with a half smile.

"Hmm . . . I'll consider that a fair trade."

I reach up and give him a hug. He pulls me closer, giving me an extra squeeze before drawing back.

"Tell your mom I said hi," I tell him.

"Tell her yourself when you come over. You still owe me a *Witcher* marathon."

"I know, I know."

As is our usual custom, I wait for him to get to his house before unlocking my front door.

"By the way, if they have inago on the menu, you might want to skip it," he calls as I step inside.

It takes a second for his words to register, and I poke my head back out into the cold.

"Kyle, wait!"

His head pops out from his own door. "What?"

"Why should I skip the inago?"

Silence. Did he hear me? As I prepare to repeat myself, a smile spreads across his lips. My eyes narrow.

"Kyle. Why should I skip it?"

Even from a distance, I can see the wicked sparkle in his eyes. He winks, and then ducks back into his house.

"Kyle!"

Chapter 10

Two days later, I'm walking home alone. Kyle plans to stay after school the rest of the week because the file for the February *Worldly* issue was somehow corrupted. After spending the past hour troubleshooting it with him, I suspect one of the emails he opened must have had a virus. No matter the reason, he's resetting the entire issue so we don't miss our deadline.

I move quickly, keeping my coat zipped high and my eyes on the ground. Nonetheless, with the amount of rush hour traffic and people on the sidewalk, it's nearly a half hour before I make it home. I walk up the front steps and am inserting my key into the lock when my phone pings. It's Mom reminding me she and Dad will be late because they accepted a last-minute invite to a fundraiser.

"Hi, Gigi!"

"Etta!"

She jogs the rest of the way to me. With how busy I've been, and Etta walking to her classes on her own, we haven't met up since Saturday. In fact, the closest I've gotten to seeing her in the clothes we picked out has been the pictures she's texted me every morning. Come to think of it, I should really talk her into posting OOTDs on her Instagram.

Despite our best efforts, however, Etta's reluctantly admitted she's still struggling to make friends. New look or not, no one is willing to give her the time of day. That's why I invited her to the house during lunch today, even if it means possibly getting into trouble for having someone over while Mom and Dad are out.

"Did it take you a while to get here from home?" I ask.

Etta walks through the wrought iron gate and shuts it carefully behind her. She then points at the subway station entry at the end of the block.

"Not long at all. I only got off the train a few minutes ago. You were steps ahead of me when I came out onto the street."

"Come inside, then, before we both freeze to death."

I unlock the door and send her in ahead of me before disarming the alarm. When I turn to face Etta, she's standing in the middle of the foyer with her mouth hanging wide open.

"You *live* here?"

"Yeah, this is my house."

"It's so beautiful." She walks over to the spiral staircase and looks up. "How many floors are there?"

"Six, if you count the basement."

I sit down on the shoe bench and tug off my boots before gesturing for her to come over.

"Here. Take off your shoes and I'll show you around."

With our coats hung in the closet, I walk her through the house, starting from the basement. Etta *oohs* and *aahs* at everything like she's at Disney World. At one point, she even asks to take pictures of my walk-in closet.

"Everything is so nice here," she says once we're settled in my bedroom. "I'm afraid to touch anything."

I pat the mattress next to me. "Don't be silly. It's a house, not a museum."

She plops onto the bed with a giggle, throwing herself onto her back with a loud moan.

"Your bed . . . it's like lying on a cloud! If mine felt like this, I'd never get out of it."

"It's a sacrifice for sure," I answer with a grin. "But we're not here to sleep. What do you want to eat?"

She shrugs. "I don't know. What's good around here?"

"There's pretty much everything you can think of around here. Plus, we can get delivery too."

We spend the next twenty minutes debating what to order for dinner. When we finally have it narrowed down, the doorbell chimes.

Etta looks at me. "Are you expecting someone else?"

"No," I answer, frowning. "Hold on. I'll check the security camera."

I pull up the home security app on my phone, and the person I see on the screen brings a smile to my face.

"Stay here. I'll be right back," I tell Etta.

Less than a minute later, I'm sliding across the marble tile of the foyer in my socked feet. I grab the handle and open the door.

"What are you doing here?" I ask, though I step aside so he can enter the house.

Kyle raises his eyebrows. "Is that any way to talk to your best friend?"

"It is when you show up unannounced," I reply, shoving him lightly on the chest. "Usually that means you want something from me."

"In that case"—he pulls an insulated bag from behind his back—"I'll find someone else to share this ramen with."

I gasp. "Is that Ippudo?"

"Do you have to ask?"

Kyle barely has enough time to slip off his shoes before I drag him into the kitchen. He puts the bag on the table and perches himself on one of the kitchen island stools.

"How did you know to bring food?" I ask over my shoulder.

"Magic." He laughs at the glare I shoot him. "Fine. My parents are at the same fundraiser yours are, so I knew you'd be home alone tonight."

"Who said I was alone?"

Kyle smirks and pulls his phone out of his pocket.

"In that case, we should order more food. How many bowls of ramen do we need?"

"One more."

He nearly drops his phone. "Are you serious? There's really someone here?"

"Yep. They're upstairs in my bedroom," I tell him, biting back a laugh. "I'll go get them."

"G, wait!"

I leave him sputtering downstairs as I climb the steps two at a time, careful to hold on to the railing. The last thing I need is for Dad to come home and find me with two broken legs. Etta's sitting on the bed when I burst into the room.

"Is everything okay?" she asks.

"It's great, actually. Follow me."

When she doesn't get up, I reach out and tug her to her feet. As soon as we're all in the kitchen, I start the introductions.

"Kyle, this is Etta Santos. Etta, this is my best friend, Kyle Miller."

It's hard to say whose reaction is more entertaining. Kyle's features morph from confusion to relief to curiosity. Etta, on the other hand, stands there with her mouth slightly agape.

"Um, hi, Etta," Kyle says, recovering first. "It's nice to meet you."

Etta makes a strange sound. I touch her on the shoulder.

"Etta, are you okay?"

She still doesn't speak, but nods. I glance at Kyle. He shrugs. Picking up the closest bowl of ramen, I open the lid and wave it under Etta's nose. Her stomach growls loudly in response, and it snaps her out of whatever trance Kyle put her in.

She hums. "Oh, that smells so good. Is it ramen?"

"Mmmhmm, from Ippudo," I tell her. "Kyle can order another bowl if you'd like some."

"Yes, please," she replies before I've gotten all the words out. "Erm, if it's not too much trouble."

"Of course not," Kyle answers warmly. "Do you want anything else? They have some good appetizers."

Apparently, the sight of his pearly whites is enough to render Etta speechless a second time. So I take matters into my own hands.

"Why don't we go ahead and grab a couple orders of the Ippudo buns while we're at it?"

Kyle quickly adds the items. "What kind of ramen?"

I spin Etta to face me. "Do you like your ramen spicy?"

"Um . . . yes?"

"Karaka," Kyle and I utter at the same time.

"I'll order another Shiromaru and Akamaru so they'll all arrive hot," he says. "We can split the ones I brought in the meantime."

Once our order is in, he carries everything to the dining table while I grab us bowls and chopsticks. Etta blushes when Kyle pulls out her chair for her. She sinks into it mumbling her thanks.

I place a bowl and a pair of chopsticks in front of her as Kyle pulls a chair for me as well.

"Thanks."

"You're welcome," he says, settling into his own seat.

He opens the containers of broth, as well as the one with the noodles and dry ingredients, then pours the first into the second before mixing everything carefully. With that done, he looks at the two of us.

"Meshiagare!"

♡

"Your great-aunt is a professional matchmaker?"

After finishing both rounds of ramen, the three of us grabbed our drinks and headed up to the third floor to hang out in the living room. Once Etta discovered it was Kyle who introduced me to *Attack on Titan*, they had a full-blown discussion about the controversial twists in its final season. I tuned out five minutes into it, unable to follow the many names and plot lines.

At one point, I excused myself to go to the bathroom, but took a detour up to my room to sneak in some work on Matchmaker 3000. Though it couldn't be my entry for the app contest, I had Miss Wu's matches to find. I was so immersed in the work that I forgot to head back, freezing at my computer when Kyle caught me in midcode.

"What are you doing in here?"

I shut my laptop. "I was . . . checking my email . . . for one of my classes."

"No, you're not," he contradicted. "You can do that on your phone. You're coding, aren't you?"

I attempted to keep a straight face, but he saw through it immediately. Grabbing me by the hand, Kyle dragged me back to the living room. We tossed around a few conversation topics before my apprenticeship with Auntie Rose came up.

"She is, and she's one of the best," I now say to Etta, who is seated on the armchair to my right. "It's something the women in my family have done for generations."

"Wow," she breathes. "Does that mean you're going to be a matchmaker too?"

"Maybe one day. I've been training every Saturday at the shop. It's why we ran into each other at Kam Hing that day," I tell her. "We were on a break between clients."

"That sounds like such a cool job," she asserts. "Helping people fall in love and all."

"It's not about love, it's about compatibility," Kyle replies, in a scarily accurate impression of Great-Aunt Rose from across the couch. "I don't get paid for romance. I get paid for marriage."

I reach out and slap him playfully on the arm. "Watch your mouth, Kyle Miller. That's my family you're making fun of."

He rolls his eyes. "Like you weren't doing it the other day."

"Totally not the same thing. I was trying to say something the way she did so you could understand the context," I defend.

"Tomato, *tomahto.*"

"Are you guys always like this?" Etta interrupts, glancing between us.

Kyle and I look at each other and burst into laughter.

"Pretty much," I manage between giggles.

"I don't think we can go more than a few minutes without arguing about something," he agrees. "Though it's never over anything serious."

"I wish I had a friend like that," she says softly.

It's not Etta's intention to dampen the mood, but her words turn the room somber. Kyle takes a long swig of his iced tea while I play with the condensation on the outside of my glass.

"So how does your great-aunt match people?" Etta asks, clearly trying to get the conversation back on track.

"Well, she collects biodata on new clients and compares their information to potential matches in her database," I reply. "It's kinda complicated."

"Didn't you say the biodata is just stuff like height and weight, though?" Kyle asks.

"It's more than that. It also includes the answers her clients give to her questionnaire." I twirl a strand of hair around my index finger. "You should see this thing. It's huge."

"Come on, it can't be *that* bad," he insists.

"Oh yeah? I'll be right back."

I pop off the couch and run upstairs at a speed that would give Dad a heart attack. Once back in the living room, I pull the printed questionnaire out of my bag and hand it to Kyle. His jaw swings open.

"Are you kidding me? This isn't a questionnaire. It's a weapon."

I squeal as he pretends to swing it at me. "Stop it! The last thing I need is a concussion."

"I can't believe you don't trust me," he says as he places it gently on the coffee table. "We've been friends our entire lives. I'd at least give you a heads-up. Get it? Heads-up?"

I groan and reach for the thick pile of paper. "Maybe I should give you a concussion instead."

He makes a grab for it first, skimming over the contents as curiosity gives way to disbelief. Eventually, he hands it over to Etta.

"She makes all her clients fill this out?" he asks me.

I nod. "She says it helps her understand them better, which helps her figure out who is most compatible with them."

"Well, sure . . . because the only questions missing are their blood type and if they're an organ donor," he quips.

"Oh, that's on page twelve."

Etta flips to the page in question. She stiffens slightly as Kyle leans closer, though I doubt he noticed.

Interesting.

"Wait, I don't see where—" He makes a disgusted sound. "I should've known you were lying."

I giggle. "Okay, but honestly, I wouldn't put it past Auntie to ask. I'm convinced that doorstop is the reason she books the most clients of all the Chinese matchmakers in the country. People fly in from other states to see her. A few even travel from Canada."

Kyle moves away from Etta, leaning back against the couch. She sways unconsciously toward him before straightening in her chair.

"It sound like she uses basic statistics. The more answers two people share, the higher probability they will be a good match," he quips.

"That's what I thought," I answer, turning my attention back to him, "but apparently she chooses different points to focus on every time she matches someone new. She insists that's why dating apps won't ever be as good as a real matchmaker."

Kyle doesn't look convinced, but shrugs. "If you say so."

"My mom always says friends make the best lovers," Etta interrupts.

She turns to Kyle as she says this. He freezes in the midst of reaching for his drink, and she turns eight shades of red. I choke back my laughter and come to her rescue.

"That makes sense. Our friends are usually people we have a lot in common with. That automatically makes you more compatible."

Etta shoots me a grateful look. A moment later, the alarm on her phone goes off. After checking it, she gasps.

"I didn't realize how late it was! I need to go, or else I'll miss the last train home."

I stand. "I'll walk you out."

"It was really nice meeting you, Etta," Kyle says, rising to his feet.

He extends his hand and she gives it a shake, her fingers disappearing in his grasp. I nearly have to carry her to the door after that. As she puts on her shoes, I retrieve her coat.

"He's so hot," she whispers, as if he can hear us from upstairs. "I don't know how you can be so calm around him."

"To be honest, I've never thought about him that way."

"Maybe you should. You two would make a cute couple."

I stare at her, my arm outstretched, her jacket clutched in my hand. An odd twinge appears in my chest as Etta claps a hand over her mouth.

"I'm sorry, Gigi. I shouldn't have said anything. You probably already have a boyfriend. I mean, how could you not? You're so pretty and popular. I bet all the guys want to date you." She winces. "I'm always doing this, blurting things out without thinking. Lola says it's going to get me into trouble one day, and I—"

"Etta, stop. It's fine." I shake off the strange sensation. "You surprised me, that's all."

For the next few seconds, the only sound in the room comes from Etta's zipper as it makes its way up to her neck.

"And no, I don't have a boyfriend. I have so much going on in my life as it is," I feel compelled to explain. "But maybe, one day, someone really amazing will come along and I'll change my mind. Until then, I'll stick to my K-pop boys."

Etta gapes at me. "Wait a minute. You listen to K-pop?"

"Who doesn't?" I joke. "But let's talk about that another day. You've got to get home, remember?"

I bundle into my warmest coat before turning to her. She grins, though no sparkle appears in her brown eyes.

"Let me know if your great-aunt decides to launch a friend matchmaking service. Especially if the friends look like Kyle. Sign me up!"

I tug her into a hug. "It's going to happen, Etta. I promise. We'll figure it out together."

We step out of my house, and I walk her to the end of my block.

"Text me to let me know you made it home safe, okay?" I instruct.

She nods, and I watch her disappear down to the subway. Then I head back to the house.

"Etta seems sweet," Kyle comments as soon as I sit back on the couch.

"You got that from the ten words she spoke to you?" I tease.

"She's just shy."

"Only if you're a hot guy, apparently."

Kyle smirks. "Gigi Wong, are you calling me hot?"

"Full of hot air, maybe," I retort. "It would explain that giant head of yours."

"Ha ha."

I grab my glass and drink some of my iced tea. For a few minutes, we sit together in silence, each wrapped up in our own thoughts. Then something abruptly comes to my mind.

"How are things going with Vivien, by the way? You haven't talked about her in a while."

"That's because there's nothing to talk about. We broke up three weeks ago," Kyle answers.

"What?! Already?" I sit up. "What happened? You two were so cute together."

He glances at his hands. "I don't know. We didn't . . . vibe."

I'm about to offer a few comforting words, but swallow them when I see his face. I expect to see sadness, maybe anger, but he's merely . . . relieved. Then again, none of Kyle's relationships ever last more than a few weeks because he inevitably finds something wrong with them. He's the kind of client even Auntie Rose would dread.

"I'm not surprised, to tell you the truth," I comment offhandedly. "You're an Aquarius, and she's a Scorpio. You were doomed from the start."

He rolls his eyes. "I don't know what that's supposed to mean, but you know I don't believe in that zodiac BS."

"You should. It tells you a lot about a person," I insist. "You'd be surprised how accurate it is."

"Okay, fine. Tell me. Who am I compatible with?"

"Anyone who is a Gemini, Libra, or Sagittarius," I quickly list off.

Kyle eyes me. "What's your sign?"

"I'm a Libra."

Kyle's glass stops halfway to his lips. He's staring at me like I've grown horns.

"Don't look so shocked," I say, grinning. "Those signs also make the best friends. That's why we get along so well."

"Oh, right. Of course." He takes such a large swig of tea some of it dribbles down his cream-colored sweater. "Crap."

I pop off the sofa. "Don't move. I'll get you something to wipe it with."

I grab a hand towel out of the guest bath and wet it with the club soda in the fridge before bringing it to Kyle.

"Thanks."

I consider him for a few minutes while he dabs at the stain. I clear my throat.

"You know, I could . . ."

"No."

My mouth falls open. "You don't even know what I'm going to say!"

"No, I don't want you to set me up," he states firmly.

"How did you guess?"

"Because you ask me that every time I break up with someone," he says as he puts the towel on the coffee table. "I don't need your help, G. I can find someone on my own."

"Yes, because you're *so* good at it."

I regret my words the minute they pass through my lips. Kyle tugs at his ear, his lips pressed together in a tight line. I reach out and lightly touch the back of his hand.

"I'm sorry. I shouldn't have said that, but I don't understand why you won't let me do this for you. I want you to be happy."

"And I *am* happy," he stresses, touching our fingers together briefly before pulling away. "Plus, who needs a girlfriend when I have you?"

Silence echoes through the room. I stare at him. Kyle laughs awkwardly.

"You know . . . because you already boss me around and tell me what I'm doing wrong all the time. That's what I mean. Since I'm older than you."

There's something unfamiliar in his voice, but I choose not to dwell on it. Kyle and I have always been honest with each other. If he had something more to say, he would.

I crack a smile. "First of all, you're only ten months older than me. And second of all, I know a lot more than you think. You should listen to me more."

"You mean like the time you dragged me to try chapulines because you thought that was some sort of Mexican pasta?"

I shudder at the memory. "I'll never forget seeing those little legs on my tacos."

"And I'll never forget how you were threatening to call the health department until I explained that chapulines were fried grasshoppers."

"It was an honest mistake! One I no longer make."

He chuckles. "Yeah, because now you google everything on a menu before ordering."

"But seriously, I haven't ever given you bad advice, especially when it comes to anything important."

"I don't know about that," he says with a half smirk.

I narrow my eyes, waiting to dispute whatever example he comes up with next. In the end, though, his mouth opens and closes without ever uttering a word.

"I knew it!" I exclaim. "You can't think of another example because there is none."

"That's not true. I'm still thinking."

I cock an eyebrow. "How about you think your way into an apology instead?"

"Like that's going to happen."

I throw a pillow at him. He catches it and tosses it back at me. It hits me square in the head.

"I'm so sorry, G," he apologizes. "I thought—"

I cut him off with a cushion to the face. "Oops."

He reaches behind him for another pillow as I prepare to make a run for it. However, our fight ends as quick as it began when Dad's voice reaches our ears.

"Gigi? Where are you?"

"I'm up here," I call down.

A few minutes later, Mom comes around the staircase banister. She's wearing her favorite black Gucci velvet-trimmed wool coat, though the buttons have been undone to reveal a sliver of burgundy from her evening gown. When she spots us, she breaks into a bright smile.

"Kyle! What a pleasant surprise."

He stands and hugs her. "It's nice to see you, Mrs. Wong."

"Kyle brought over some ramen from Ippudo," I explain.

"Thank you for doing that," Dad adds as he joins us in the living room, tugging at his tie to loosen it. "And for keeping Gigi company while we were gone."

Under normal circumstances, he would be furious to find a stranger in the house, much less a boy, but this is Kyle. He's the only guy outside of James he knows I'm safe with. I silently thank the universe for sending Etta home first, since that wouldn't have gone over as well.

"No problem, Mr. Wong. I was stuck at home by myself anyway," Kyle answers after shaking Dad's hand.

"So you decided to annoy me instead?" I tease. "Thanks a lot."

"Don't get it twisted," he retorts. "I made your night way less boring and you know it."

"Whatever."

"Okay, I'm glad you two had fun," Mom interrupts smoothly. "But you should probably head home before the storm gets any worse, Kyle. The temperature has already dropped quite a bit."

He nods. "Thank you for letting me know, Mrs. Wong. Have a good night."

"I'll walk you out," I offer.

Mom and Dad head upstairs while Kyle and I make for the door. He takes his coat out of the front closet and slips into it before putting on his shoes. I reach up and throw my arms around his neck.

"Thanks for dinner."

"You're welcome," he says into my ear as he gives me a squeeze. "As long as you swear not to hit me with another pillow."

"I make no such promises."

Kyle laughs as I pull back, but he doesn't let me go. His expression turns serious.

"You know I'm here for you, right?"

"Yeah, of course," I reply slowly.

"I mean anytime. You only have to ask."

I raise an eyebrow. "Why are you being weird right now?"

"I'm not trying to be—" He stops and starts over. "Look, James has been in college for a while now, and you've mentioned that he's been super busy lately. I know I'm not your brother—"

"*Obviously.*"

He gives me a stern look before continuing. "But you know you can talk to me, right?"

It's times like these that I'm grateful for Kyle's uncanny ability to sense when something's bothering me. I thread my arms back around his waist, and his come up to envelop me.

"Thank you," I murmur against his jacket. "Seriously."

He nods against the top of my head before releasing me. I unlock the front door, and a blast of cold air greets us both. With a parting smile, he launches himself out the door and into the night.

Chapter 11

By the time Friday rolls around, I'm no closer to an idea for Quizlr than before. Instead, I'm watching Mr. Sanchez go over the Krebs cycle for the third time in biology. We recently had a test on the subject, and over half the class failed. Needless to say, Mr. Sanchez dropped to dead last on the school's unofficial teacher ranking list the minute the grades came out. I had to stop reading the comments in the thread because they were becoming vicious.

It's tough enough attending an elite preparatory like Superbia, but the competition to rank at the top of the class recently caused a cheating scandal that nearly made it into the local news. I don't know the exact details, but someone was caught sneaking snaps of their test questions to other students. Ever since then, all our teachers have been super careful during test periods, confiscating any technology and walking around the room.

I was one of the lucky few to escape the Krebs curse, having spent hours drawing and redrawing the steps for three days straight to make sure I remembered it correctly. Even so, I was convinced I was in that failing 50 percent until I saw the A on my paper. With my GPA safe for the time being, I'm currently staring at my laptop, pretending to take notes on how ATP is produced along with the rest of my classmates.

Keeping one eye on Mr. Sanchez, I open the IDE—integrated development environment—and load the app. Despite Ms. Harris's suggestion that I take a break for a few days, I can't resist chipping away at the boulder-size block in my brain. As my eyes skim the lines of code I haven't looked at since winter break, my mind suddenly flashes to something Etta said.

I wish there were an easier way to meet friends.

I've never had trouble with making friends. Mom says people are drawn to me because I have warm energy, whatever that means. Dad thinks I'm good at reading others and knowing what to say. Either way, it's hard for me to understand what Etta's going through.

I know not everyone's going to like me, but people could at least give me a chance.

There's got to be another way to help her . . . but how? Superbia might have been the first New York City prep school to announce a diversity initiative in their admissions, but it's money that decides who you sit with at the lunch table. As much as I hate to admit it, I've heard more than one person snidely ask why the help was in their class.

As my brain tries to untangle the mess of thoughts in my head, I flip from one program window to the other. Back and forth, back and forth, until the lines of code start blurring together.

. . . if your great-aunt decides to launch a friend matchmaking service . . .

I gasp. Mr. Sanchez freezes in midsentence, turning to me with a questioning stare.

"I'm sorry. I . . . had something in my throat," I manage to say.

I'm not sure if he believes me, but he resumes his lecture. I let out a breath and return my attention to my laptop with a pounding heart.

I'm going to turn Quizlr into a friend matching app!

I can't believe I didn't think of it before. All I have to do is convert Auntie Rose's behemoth of a questionnaire into smaller, fun quizzes that users can take. Once someone finishes the quizzes, the app will collect the answers into a database like the one I created for her clients. From there, it's a matter of commanding the computer to match people based on the highest percentage of compatibility.

Oh, but wait.

There's a problem.

Matching potential friends is only half the solution. Unlike Auntie Rose's clients, I can't set up people on playdates. I have to come up with something else if I want to show Ms. Harris—and the judges—that my app works.

So much for that bright idea.

I absentmindedly click the add-on section in the open-source framework I built Quizlr on. The first few are superficial features like skins and font options, but I straighten in my seat when I spot something I hadn't noticed before.

There's a chat add-on.

I pull up a browser window and search for more information. After a few minutes, I discover the chat doesn't allow for GIFs, video, or manipulation of the font using third-party apps, but it does allow for emojis and basic text. A slow smile spreads across my face as a new, even better idea forms in my head. I switch back to the IDE and scroll to the bottom. I add a call to the chat API, essentially turning it on for Quizlr.

Leaning back in my chair, I skim over the new section of code. It's not much, but it's a solid start.

Actually, it's brilliant.

It's foolproof.

It's going to win me that contest.

♡

"G, wait up!"

I force myself to slow down. The minute the bell rings at the end of the school day, I practically run out of the classroom. I'm so absorbed in my plans for Quizlr that I fly past Kyle, who is waiting to walk me home as usual.

"Where are you going?" he asks when he catches up. "What's the rush?"

"Sorry, I want to get home so I can put some code down," I explain. "I figured out what I'm going to do for the contest."

Kyle frowns. "I thought you were going to submit that matchmaking app."

"I can't. I mean, I am . . . kind of. It's technically not Matchmaker, but it'll use the same algorithms to do the matching. There's still a lot of code I have to write, so I need to get started right away."

"I haven't learned how to read minds yet, G."

I glance over at him. "Sorry. I talked with Ms. Harris about Matchmaker, but she reminded me that I would have trouble testing it in time for the contest. She suggested I modify Quizlr instead, and I finally figured out how to do it."

"By turning it into Matchmaker," he deadpans.

"By adding a matching *function*," I clarify firmly. "I'm going to turn Quizlr into an app for making new friends."

He stares at me for a long moment.

"A social media app," he comments slowly. "Don't we have enough of those already?"

Whatever reaction I expected to get from Kyle, it's not this. I roll my eyes and pick up the pace. A few steps later, I feel his fingers around my wrist, and he tugs on it gently until I stop and face him.

"I'm sorry. That didn't come out right," he says. "I just wasn't expecting you to say what you did."

He sticks out his lower lip and gives me his best puppy eyes. It's surprisingly effective for a guy with shoulders broader than half the swim team. Kyle tenses as I slide my hand up his forearm, but relaxes as I hook it around his elbow.

"It might not be the next Twitter or Instagram," I acknowledge as we start walking again, "but mine will be something no one has ever seen before."

"In what way?"

"Well, instead of people following others randomly, or only following their friends, my new app is going to connect users to each other based on compatibility."

We continue on the sidewalk off Lexington, weaving our way between pedestrians while rush hour traffic inches forward on the street beside us. Once we've settled on a pace that's comfortable for us both, he glances down at me.

"Wait. Will you be using your great-aunt's questionnaire?" He frowns when I nod. "But that's for matchmaking."

"That's what I thought at first. But the truth is, a lot of what she asks about can apply to any kind of relationship. Questions like interests, hobbies, personalities . . . if I take those and turn them into quizzes, in theory, anyone whose answers match are compatible as friends. So why not use it to connect people who otherwise might not talk to each other?"

We come to a red light and stop to wait. Kyle scrunches his nose in thought.

"Okay . . . I can go with this, but if your app only takes people's quiz answers and matches them, how will that make them friends?"

I grin. "I was getting to that. Turns out there's a chat function add-on in the framework I built Quizlr on. I can set it up so people can message each other."

"If you do that, won't anyone who uses the app be able to message?"

"I'm going to set it up so the app controls who gets to be in the same chat rooms. The users won't be able to access a specific chat without an invitation that you'll only get if the app finds you compatible."

Kyle's brows furrow. "But what if people want to chat with their friends, and your app doesn't deem them compatible?"

"That's what text messages are for," I remind him. "This app is for people who want to make *new* friends. Not make friends based on what you look like, what you have, or where you're from, but on true compatibility."

We make it a whole block before he speaks again.

"Why do I get the feeling there's a reason you're doing all this?"

"I am. For the contest."

"Gigi, that's not what I mean and you know it. Spit it out. Why are you *really* doing this?"

To give Etta a chance to find friends.

I'm tempted to keep that to myself, but in the end, I tell him the truth.

"Remember the girl you met at my house Wednesday night? The new merit scholarship student?"

Kyle nods slowly. "Yeah, Etta."

"I got the idea from something she told me. She's had a really tough time making friends at Superbia." I sigh. "I know I can't expect everyone to love Etta, but I'm honestly surprised at the way people have been treating her."

"I know you want to see the best in everyone, G, but a lot of the students at Superbia are clout chasers," Kyle states without hesitation. "They don't want friends. They want fans."

"But *we're* not like that. We're nice," I protest. "And people are nice to us. Why should it be any different for Etta?"

A tiny voice pops into my mind. *You know why.*

But she's fun, and sweet, and . . .

She's also loud, too direct, and doesn't know when to stop talking. The voice continues. *She dresses like she shops in her mom's closet. Oh, and she's . . .*

"Shut up."

Kyle rears back. "I didn't say anything."

"Sorry. That wasn't meant for you. I was talking to myself."

"You were telling yourself to shut up?"

"Yes. I mean, no. Well, sort of. I was thinking something and I didn't like what it was, so I told . . ." His barely veiled amusement stops me. "Never mind."

Good lord, is rambling infectious? Maybe *I* should stop hanging out with Etta for a bit.

My heart drops into my stomach. What am I saying? I sound exactly like the people I was judging a moment ago.

My thoughts evaporate when Kyle leans down, his eyes zeroing in on the jewelry around my neck. An unfamiliar expression flits across his features as he touches the locket I put on this morning.

"Is this new? You don't usually wear jewelry."

"Not exactly," I squeak before clearing my throat. "My āmà gave it to me last year on my birthday. I thought it went with my outfit."

The lines around his mouth relax. "Oh . . . that's nice. And it does. Go with your outfit, that is."

I exhale as he straightens and rubs the back of his neck. Not wanting to dwell on the strange moment, I continue down the sidewalk. He falls in line with me after a few steps, until we pause outside the gate to my house. Kyle opens his mouth as if to speak, but I spy Dara getting out of a car. She's our family's personal chef. Mom usually calls her if we're having dinner guests or hosting a party. As she starts unloading a cooler from her trunk, the front door opens and Mom steps out.

"Dara, can you please—" She stops in her tracks when she sees me. "Gigi! You're just in time! You won't believe who's coming to dinner."

"I guess that means I should go," Kyle says. "Hi, Mrs. Wong! Bye, Mrs. Wong!"

"Oh goodness, Kyle. I didn't mean to be rude," Mom replies. "Please say hi to your parents for me."

"Will do."

He winks at me before heading up the street. I turn and walk into the house, stepping around Mom as she descends the steps to talk to Dara. I push the door mostly closed to keep the wintry air out before dropping my school bag in my bedroom.

"So who's coming to dinner?" I ask once I join Mom in the kitchen.

She holds up a hand. "Hold on, bǎobǎo. I need to go over the menu with Dara."

I sit on a stool next to the island and wait for her to finish. Eventually, she comes back to me and presses a kiss to my cheek.

"How was your day?"

"It was fine. Who's coming to dinner?"

She beams. "The Kwans! You remember them, right?"

I nod. "I didn't know they were back from Singapore."

The Kwans have been friends with my parents for almost as long as they've known each other. Mr. Kwan met Dad in college after joining the same Chinese student organization. Dad was supposedly a big gamer back then, and after a friendly round of *StarCraft*—which turned into three because neither would let the other win—they became fast friends. In fact, it was Mom who introduced Mr. Kwan to his wife a couple of years later. She was a regular at the bakery and would pick up pastries for her co-workers every morning.

The Kwans moved to California for a while after they got married, but came back to New York when Mr. Kwan sold his tech start-up seven years ago. I guess he got restless, since he moved the entire family to Singapore after he was offered the job of CFO of an up-and-coming tech company there. The Kwans have been living there for the past three years.

"They just got back a week ago and have been trying to settle in," Mom tells me. "But Susan reached out to see if I was free to catch up, so I invited them over for dinner. I'm pretty sure Joey's coming too."

Joey is the Kwan's only son. I met both him and Kyle through our families, but that's where the similarities end. Kyle couldn't walk down a hall at Superbia without girls trailing behind him because he was tall, athletic, and handsome. Meanwhile, Joey couldn't because he saw barely five feet in front of his face without thick glasses. He always looked like he'd just rolled out of bed, and he had a mouth full of metal. Besides that, he never quite lost his baby fat, and was so shy he either blurted out the first thing on his mind or said nothing at all. Anna and I were probably the only girls he had the courage to talk to, and only because we were in the same honors classes before he moved.

I wonder if Anna stayed friends with Joey after we . . .

"They should be here in about a half hour," Mom continues, interrupting my thoughts.

Damn it. That doesn't leave me much time to get started rewriting Quizlr. I was really hoping to spend tonight doing that, but Mom will undoubtedly expect me to entertain Joey.

"Okay. Well, I'm going to go upstairs and get some homework done, then," I tell her. "Let me know when they get here?"

"Sure, bǎobǎo."

I leave her in the kitchen with Dara and go up to my room. Once my laptop has powered on, I enter my password and open the editor. After a quick stretch, I put fingers to keyboard and start typing.

Chapter 12

It's been nearly an hour since the Kwans arrived for dinner, and I remain speechless. We're sitting around the rectangular mahogany table in our formal dining room on the second floor. Dara's mouthwatering spread of sweet chili and soy beef tenderloin, garlic mashed spring potatoes, caramelized carrots, and long-grain rice has filled our stomachs, but that's not why I'm finding it hard to come up with words.

It's Joey.

He's so . . . different.

The Joey I last saw three years ago preferred staring at the floor or his phone to making eye contact. Though we were friends, the truth was we rarely spent any time together unless Anna was with us. The two of them had known each other longer and spent a lot of time together, while he and I mostly bonded over what TV shows we both liked watching, or the places we would visit on vacation. A part of me wondered if this is the reason they stayed friends while she and I fell apart.

At any rate, that's why the guy sitting in front of me has shocked me into silence. I was convinced the Kwans were playing a joke on me. At six foot one, Joey was the tallest one in the room when he walked into the house, easily towering over me. His unruly locks had been tamed into sleek black strands, and those old hamster cheeks? His cheekbones could cut glass now. The pimples that used to cover his forehead and whole face had been replaced by smooth golden skin. When he greeted me with a smile, I was nearly blinded by the whitest, straightest teeth I've ever seen.

Whatever they put in the water in Singapore—they need to bottle it.

It's not only his appearance, either. Joey came back to New York with a whole new personality. He's grinned more in the last sixty minutes than I ever saw him do in the entire four years we knew each other before his family's big move. I'm the one who glances away now if our eyes meet. Even the way he sits, slightly slouched, but with one arm on his mom's chair, screams confidence.

Joey looks across the table and smiles. "Do I have something in my teeth?"

"Oh, no. I was . . . thinking," I manage to say.

"About me, hopefully."

For a moment, all I can do is gawk at him. How is this the same boy who used to blink both eyes when trying to wink? As if reading my thoughts, Joey executes a wink worthy of the flirting hall of fame.

"Actually, I was thinking about the app I'm working on," I lie. "It's for school, but I'll be submitting it for a programming contest too."

The old Joey reappears. His brown eyes light up like they used to when we would talk about our favorite Avenger.

"Oh really? What does it do?"

"It's a new type of social media app. Nothing like Facebook or

Twitter, but with similar features," I explain. "Basically, it allows you to take pop culture quizzes for fun, but the program will compare your answers to other users and suggest new friends for you to meet."

"That sounds pretty cool. I could've used that when I first got to Singapore." He laughs, waving a hand dismissively. "What am I talking about? I could have used that, *period*."

"It's not your fault that you were shy," I reply.

Joey shakes his head. "That's very nice of you to say, Gigi, but we both know it was more than that. I was a geek . . . a hot mess. I was lucky you were willing to be my friend."

"Don't be silly. Our families have known each other forever. How could we not be friends?" I insist. "And now that you're back, hopefully we can get to know each other again."

"I'd love that. I'll need a friend when I start at Superbia next week. Three years is a long time to be gone. I'd finally gotten used to the school system in Singapore, and now I have to start all over again."

I sweep my gaze over him again. Old Joey might have watched from the sidelines, but the new, improved version?

I raise an eyebrow. "I think you'll be surprised how different things will be this time around. In fact, I'd bet that you'll be too busy to hang out with me soon."

His reply is put on hold as Dara arrives with a tray of crème brûlée. After everyone has received theirs, Joey leans back across the table with a slow smile.

"That will never happen, Gigi Wong. If there's one person in the world I will always make time for, it's you."

Once again, he renders me incapable of speech. Needing a minute to collect myself, I pick up my spoon and crack the sugar on my crème brûlée. Scooping up a bite, I put it in my mouth and savor the contrast of the slight bitterness from the burnt sugar with the heavy sweetness of the crème. I hum and take another bite, then another, until I'm scraping the edges of the ramekin for the last tiny bits. I glance up to find Joey staring at me, and he grins when our eyes meet.

"You obviously hated it."

I press my lips together. "I did. I only ate it out of spite."

He starts laughing, and I join in. Our parents, who up until now have been deep in their own conversation about business in Asia, turn to look at us.

"What's so funny?" Mom asks.

"Nothing," we answer simultaneously, which sends us into another fit of giggles.

The corners of Mrs. Kwan's mouth twitch. "I'm glad to see you two getting along so well."

I tense. I know that tone. It's the same one Auntie Rose uses whenever she meets people in public she wants to match.

"Gigi, I hope you'll make time to help Joey get reacquainted with the city," his mom suggests, confirming my suspicions. "It's been so long since we've been home. Besides, I'm sure he would appreciate the company, right, son?"

"I couldn't imagine a better tour guide," he answers, winking at me.

His mother smiles brightly. "How about this weekend? Mr. Kwan and I have commitments, so Joey will be on his own."

I look helplessly from Mom to Dad. The former is too busy trying not to laugh at the obvious setup, but the latter clears his throat.

"I'm sure Gigi will be happy to spend time with Joey, but she has lots of schoolwork to focus on right now. Why don't we let the two of them figure things out on their own?"

"I agree," Mr. Kwan says. "Now, tell me more about Wong Consulting's expansion into Asia. You mentioned you came back from Japan a few days ago?"

Mrs. Kwan clearly wants to say more, but she presses a polite smile onto her face and turns her attention back to the adult conversation. I sneak a peek at Joey. If he's disappointed that his mom's attempt to put us together didn't pan out, he doesn't show it. Instead, he changes chairs in order to sit in the empty one next to me.

"So," he drawls, "since you're going to be busy this weekend, how about you let me try out that app of yours?"

"It's not ready yet," I hedge. "I need to finish working on it."

"Then sign me up to test it when it is," he insists. "I'm the perfect candidate."

Flirting aside, I will need someone other than Etta to test out if my new app is going to be ready in time for quality assurance.

I stick out my hand. "Deal."

When he wraps his fingers around mine, I'm startled by the unexpected static.

He smiles. "I'm looking forward to it."

Early Saturday morning, I call Auntie Rose and tell her I won't be coming to the shop like usual. I explain I've got too much homework, which isn't a total lie, since I plan on spending the day coding. The conversation last night with Joey only increased my motivation to get the app modified and working as quickly as possible.

In a stroke of luck, Miss Wu had to push back her session because she got called into work, so Auntie Rose readily agrees. Not having to turn in my matches for an extra week is icing on the cake. After hanging up with her, my plan is to get out of bed and start working. When I check my alarm, I see there's fifteen more minutes before it's due to go off.

I yawn. "Might as well get a little more sleep."

The next time I open my eyes, Mom is hovering over me, her face so close I can count every crease on her forehead.

"Thank heavens you're okay!"

I push myself up onto my elbows. "Why wouldn't I be? It's only been a few minutes since I closed my eyes."

"Bǎobǎo, it's almost eleven o'clock. I came up because I thought you weren't feeling well." Mom sits on the side of my bed. "I checked in with your auntie, and she told me you called to say you weren't coming."

She touches the back of her hand to my forehead, then my cheeks, and finally, the back of my neck. Apparently not satisfied, she proceeds to prod her fingers along my jaw, checking for swollen lymph nodes.

I pull out of her grasp. "Auntie didn't tell you why I canceled on her?"

"I didn't ask," she replies, tugging me forward again. "I came upstairs right away to make sure you were okay."

"I canceled because I have a lot of work to do on my app for school," I explain. "It's not because I'm sick, okay?"

I give up fighting and allow Mom to brush the hair off my face and cup my cheeks. I wait patiently for her to examine every inch of me. Finally convinced I'm not going to keel over, she releases me.

"How about I make you some breakfast, then?"

I frown. "Haven't *you* been feeling really tired lately?"

Mom pulls me into a tight hug, planting a kiss on my cheek. "I'm never too tired to spend time with my bǎobǎo.*"*

"I don't want to make you late for anything, Mom. Don't you have somewhere to be today?"

"I do, but not until the afternoon. Amy Chang asked me to stop by and look at the auction items that were donated for the Society of Asia dinner next weekend." She bops me on the nose. "So how about it? I can make you my famous Hello Kitty pancakes."

I can't remember the last time she made me breakfast, much less the pancakes I used to look forward to every Sunday. Mom takes one look at my face and smiles.

"I knew you couldn't say no to those. Come downstairs when you're ready."

She leaves the room and shuts the door. I bounce off the mattress and head into the bathroom, washing my face and running a brush through my hair. After making my bed, I put on slippers and go down to meet Mom.

The aroma of butter hits me the minute I reach the bottom of the stairs. Following it through the foyer and into the kitchen, I slide beside Mom to watch her make the pancakes. No matter how many times I've seen her do it, it always seems like magic. She's preheated the griddle and poured pancake batter into a squeeze bottle. Now she draws the outline of the kitty head before adding the face. Once the bottom of the pancake firms up, she fills in the rest of the head with batter. A couple of minutes later, she flips the whole thing onto the other side before transferring it to a plate.

Mom makes five more pancakes like this before turning off the griddle. After splitting the pancakes onto two plates, she carries them to the breakfast table. I grab both the honey and the maple syrup out of the cabinet and hand her the latter before sitting down. I pour a thin layer of honey on top of my pancakes before cutting them into bite-size pieces.

"Bon appétit," she says.

We clink forks before digging in. The minute the fluffy cake hits my tongue, all the memories come flooding back. Each sweet, soggy bite reminds me of a different moment—my first day of kindergarten, Mom crying the night she missed seeing me walk my first fashion show because she was in the hospital, Dad telling us he was starting his own consulting firm, and James announcing he was staying in Houston for college.

The last memory is bittersweet. James called to catch up right after I flew home from studying abroad last summer. He mentioned he had some news, but I assumed it was about the girl he'd met while he and my cousin Ben were spending the summer in Houston. I'd never heard him talk about anyone the way he talked about Liza. I knew they'd end up together, long before he did. Now I can't imagine them apart.

"Penny for your thoughts?" Mom asks, pulling me out of my reverie.

"Oh, I was just thinking about how busy James has been this year."

"Tell me about it. Ever since he started dating that Liza girl, he's forgotten I exist."

I'm about to defend him when I catch the sparkle in her eyes. I cradle my chin in my hand. "I miss him a lot."

Mom pats me on the head. "I know you do. We all do. But it's only a few more months until summer, and then he'll be back."

"I can't believe Dad's handled James being gone so well."

"He still has you, doesn't he?" she points out. "As long as you're home, he'll be happy."

"What's he going to do when I go off to college too?" I ask without thinking.

Mom's fork clatters to her plate. She murmurs something about being clumsy, but I quickly amend my statement.

"I mean, because I'll probably be as busy as James."

There's a long pause before she answers. "I'm sure you'll have more downtime. I can't imagine psychology being as time-consuming as engineering or premed."

I bite my tongue. I first threw out the idea of majoring in psychology because I thought that learning about the way people think would help me make better matches. But now that I've spent time apprenticing under Auntie Rose, I'm starting to wonder if that's the best decision. With dating apps being match-making's biggest competition, wouldn't it make more sense to major in something like . . .

Computer science?

I give myself a shake. Where did *that* come from? It's one thing to update Auntie Rose's methods, but it's another to invest in a whole new field of study. Only one Wong can pull off that drastic of a change, and James has already done it.

We finish our pancakes in silence, and I help Mom clean up afterward. She goes upstairs to change, and I pull out my laptop and get to work. The first thing I have to do is make sure I have quizzes that match up to the compatibility questions I'll be using from Auntie Rose's questionnaire. That means I have to filter out the parts that ask about physical preferences, relationship style, and family goals.

It doesn't take me more than twenty minutes or so to do that. Thankfully, having spent so many weekends with Great-Aunt Rose, I know just what to look for. With that done, I've managed to whittle down the questionnaire from *this is going to take me forever* to *haven't I answered this yet?* Next up, the quizzes. After searching through the app, I groan aloud. Most of the ones in my database don't ask the kind of questions I need. The only way to make this work will be to create all new ones.

"I'm heading out," Mom tells me, popping her head in the door.

"I'll be here."

She spies the laptop and steps closer. "What are you working on?"

"Um, this is the app I was telling you about. The one that I'm working on for AP Computer Science."

"But it's just a bunch of words and symbols," she says.

"That's because this is the raw code. Once I'm done, I'll run the program, and it'll look like a real app. These lines you're looking at now are for the part of the app that downloads quizzes for the users to take."

"Oh, I see."

It's pretty clear from the look on her face that she, in fact, does not see. The last time her eyes glazed over like this, Dad had droned on for nearly an hour about how his firm used established patent law to push through one of his client's medical device designs. I don't blame her, really. I didn't make it past the first fifteen minutes. Only James followed the whole conversation.

"You should probably go," I comment. "I think Fernando's pulling up downstairs."

I have no idea if that's true, but it's better than the two of us staring at each other like two cats meeting in an alley.

She makes for the door. "Okay, bye, bǎobǎo! Have a good time with your lines."

"Code, Mom. It's called code."

"Yes, yes. Whatever you say!" she shouts as she descends the stairs.

Thankfully, I've guessed right, and a moment later, I hear the front door shut behind her. Heaving a sigh, I turn back to my laptop and pull up my favorite quiz-making site.

Question one: Would you rather . . .

Chapter 13

"All I have to do is take the quizzes?" Etta asks.

I nod. "Yes, but make sure you answer all the questions as honestly as possible."

After two straight days of grueling work, I finished creating the quizzes to include all the questions I needed. I feel bad for the FBI agent monitoring my Google searches. They're probably super confused about the world-traveling foodie K-pop stan with a weakness for fantasy heroes and magical creatures.

I still need more time to fine-tune the chat function, but I'm eminently grateful that the framework I chose made it an add-on. If I had to write all of the code myself, it would have taken months to get right. In the meantime, the only data points I have so far are my own, and it's obviously not enough to make a compatibility match.

That's why I invited Etta over tonight, sweetening the deal with pizza from San Matteo. I could have uploaded the app to my drive and shared the link with her, but I completely forgot about my shift at SYC on Sunday. After she texted to find out if I was okay, it was the perfect opportunity to catch up with her *and* test the new and improved Quizlr.

She pops the last bite of margherita into her mouth and stands up.

"Let me wash my hands real quick. I'm sure you don't want tomato sauce all over your keyboard."

I load everything on my laptop while she's gone. When she returns, I gesture at the chair by my desk and she drops into it.

"Start with this quiz, and keep going until you're done."

Once she's clicked through the first few questions, I sit down on the bed and text both Kyle and Joey, asking them to take the quizzes as well. The more users I have, the better. A few seconds after I hit send, Kyle texts back.

Where's your electronic agreement? I need to make sure you're not going to sell my info to a third-party vendor.

Don't worry, I text back. **You're not that interesting.**

I am offended. Just for that, I need you to send me the download link.

I let out a giggle before copying and pasting the link into the chat. Etta turns around and looks at me with wide eyes. "What's so funny?"

"Nothing. Don't worry about it," I say. "I was texting Kyle."

At the mention of his name, Etta's cheeks tinge with color. She faces the screen while I suppress a smile. Another name to add to Kyle's list of hopeless admirers. Too bad his list of exes is even longer. A few seconds pass before Etta turns around again.

"I like these quizzes. They're super interesting, but some of the questions are hard! Like, how do I choose between a beach and forest? I love them both."

"Don't think too hard about it. Just go with the first choice that comes to your mind," I instruct.

My phone pings. This time, it's from Joey.

What do I win if I get all the questions correct?

I frown. **Nothing. It's not a real test.**

Damn. I was really hoping to win something.

Like what? I ask.

That's for me to know and you to find out.

I roll my eyes even though he can't see me. **You know that doesn't make any sense, right?**

No? And here I thought I was being smooth. ☺

I stare at the screen for a while. I haven't decided if I like the new Joey. While there are definite perks—the hair, the face, the body—I kind of miss the awkward nerd I used to know.

Wait. Did I say . . . perks?

I clear my throat, distracting Etta again. She glances over her shoulder.

"Are you okay?"

"It's just allergies," I assure her.

"I think I finished this quiz. Should I hit submit?" she asks.

"Yes, but don't move on to the next one yet. Let me check to make sure everything saved properly."

I climb off the bed and move the laptop to face me. After

finding her answers stored on the server like I wanted, I shift it back to her.

"Looks great. On to the next one!"

When I pick my phone off the bed, I notice two new messages from Joey.

I'm sorry if I upset you. I was just joking.

Hello? Please text me back.

Now that's the Joey I remember. He used to get so nervous whenever I didn't reply right away. I send a quick message.

> **No, it's not you. My friend Etta's here.**
> **She's taking the quizzes too.**

Does that mean I can come over and take them in person too?

Well that lasted for all of five minutes.

No, I type back. **But if you take the quizzes, I'll reconsider your request for a tour of the city.**

Three little dots taunt me for several seconds before his reply appears.

How do I find it? Is it in the app store? I'll download it before you change your mind.

I heave a sigh, but send him the link to my drive before going to check on Etta's progress. Not too bad. She's made it through half the quizzes already.

"Can I be honest?" Etta says, deep channels forming between her brows.

"Of course."

"The quizzes are fun . . . but there're *a lot* of them. I'll make sure to finish, of course, but I can see someone else getting tired and giving up," she admits.

"That's a really good point," I tell her, frowning. "I need the users to complete the entire set if the app is going to work like I want it to."

For a few minutes, we sit without speaking—Etta in my desk chair, and me on the bed. My eyes wander around the room, searching for inspiration. Unable to find any, I unlock my phone and stare at the screen. When I spot one of my favorite hidden object game apps, something clicks.

"What if . . . what if I did something like a prize? You know, where every time you finish a quiz, you earn something that will help you unlock it?"

"Oh, you mean like a puzzle? Or a quest?" Etta asks, her eyes shimmering with excitement.

"Kind of, yeah." I rub my face. "I just have to figure out what the prize is."

"Why don't you make the chat the prize?"

I grin. "You're a genius, Etta! I'll make it so you can't unlock the chat feature until all of the quizzes are done."

Etta preens. "I don't know about being a genius, but I'm glad I could help."

"I think this calls for some bubble tea."

"I love bubble tea," she gasps.

I open Grubhub and place an order at my favorite shop nearby. While Etta tackles the rest of the quizzes, I wait for the delivery. By the time I carry the cups up to my room, Etta's done.

"Right on time," I say.

She turns the chair around so she's facing me. I hold out her Thai tea with boba, and she accepts the cup with a toothy grin.

"Are you getting used to your class schedule now?" I ask.

She takes a large sip before answering. "Yeah, for the most part, but it still feels like I'm behind."

"You'll get it," I assure her. "Not just anyone can win a merit scholarship from Superbia. You must have been at the top of your class at your old school."

"But the classes at Superbia are so much more intense. I thought the classes I was taking at Mastil were advanced, but the material my teachers would take a whole semester to teach there is only going to take a month here."

She slumps against the back of the chair. "I guess it's not the worst. At least I can pretend school's the reason I don't have a social life."

"Don't say that." I reach out and touch her arm. "We've been hanging out."

"I know. And it's not totally accurate to say I have *no* social life. I still text my old friends from Mastil. I'm hoping to meet up with them soon. Plus, there have been a few people at Superbia I've been talking to."

I smirk. "Oh?"

"It's not like that," she immediately denies. "Just a couple people from class."

"I want names."

"You already know Anna. She's in my world history class."

"You two like a lot of the same things. I'm not surprised you're getting along," I answer truthfully. "What's the other name? You said there were a couple."

Etta freezes, her cheeks bulging with tea and tapioca. She chews and swallows the little black balls before finally replying.

"I . . ." She scoots closer, her eyes imploring. "Please don't be mad. I know you told me to stay away from him, but he kept talking to me in class. I even told him I was too busy to watch anime anymore, but he wouldn't let up and—"

"Hold up! Stop."

I put my tea down and look directly into her eyes. "Are you telling me you're still talking to Tyler?"

She nods. I reach up and rub my temple. "Etta . . ."

"I know, Gigi, I know. But he's the only one who likes anime as much as I do. I mean, I'm so happy we're friends, but we don't have any classes together. When I'm at school, I feel really, really alone."

She pauses to take a breath. I'm startled to see wetness at the corners of her eyes. I get up and wrap my arms around her. Etta leans against me as I give her a gentle pat on the shoulder.

"I'm sorry I got upset. You're allowed to be friends with whoever you want. But from now on, you won't have to worry about saying yes to anyone who asks, because I have a plan."

She tilts her head. "What do you mean?"

"Quizlr. Once I'm done, you'll be able to make new friends with it!"

She stares at the laptop screen for a moment before glancing back at me. "I don't think I understand."

I extricate myself and sit back on the bed before explaining how the new Quizlr will work.

Etta's lips part. "You . . . you did all this for me?"

That's not what I expected for her to say, and it takes me a full minute to respond. Yes, I was thinking of her when I came up with the final idea, but it's obviously not the entire reason why I wanted to do this. I start to explain, but the Bambi look on her face changes my mind.

I smile. "Of course. What are friends for?"

♥

With the deadline for quality assurance looming in a little over a week, I spend every free moment frantically coding the rest of Quizlr 2.0. In fact, for the next three days, my life consists of waking up, going to school, having dinner, and then tackling the program until I pass out with my fingers positioned over the laptop keyboard.

Even my walks home with Kyle morph into twenty minutes of utter silence, at least on my end. The first couple of days, he tried chatting with me, but my brain only heard Sims-like gibberish as it pieced together more code. Once he figured out I would only offer a series of vague grunts in reply, Kyle gave up.

To his credit, he doesn't get mad. I suppose that's what years of friendship buys you—automatic forgiveness.

I finally finish Quizlr at three a.m. on Friday morning. I manage to squeeze in a short nap before getting ready for school. I would have been done sooner, but there was something about turning in a basic message box that didn't sit well with me. I wanted it to look as nice as possible, while also making sure the app successfully kept each chat private and only accessible to those with the direct link.

When my alarm goes off three hours later, it yanks me out of the grasp of a horrible nightmare. In it, Ms. Harris called me to the front of the class to announce my app was nothing more than a figment of my imagination. When she revealed the big fat zero next to my name in her grade book, the ground opened up and I fell into a pit of scalding-hot lava. It's a wonder I didn't wake up screaming.

Taking a deep breath, I throw my legs over the side of the bed and drag myself into the bathroom for a shower. I barely catch the two different-colored socks I put on while getting dressed. Terrified that Quizlr might be a product of late-night sleep-coding sessions, I send a private chat link to both Kyle and Etta, and a different one to Etta and Joey. Hopefully, having two separate chats will expose any weaknesses in time for me to make last-minute changes.

Once I show up at Superbia, the morning passes in a flood of yawns and desperate attempts to keep my eyes open. The only burst of adrenaline I get happens when Etta texts me in third period to let me know the chats are working. Despite this, I'm so tired I hide in one of the library cubbies to take a nap during lunch. By the time Ms. Harris greets me as I walk into computer science, I'm human enough to take note of her gold combat boots and new purple ombre braids.

"You look really nice today, Ms. Harris," I offer with a faint smile. "Especially your hair."

"Thank you for noticing, Gigi! I had it done this weekend."

I move on to my desk, sinking into the chair like it's a lifeboat. While the rest of the class trickles in, I run one more check on Quizlr. A horrid thought crosses my mind.

What if I did all this work for nothing? What if people hate it? What if they laugh at me?

My chest tightens to the point it's hard to breathe. Ultimately, I don't have time to dwell on it, because the bell rings to signal the start of class. Ms. Harris walks up to the front of the room.

"Good afternoon, everyone. As you all know, today is the last day before we begin stage three: quality assurance. Before Monday's class, I'll send you a link to the shared drive to upload your apps. I will also lend each of you an Android device to perform the testing. As these phones are school property, I will need a permission slip signed by a parent from each of you by Monday."

She pauses to have us pass down the permission slips before continuing.

"To make this both fair and objective, your apps will be randomly assigned among the students in my five classes. Each of you will also be expected to review three apps from other students. You'll be checking for usability, reliability, and efficacy."

That statement earns Ms. Harris a room full of blank looks, and she sighs.

"It means you're going to check to see if the app works and if it does what it's supposed to do."

Tyler raises his hand. "I already have an Android phone. Can't I just use mine?"

"No, for two reasons. The first is to protect your privacy. Some of these apps will have data stored on the school's open server. Second, given what happened in the fall, the only way Superbia would agree to letting you have phones out during class is if they only had approved apps on them."

While she avoids specifics, it's clear from the glances being snuck around the room that everyone knows she's talking about the testing scandal.

"I will check your phones every day to make sure no outside apps have been downloaded," Ms. Harris continues. "We're teaching you about quality assurance, not helping you get to the next rank in PUBG."

She sweeps her gaze across the room, and she's met with more than one guilty expression.

"Make sure you use the apps you're assigned at least ten to fifteen times for consistent results. Be rough with them; don't handle them with care. Click on every button and check every link. Keep track of any crashes, system errors, or difficulty while trying to use the app, and write it all down on the evaluation sheet. Remember, these are the things that will make the difference between a success and a flop."

She pulls up her lecture for the day and switches to full screen, but pauses before launching the first slide.

"One more thing. Please double-check your link before sending it to me. If it or the file is corrupted, you'll lose ten points."

Ms. Harris waits for those of us taking notes to write down that piece of information. Then she takes a deep breath and smiles.

"All right. Now, who wants to tell us the first rule of quality assurance?"

Chapter 14

"I like the update you made to Quizlr," Kyle tells me when I meet him after school. "The chat feature is a really nice touch."

I smile so wide my cheeks hurt. "You have no idea how nice it is to hear that. I've spent so much time on it I'm starting to wonder if *I'm* made of code."

"Technically, you are. You're made of DNA—a genetic code."

I groan loudly. "Nerd."

"I can say the same for you," he teases back. "I saw what time that invitation was sent. You were up super late working on it."

Kyle tucks his phone back into his pants, and we head out the front door. As we step into the cold, I shove my hands into the pockets of my jacket to protect them from the wind.

"Etta seems nice," Kyle says after a block.

I hide a smile. He said the same thing the night they first met at my house.

"Did she tell you how much she loves anime?"

"Are you kidding? You should see the paragraphs she sent me in the chat," he replies, laughing. "They're whole tomes."

"That's definitely her." My shoulders slump. "It's why I wanted to help her find more friends. She's kind of a lot at first, but she's super sweet."

"Well, you can count me as a new friend. I told her the next time I hit Forbidden Planet, I'll take her with me," Kyle states.

"Is that the comic-book store you like so much?"

He squints at me. "They don't just sell comic books, but yes. I always ask you to come, but you never want to."

"It's not my thing. I would be the only one there who wouldn't know what was going on," I reply.

"You can always learn."

"Nah. You'll have way more fun with Etta." I sidestep an older couple walking a little too slowly in front of us. "She already knows what you're talking about. Besides, there're lots of other things we do together."

"Yeah, I guess."

He turns away from me, and my stomach knots, but then the light changes at the intersection. We're about two blocks from home when my phone buzzes. I take it out of my back pocket and glance at the text.

♥

You still owe me a tour.

I burst out laughing. Kyle looks over at me, brows furrowed.

"What's that for?"

"Sorry. Joey texted me."

His eyes widen. "Joey? Joey Kwan? I thought his family moved to Singapore."

"They did, but they're back. Remember when my mom said we had guests for dinner?" I wait for him to nod before continuing. "It was the Kwans. In fact, I'm surprised you haven't run into Joey at school."

Kyle shrugs. "I heard that someone enrolled late this year, but I thought they were talking about the new guy."

That takes me by surprise. I'm so busy trying to figure out who it might be that I don't notice I'm heading right for a bicycle chained to a pole. I yelp as Kyle pulls me against him, saving me from a painful encounter with its back tire.

"Thanks," I say.

"What would you do without me?" Kyle teases.

"Become one with a bike, apparently," I answer, shaking my head. "Can you imagine if I had hurt myself? My dad would kill me."

Kyle chuckles. "Would he, though?"

"You're right. He'd make sure I was okay first. *Then* he'd kill me," I correct.

This time we both laugh. He offers me his arm. Though my feet feel steady, I take it, and we continue on. After a few minutes, my heart stops pounding, but every time I move closer to Kyle to avoid another bike on the sidewalk, it skips a beat.

"Anyway, like I was saying, I've been hearing the girls in my classes talk about some Korean dude they think looks like a K-pop idol," Kyle pipes up. "They're all obsessed with him."

Come to think of it, I remember the same. I never did catch a name, though.

"I'm sure we'll find out who it is sooner or later," I say, half to myself. "Superbia's not exactly a big school."

As we turn down our street, I look up at him and smile. "Thanks for being sweet to Etta, by the way."

"Wait, you wanted me to be mean?" He sighs dramatically. "You should have told me this *before* I started talking to her. Now I have to be twice the jerk to make up for it."

I poke him in the side. "Don't you dare. I know where you live."

"Yes, I know. You never let me forget it." We stop in front of my house, and he winks at me. "Just you wait. The next time you actually come over, there'll be a moat."

"With alligators?" I ask, grinning.

He waggles his eyebrows at me. "With sharks. Sharks wearing missiles on their backs."

I press a hand to my chest and gasp. "All those teeth to keep me out of your house? I feel so special."

"I'm glad you approve of my deadly ways."

My phone goes off a second time. It's another message from Joey.

I'm having a problem with the chat.

The world comes to a halt. I suck in a breath before typing back a reply.

Is it lagging? Are the emojis not showing up? What's the problem?

"G? Everything okay?"

I glance up and find Kyle staring intently at me. I shake my head.

"I need to get inside. Joey's having an issue with Quizlr."

"Oh . . . okay. Bye."

I race up the steps and into my house, keeping my eyes pinned on the three blinking dots at the bottom of our chat box.

Please let it be something simple to fix. Please please please please please . . .

My mind runs through a thousand possibilities. It can't be the actual chat add-on. That's part of the framework. It has to be something in my code, but what? Too nervous to go upstairs, I traipse past the kitchen and into the dining room. His answer comes through, and I have the sudden urge to throw my phone out the window.

Correction: I want to throw Joey Kwan out the window.

I sink into one of the dining chairs, waiting for my heart to slow while glaring at the four little words that nearly sent me into a tailspin.

You're not in it.

I let out a string of loud curses, but zip my mouth shut after belatedly remembering I might not be alone. I hold my breath and listen for several minutes, but only silence answers back. I count to ten, then to twenty and thirty before finally allowing myself to type back a G-rated reply.

That was way less heart fluttering and more heart-attack inducing, Joey.

My phone rings. I pick up.

"I'm sorry," Joey says as soon as I answer. "Please forgive me?"

"That depends. Is the chat working?"

I can't keep the edge out of my voice, and I can almost see Joey cringe on the other end of the line.

"I'm really sorry, Gigi. I didn't mean to worry you," he apologizes again. "And it totally is. In fact, I've been talking to your friend Etta all day."

"Really?"

"Yeah, she's pretty cool. I've never met a girl who genuinely likes anime and gaming like me. Etta actually knows what I'm talking about."

Despite my irritation, something in his voice triggers the wheels in my brain to start turning.

This is good.

This is *very* good.

"I'm glad to hear that," I say aloud. "You should get to know her better. She's new to Superbia."

"She told me that. Something else we have in common," he answers. "Besides knowing the amazing Gigi Wong, that is."

It takes several seconds to retrieve my eyes after they roll to the back of my head.

"Well, that flopped spectacularly," Joey says when I offer no reply. "But it's okay. I have more. You want to hear them?"

"No, not in the least."

"Really? I was kind of hoping to collect on that tour you promised me."

I can't see him, but somehow I know he's pouting. I'm not ready to forgive him for nearly scaring me to death, but I do have an idea of how he can make it up to me.

"To be honest, I'm swamped trying to get Quizlr ready to turn in next week," I say. "But if you promise to keep using the app and chatting with Etta, I'll see what I can do."

There's a long silence on the other end of the line, and I wonder if I misread him.

"And here I thought you were going to make me work for it. Done."

I break into a grin. Perhaps Etta's getting more than a new friend. I glance down at my watch.

"Sorry, Joey. I need to go. I've got an essay to finish before to-morrow."

He sighs. "One of these days, you won't be too busy for me."

I hesitate. Why is Joey still flirting with me if he likes Etta? I choose my next words carefully.

"In the meantime, I guess you'll have to settle for Etta."

"Who's settling? She's great to talk to," Joey volunteers. "I'm glad you introduced us."

I relax. Clearly, I was worried for nothing.

"I am too, Joey. Talk to you later."

After I hang up, I let out a whoop. My app hasn't been turned in and it's already claimed its first success. There's no way I won't get nominated for the contest now. In fact, I might really have a shot at winning.

I can't wait to tell Etta.

I sneak a peek at Great-Aunt Rose for the fifth time since she sat down opposite me for our lunch break. She pulls the aluminum container of baby bok choy closer with her chopsticks, picking up a generous amount and dropping it on top of her rice. My own bowl sits half-eaten, my appetite overtaken by the butterflies that keep fluttering in my stomach.

"Are you sick?" she asks without raising her eyes.

"No, Auntie. I'm not sick."

"Allergies?"

"No," I repeat.

"Hmm."

Auntie Rose transfers a couple of pieces of char siu pork into her bowl and continues eating. Straightening in my chair, I summon the courage to speak.

"Auntie—"

She cuts me off. "You need to eat more. You're too skinny. That's why you're cold all the time. Eat."

I press my lips together tightly. She was complaining my cheeks were getting too round barely three weeks ago. Rather than argue, though, I pluck a few string beans out of another container and shove them into my mouth.

When I arrived this morning, I expected Great-Aunt Rose would sit me down and ask which names I came up with. After all, Miss Wu is supposed to come in this afternoon to go over her newest matches. To be honest, part of me was hoping she forgot, because I nearly did. With all the extra work I put in these last few days, I'd been too distracted to go through Auntie Rose's database. I ended up running a search using the same program I used for Quizlr 2.0 to pull the three names I needed.

Instead, she asked me to help unpack a shipment of silk scarves. By the time I finished folding each in a way that displayed their printed patterns and arranged them on the multilevel wooden rack she bought, Great-Aunt Rose was in session with her first client. I tried to broach the topic as soon as she was done, but then she disappeared into the bathroom for nearly fifteen minutes.

When she returned, I had to help a Russian tourist intent on buying one of every ceramic figurine we had in the shop. It took nearly twenty minutes to carefully wrap each one in tissue paper so they wouldn't fracture when packed. Then, while I was ringing her up, she spotted the embroidered boxes. It would be another half hour before she happily lugged five plastic bags of souvenirs out the door. When I went in search of Auntie Rose, she quickly sent me to prepare another tray of tea and cookies.

Now, almost three hours later, I'm convinced she's stalling for time. In fact, right before we took our break, I wanted to observe her session with Mr. Tsai, but she sent me to pick up the lunch I'm pretending to enjoy. It doesn't help that Auntie Rose tends to eat with her mouth open, something she swears is supposed to show how delicious the food is. I get more impatient with every lip smack and hum, until I am no longer able to hold back.

"Aren't you going to ask me about Miss Wu's matches?"

Great-Aunt Rose freezes, the piece of fried tofu pinched between her chopsticks slowly being dissected from the pressure. It only takes the slight narrowing of her eyes to make her feelings known, and the apology spills out of my mouth before I realize I've spoken.

"I didn't mean to be rude, Auntie. I've been waiting all day to talk to you about them, and—"

"And you can wait fifteen more minutes for me to finish eating," she interjects calmly. "We have plenty of time before Miss Wu arrives."

I don't have a comeback, at least not one that won't have Auntie Rose calling me by my given name, so I nod. I sneak my phone out of my pocket to check my social media under the table. That's when I notice I missed two calls from Mom. I quickly excuse myself and dial her number, walking out of the break room while waiting for her to pick up.

"Why didn't you answer your phone earlier, bǎobǎo?" she asks the minute the call connects. "I thought maybe something had happened to you two."

Only Mom would assume a missed call meant catastrophe. I take a deep breath.

"I'm sorry, Mom. I forgot I had my phone on silent, and we were busy all morning at the shop."

She hums. "Well, I'm glad you're okay."

"I am. I didn't mean to worry you." I walk down the nearest aisle. "So why did you call?"

"I wanted to tell you that I won't be able to go to the Shibui preview tonight," she informs me.

"What? Why?"

"Remember how I told you I've been having more palpitations the last few days?"

How could I not? Dad's had both of us on lockdown all week—Mom because she's had a couple of near-fainting spells, and me because he wanted someone at home with her. I didn't complain, since I got to spend the time getting Quizlr ready.

"Uh-huh."

"I went to see Dr. Samuels yesterday, and he switched me to a new medicine. He warned me there might be side effects, but I never expected to be so tired. I think it's best if I take it easy until my body adjusts."

"I was really looking forward to going with you tonight," I reply, wincing at how childish I sound.

"I know, bǎobǎo, I was too. I already explained the situation to Amelia, and she promised to take good care of you." There's a short pause on the other line. "One more thing. Your dad doesn't know if he can make it either. He's scheduled for a conference call with his partners in China tonight, and with the time difference, he doesn't want to risk missing it."

With the Asia branches of Wong Consulting opening their doors in two days, I'm not surprised to hear this. Every time he expands, Dad is more ghost than man.

"Okay, then," I answer in a low voice.

"I know you're disappointed," Mom states. "But I'm sure Kyle will be there."

"Actually, he's going to *Hadestown* with his mom tonight."

"Oh, well, if you'd like to invite any of your other friends, we have those seats already reserved." I hear her speak to someone before coming back on the phone. "Bǎobǎo, I need to go. Have a good time tonight."

"I'll try. Bye."

After hanging up, I duck back through the curtain. Auntie Rose is waiting at the now-cleared table, and she cocks her eyebrow at me.

"That was Mom," I say. "She has to stay home tonight because of heart stuff, and Dad's going to be working late."

"I'm sorry to hear that, xiǎojī."

I shrug. "It's okay. I'm used to it."

Outside of James, she's the only one who knows how much I wish my parents had more time for me. I've never even talked to Kyle about it, though I suspect he knows. It can't be a coincidence Mrs. Miller invites me over to their house whenever I'm by myself too many days in a row.

"I know it doesn't always feel like it," Auntie Rose tells me, "but nothing is more important to them than you. Remember that."

I do my best to smile, but there's no fooling her. She takes my hand in both of hers.

"Would you feel better if I came with you?"

Though she offers, I know it's the last thing she'd want to do. Great-Aunt Rose might enjoy the finer things in life, but fancy dinners are not one of them. I still recall when Mom and Dad took her to Atomix last year for her birthday thinking she would enjoy the Korean tasting menu. Instead, they listened to three hours of Auntie Rose griping about the uncomfortable chairs, boring decor, and minuscule portions. In fact, she shamed them so much they spent another hour sitting across from her in Joe's Dumpling, watching her shovel dumplings to her heart's content.

"No, you don't need to do that, Auntie. I'm sure there will be people there I know. Plus, Mom said I could invite a friend."

"That's a great idea," she agrees, a little too readily. "I'm sure you would have more fun with a friend than your cranky old auntie."

"That's not true," I deny. "But the dinner is probably going to last a while, and I know how you like to go to bed early."

Great-Aunt Rose nods. "I need my beauty sleep. I like my bags on my arm, not under my eyes."

That gets a giggle out of me. She smiles before rising to her feet.

"I'm going to stop by the little girls' room, xiǎojī. Why don't you call some of your friends and find out who can go to the dinner with you tonight?"

To be honest, most of the people I would invite are probably already on the guest list, so only one name comes to mind. I shoot off a text message.

Hey Etta! What are you up to today?

It takes only seconds for a reply to come through.

Hi Gigi! I'm hanging out with Anna at Kinokuniya.

She's hanging out with Anna? Why didn't she tell me? I wince at the sharp sensation in my chest before I receive another message.

What about you? Whatcha up to?

I'm at my great-aunt Rose's import shop right now.

Oh! The one in Chinatown?

Yes, I type back. By the way, I know it's kind of last minute, but I have an extra seat at Shibui's soft opening tonight. You wanna come?

I hold my breath, strangely tense as I wait for her reply.

Yes! A beat goes by. What's Shibui?

I grin before searching for a press release online. Once I send her the link, it takes ten more minutes before I get another message.

It sounds amazing! I'd love to come!

Great, I type back. I'll have my driver pick you up. Dress to impress.

Etta surprises me again with her next text.

Can Anna come too? We were going to eat in Chinatown,
but this sounds way more fun.

Under normal circumstances, there's no way Shibui would open up another spot. But since Dad isn't going to make dinner either, I technically have two extra seats at our table. There's no reason I can't include Anna . . . so why am I hesitating? My phone pings again.

Pretty please?

I sigh. It obviously means a lot to Etta to have her along. Besides, I've been meaning to make amends for not being there when Anna was having a hard time.

Sure, but she'll have to meet us there. My driver won't have time to pick up both of you.

Three dots appear, and I find myself holding my breath until the words appear.

Thank you so much! I'll tell her right now!

I send Fernando a text to update him on the additional stop. Auntie Rose returns the minute I finish, as if she was spying on me from the other side of the beaded curtain. She settles back in her chair and takes a sip of the oolong tea she had with lunch.

"All right, you've been waiting long enough. Miss Wu is going to be here soon, so let's see who you matched her with."

I pull up the note with the saved names and slide it across the table for her. Auntie Rose opens her client notebook and cross-references them with the biodata she has listed for each. To her credit, her face remains impassive the whole time. The only reaction I can discern is a slight twitch in the corner of her mouth as she sits back in her chair.

"Well?" I ask when minutes pass without her saying a word. "How did I do?"

"You've made some . . . interesting choices."

"Interesting as in 'I like where this is going' or 'did you sleep through all our training?'"

She laughs. "It means that I did not write down the same

names, but I can see potential in the men you chose."

"What does that mean, then?" I ask.

My stomach churns as I await her answer. Except . . . there isn't churning. There's only the slightest gurgle of discomfort. Hmm.

"I know I said otherwise," Auntie Rose states, "but I'm going to present your top two names along with mine."

Now that gets me excited. I circle the table and throw my arms around her, squeezing her tight.

"Thank you!"

"Don't thank me yet," Great-Aunt Rose chides, but she presses her cheek against mine. "Miss Wu has to choose one of your names *and* have successful dates with him before you can call it a win."

That does little to dampen my excitement. I had run the program multiple times to make sure the results were the same. If Miss Wu agrees I made the best choice, I'll have definitive proof Quizlr 2.0—and Matchmaker 3000—works.

"Don't get ahead of yourself now."

I stare at Auntie Rose. "Huh?"

"I recognize that look. It's too soon to know for sure how things will work out. Love has a way of surprising us all."

Not if I have anything to say about it.

Chapter 15

"Are you sure I look okay?"

I glance at Etta as she twists and turns to look at her reflection in the mirror. Beneath her bright orange winter coat—which I have somehow come to love—she's paired an ill-fitting, plum-colored sweater dress with sparkly black tights. It does nothing for the figure I know is underneath. I would've helped her find something else, but there was no way I could make time for another shopping marathon while working on Quizlr.

Fernando dropped her off at the house about twenty minutes ago after driving her into town from Woodside. I originally planned for him to swing by and pick me up so we could head straight downtown, but I had to leave Rose and Jade later than expected. Miss Wu called about thirty minutes before her session to say she was stuck on the train because of a fire up the track.

I waited around for as long as I could, but nearly an hour later, she called to say the train hadn't moved. Before sending me home in a taxi—something she swore she wouldn't tell my parents—Great-Aunt Rose promised she would let me know who Miss Wu decided on if she showed up. I made it home ten minutes before Etta appeared at my door. Now she's standing in my closet, waiting for me to finish getting ready.

"I feel really underdressed," she bemoans after inspecting herself. "But this is the fanciest thing I own."

I cock my head to the side and take her in. Etta's face is covered with a layer of foundation that doesn't quite match her skin tone, making her ashy under the bright lights. The purple eye shadow and thick liquid liner on her eyelids are no better, clashing with the nude pink color painted on her lips. Still, I can't help but smile at the stars in her dark brown eyes, or the playful tint of pink the cold brought to her cheeks. Etta has this irresistible bubbly personality that shines through the worst makeup job.

"I admit, it's not the best for the occasion, but I can work with this." I look her up and down. "Maybe we can lose the tights and add some accessories."

"Won't I be cold?" she asks.

"You can borrow one of my long winter coats. We're not quite the same size, but I'm sure we can find one that'll fit. Now . . ." I spot a tiara from last year's Halloween party and put it on my head. "Off with your tights!"

Etta bursts out laughing, and I join her before walking out of the closet to give her some privacy. A few minutes later, she comes out with a mass of sparkly material in one fist.

"That looks better already," I tell her. "Time for the accessories."

I move over to where my belts are hanging and pull out a skinny patent one.

"Here. Try this."

Etta wraps it around her waist, and I help secure it in the back. A quick tug here and a small tuck there, and voilà—she goes from lumpy to curvy. I spin her around to face the mirror, and her face lights up.

"I can't believe how much difference that makes!"

I grab her by the wrist. "I'm not done yet. Come on."

Tugging her into the bathroom, I make her sit on the stool at my vanity while I unpack my makeup case.

"Close your eyes," I instruct.

She stares at me warily. "What? Why?"

"Just trust me."

It takes another second for her to comply, but she does. After soaking a cotton pad with makeup remover, I carefully wipe away the heavy eye shadow and eyeliner. Giving it a minute to dry, I apply a soft smoky eye and reline her eyes with a pencil. A coat of mascara later, I clean up the area under and around her eye. Then I take my contour kit and dust the closest color to her skin over her entire face, taking away as much of the ashy foundation as possible. Satisfied, I take a step back.

"Not bad, if I do say so myself," I say. "Take a look."

Etta blinks a few times before standing and facing the mirror. Her brown eyes grow wide, and she abruptly throws her arms around me.

"I love it! Thank you! You're like my very own fairy godmother."

I laugh. "I'm not sure that's a good thing. If the best my fairy godmother could come up with was a belt and some eye makeup, I'd be pretty sad."

"Trust me, it's great. No one's had the time to help me look my best." Her smile falters. "Mom tries, but she has a full-time job and five kids. And with Dad working twelve-hour shifts, six days a week, I do my best to help out. I cook dinner and clean up around the house, but it's still tough."

I haven't forgotten Etta's family isn't well-off, but hearing her talk about it firsthand and seeing the light fade from her eyes hits me hard.

My arms tighten around her. "I might not be able to perform real magic, but I can promise to be a friend who will always fix your makeup. How about that?"

Etta giggles. "I can live with that."

"Great. Now let me finish getting ready too and we can go."

I assume she'll head back into the bedroom, but she plops down on the stool again. I quirk an eyebrow at her, and she shrugs.

"How often do you get to watch a master at work?"

I roll my eyes. "Flattery will get you everywhere. Which apparently in this case is a free dinner at Shibui."

I ignore Etta's loud cackles as I apply my makeup and run a brush through my hair. I opt to leave it down, parting the straight black strands to one side and pinning it back with a set of rose gold hairpins. Satisfied, I leave the bathroom and head back into the closet, where I take one last look in the mirror at the powder-blue silk blouse with a neck bow I've paired with black leather leggings. I pull my favorite black Chanel tweed jacket off the hanger and put it on. Finally, I grab the Alexander McQueen skull clutch James gave me for Christmas last year.

When I stick my head back into the bathroom to check on Etta, I find her engrossed in her phone.

"What's so interesting?"

She presses the phone against her chest. "Oh, I was chatting on Quizlr."

"With who?" I coo.

"Um, with . . . Joey."

Not wanting to show my cards yet, I merely smile. "I'm glad you're getting to know each other better. I'm ready to leave if you are."

"Yeah, yeah. Let's go!"

After I run upstairs to say goodbye to Mom, we make our way downstairs. I help Etta try on a few winter coats until we find a three-quarter-length Ralph Lauren that fits her perfectly. While she dons a pair of weathered booties, I slip my feet into my favorite pair of black suede Louboutins. I set the alarm, and we step out into the chilly night. Fernando has pulled the car right up to the front of the house, so Etta and I slide into the back seat.

"Ready to go, Miss Gigi?" he asks, meeting my eye in the rearview. "Miss Etta?"

I smile. "Whenever you are."

♥

Thirty minutes later, Etta and I are seated at a horigotatsu in one of the private dining areas in Shibui. We're waiting for Anna to arrive, along with some of the other guests assigned to our room. The table with recessed seating is one of four in the space, which is surrounded on three sides by shoji screens and contains a tatami floor. Carved wooden lamps hang from the ceiling and line the walls, casting a warm golden glow over the diners.

"This place is so fancy," Etta stage whispers at me. "It's like a movie set."

I have to agree. When we first walked through the front entry, we found ourselves in a small Zen garden. Cherrywood planks carried us across a shallow koi pond, with living walls of moss surrounded by bamboo. On the other side were a pair of stone tōrō, standing guard amid swirls of light-colored gravel. Japanese calligraphy and brush paintings were splashed on the walls where the hostess stand was located, and a sign requested all diners silence their phones and keep voices low to maintain the ambience of the space.

"Irasshaimase. The name on your reservation, please."

Once the hostess checked us off the list, another guided us down a long, dimly lit corridor with the same cherrywood plank serving as a walkway. Between each dining room and on either side of the walkway was an artificial creek, where a constant but gentle stream of water trickled over rounded black rocks. Before we were allowed to step inside our assigned room, the hostess directed us to take off our shoes and place them into wooden cubbies just inside the door. She pointed out the disposable slippers to wear if we needed to use the restroom, and then we were seated.

Now Etta frowns as she glances at her watch. "I wonder what's keeping—"

The door to our dining room slides open, and the hostess who showed us to the table escorts Anna inside. She's arrived in a knit dress similar to the one Etta is wearing, though it's clear the simple charcoal-gray material is far nicer. It hugs her slender frame in the right places, ending above her knee so as to show off the brown leather riding boots she's currently taking off. A maroon silk scarf is tied loosely around her neck, and her straight black hair has been left down.

"Anna!"

Etta climbs out of the horigotatsu rather clumsily, but Anna waits patiently for her to stand before hugging her. I also rise to greet her, though we opt to exchange polite smiles.

"I'm glad you could come," I tell her.

"Thank you for including me," she replies. "Especially on such short notice."

The three of us settle into our seats. There is an awkward lull in the conversation at first, but then Etta smiles brightly.

"We had a really good time at Kinokuniya today. The last time I visited was almost a year ago. There's so much new stuff!"

"It's been a while for me too," I admit. "I always pass by the store, but I never go inside."

"We should all go next time! But not right away . . . I need to save some money," Etta says with an unhappy moan. "There's so much I want to buy there."

We lapse into silence again. Searching for something we can talk about, I look across the table at Anna.

"I'm glad we're finally getting a break from our apps. I was starting to dream in code."

A small smile appears on Anna's lips. "Yeah. It's been a pretty intense few weeks."

"Are you happy with how yours turned out?" I ask.

A crease appears between her eyebrows. "I guess so? It still needs quite a lot of work before it'll be ready for the contest."

"Is this that programming contest you were telling me about?" Etta blurts, looking at me.

I nod. "Our teacher, Ms. Harris, is going to nominate one student from her class to represent Superbia. She'll decide who based on our apps."

Etta stares at both of us with wide eyes. "That sounds so exciting! You're going to enter Quizlr, right, Gigi?"

I nod, and she turns to Anna. "What does your app do?"

"Well, it—"

Our conversation is put on hold when the door opens for a third time as Amelia steps in. Dressed in a sleek black Armani tube dress, and with her dark brown curls tamed into a French twist, she looks every bit as serene as her surroundings. Her hazel eyes land on us, and she pads across the tatami to our table. I rise from the horigotatsu and give her a hug.

"Hi, Amelia."

"Konbanwa," she replies with a warm smile. "Welcome to Shibui."

I turn to Etta and Anna, both of whom have stood up behind me.

"These are my friends, Etta and Anna. Etta, Anna, this is Amelia, my mom's friend and one of Shibui's owners."

Etta instantly launches into a speech. "This place is . . . I don't even have the words. I feel like I'm in a dream. Everything is so beautiful, and the garden outside? Oh my gosh! Those fish in the water . . . and the lanterns!"

With every word, her voice rises in volume and octave, until I'm forced to wrap a hand around her wrist to get her attention. I shift my eyes to the sign by the door, the same one we saw on the wall next to the hostess stand.

Etta immediately bows her head. "I'm so sorry. I . . . I get a little too excited sometimes."

"That's quite all right," Amelia tells her with a gentle smile. "I understand. I felt the same way the first time I walked through the finished restaurant. It feels like you're being transported to another world. And welcome to both of you."

"Yes, exactly!"

"It's absolutely stunning," I add. "And I can't wait to try the food."

Amelia beams. "Oh, the food. The food is sublime. Our chef actually spent a lot of time with the Buddhist monks and nuns in Japan and Korea, learning about their approach to food and cooking."

A murmur of voices directs our attention to the open doorway. Soon another familiar face enters, followed by two others. A gasp goes up beside me, and I turn in time to see Anna slap a hand over her mouth. She averts her gaze when I make eye contact.

That's weird.

"Excuse me. I need to go say hi," Amelia tells us.

I watch her walk over to the trio and greet them with a slight bow. Mr. Kwan is dressed smartly in a well-tailored business suit, and Mrs. Kwan in a magenta sheath dress. As they interact with Amelia, it's obvious that, as usual, Mrs. Kwan is doing all the talking.

"Do you know them?" Etta asks in a low voice.

"They're the Kwans," I reply. "They're friends with my family."

Her jaw drops. "Who's the hot guy?"

I bite back a laugh. It's not hard to guess who she's talking about. Etta's eyes are pinned on Joey, who's wearing a pale blue button-up. The collar of the shirt is opened enough to expose his neck and throat, and the black slacks he's wearing show off his toned physique. This is better than any meet-cute I could have planned.

I reach over and close her mouth. "That's Joey."

Etta gasps. "Wait. The Joey I've been chatting with on your app?"

"One and the same," I answer, grinning.

Amelia gestures for them to follow her to their table. I wait for them to pass before waving at Mrs. Kwan. She claps her hands together.

"Gigi!" She pulls me into her arms. "I didn't know you were going to be here tonight! Is your mom feeling any better?"

Since Mom and she have been talking on the phone nearly every day since the Kwans came back, I merely nod.

"She's resting at home, but she didn't want us to miss the opening."

"Well, I can understand that. But what luck for us to end up in the same dining room," she comments.

I turn to her husband. "It's nice to see you again, Mr. Kwan."

"It's lovely to see you too, Gigi," he answers in a quiet voice. "Will your dad be joining you?"

"I'm afraid not. He's working late tonight."

"That's too bad. We would have loved to see him, but no rest for the weary, I suppose," Mrs. Kwan interjects. "And who's this you've got with you?"

"I'm Etta," she tells them before I can introduce her. "I go to school with Gigi."

Mrs. Kwan rewards her with a brilliant smile. Joey steps forward with one of his own.

"It's great to finally meet you in person, Etta."

He sticks his hand out toward her, and she gives it a shake. When he winks, Etta positively melts. I slip an arm through her elbow, convinced her legs will give way any moment. Only then do I notice Anna standing behind Etta in complete silence, watching the whole exchange with keen interest. She must feel my eyes on her, because she turns to me. Her cheeks flush when Mrs. Kwan spots her.

"Anna? Anna Tam! I almost didn't recognize you. You've grown so much!"

She stiffens as Mrs. Kwan puts her arms around her, only relaxing when the older woman lets go.

"Hello, Mrs. Kwan, Mr. Kwan," she utters, bowing slightly.

"I hope your parents are well," Mr. Kwan says, smiling softly at her. "Are they somewhere nearby?"

Anna shakes her head. "They are well, thank you, but I'm here with Etta and Gigi tonight."

Mrs. Kwan angles her eyes at her son. "Joey, aren't you going to say hi to everyone?"

"I was just waiting for you to finish, Mom," he answers smoothly before turning to us. "Hi, Gigi."

I'm surprised at his subdued greeting, but smile nonetheless. "Hi, Joey."

Anna doesn't quite meet his eyes when he shifts his gaze to her. "Hello, Anna."

"Hello," she mumbles.

That's . . . interesting.

"Well, we should take our seats, sweetheart," Mr. Kwan suggests to his wife. "They'll be starting soon."

"Oh, yes, of course!" Her eyes move from Joey to me and back. "Darling, why don't you keep the girls company so they don't get lonely?"

"I wouldn't want to bother them," he replies.

"No bother! None at all! We'd love for you to join us!" Etta practically shouts before remembering the rules. "That is, only if you want."

He stares at me. "Gigi? It's up to you."

Even without Etta boring a hole in the side of my head, I would have agreed. It'll be nice to catch up about what he's been doing. I sneak a peek at Anna, but she's busy staring at the tatami at her feet. I gesture at our horigotatsu.

"Welcome to table three."

Chapter 16

"Hold up. You've *never* heard of *Rampant*?" Joey asks, incredulous. "How is that possible?"

He and Etta are staring at me as if I've told them I'd been abducted by aliens. Even Anna, who's spent the first two courses of dinner with her eyes glued to the table, snaps to attention.

"It's only one of the best period zombie movies Korea has ever put out," he continues as he swallows his last bite of Wagyu beef sashimi. "I thought you said you loved *Kingdom*."

"I do! I just didn't know it had a spin-off movie," I insist.

"It's not a spin-off," Etta explains, taking a sip of her lemon pomegranate mocktail. "But they're both zombie stories set during Joseon-era Korea."

Joey waves his chopsticks at me. "By the way, don't pay attention to the critics' reviews. They were totally off on this movie."

"Maybe we could watch it together," Etta suggests. "Have a movie night."

"That's a great idea!" he agrees. "We can do it at my house. We've got a theater room that hasn't been used in three years."

Etta claps her hands together, drawing the ire of the other two tables nearby. She turns bright red and apologizes profusely. To his credit, Joey doesn't bat an eye.

"So? How about it?" he asks.

"Please say yes, Gigi. You have to watch it. It's so good!"

To be honest, I was ready to agree when Etta suggested the idea. Listening to her constant chatter and Joey's stories about his time in Singapore has been a nice distraction from not having Mom and Dad here. The fact we're discussing a zombie apocalypse in the middle of our meat entree makes me smile even more.

I nod. "I'll bring the snacks."

"Yay!" Etta turns to Anna. "You'll come too, right?"

"Sorry, I can't," Anna murmurs. "I'm super busy with school, plus I'm running Flowers for Dollars next week."

"Oh! I forgot to tell Gigi I'm helping out with that," Etta exclaims before turning to me. "We stopped by the shop to pick out the flowers before we went to Kinokuniya. It must be so nice to get flowers for Valentine's."

She sighs the last part, while I swallow a groan. Flowers for Dollars is a fundraising event Peer Squad runs during the week leading up to Valentine's Day. Students can buy flowers to send to their friends, crushes, or significant others. They're delivered by volunteers—like Etta, apparently—during the school day. The money that's raised is then donated to a different charity each year.

Of course, it never takes long for it to turn into a popularity contest, with students vying to receive the most flowers every year. It's because of this I don't normally participate, but Mrs. Brown had asked me to spearhead it this year. Unfortunately, I was so caught up with Quizlr I completely forgot to email her back. Now, with Valentine's Day coming up on Thursday, there's no point in offering to help.

"So you'd rather slay homework than bloodthirsty zombies?" Joey teases Anna.

"Yes."

Even I feel the chill. If the tension between them was interesting before, it's an irresistible mystery now. It's begging to be solved, and I'm up for the challenge.

"By the way, I've never asked, but how long have you guys known each other?" I lean over to Etta. "I met them in class the first day of fourth grade, but they were already friends."

"Our parents go way back. Not as far as yours and mine, of course," Joey explains. "But we met at my eighth birthday party. I had it at Wollman Rink."

"You can ice skate?" Etta asks.

"If you call flapping like a chicken and falling on your butt skating, then yes," Anna answers first, the hint of a smile on her lips.

"I only pretended to be bad so you would talk to me," Joey insists. "And it worked."

Anna rolls her eyes. "Yeah. I told you to get off the rink before you hurt someone."

"That's not how I remember it."

"But that's what happened," she retorts.

Joey folds his arms over his chest. "Well, I like my version better."

Anna cracks a smile, and he grins back at her. For a second, the air between them thaws, but it ices back over so quickly I wonder if I imagined it.

"Everything we've eaten so far is mind-blowing," Etta comments, unaware of the tension. "I've never tasted anything so delicious in my life. And we're only getting started."

For once, her tendency to blurt out the first thing on her mind comes in handy. Our two dinner companions seem to snap out of their trip down memory lane.

Joey nods. "I agree. I ate at many award-winning restaurants while I was in Singapore, and this easily rivals the best of them."

I feel the same. Amelia has really gone all out on the menu. I never thought I would enjoy food that avoided using any garlic, onions, or heavy spices, but the way Chef Ferr prepared everything so far has made me forget I ever cared for those seasonings.

"Excuse me. I need to use the restroom," Anna says, standing up.

She doesn't wait for anyone to acknowledge her before leaving. Joey's eyes follow her out the door before returning to the table. His gaze lands on me briefly, but I find it impossible to guess what he's thinking.

"The instructions they gave us on how to savor everything really add to the experience too," I finally add.

Before each of the last two courses, our waitress encouraged us to use all our senses before tasting the food—examining the way each dish is built, taking a deep breath to inhale the aromas, and then, finally, putting the bites in our mouth. Between courses, we also receive a palate cleanser.

As if on cue, our waitress stops by to collect our empty plates. Based on how much time there was between the earlier courses, the next one isn't due to arrive for at least twenty minutes.

"Since we have a break, I'm going to take a look around." Joey pushes back from the table and draws his legs out from beneath it. "Either of you want to join me?"

Predictably, Etta volunteers. "I would!"

He offers a hand to help her up. When her foot snags on the edge of the seating, Joey saves her from tumbling to the ground by catching her in his arms. The whole thing practically happens in that K-drama, slow-motion way, right down to the stunned look in Etta's eyes.

"You okay?" he asks her.

She follows the movement of his lip, but doesn't hear his question. He repeats himself.

"Yes!" Even Etta cringes at how loudly she answers. "I mean, yes, I'm fine. Thank you."

"What about you?" Joey asks me. "Why don't you come too?"

"Oh, I—"

I peek at Etta, expecting her to offer resistance, to send some sort of signal to stay behind. Instead, she gestures frantically for me to stand up. I sigh and push myself onto my feet, though I still hesitate.

"Shouldn't we wait for Anna to come back?" I ask.

"She'll find us," Joey answers, a little too casually. "It's a small restaurant."

With no other excuses not to leave, the three of us put on the guest slippers and step out of the room, turning to our left to head deeper into the restaurant. Once we make our way past the row of private dining rooms, we discover a staircase leading up to the second floor of Shibui. Joey starts up the steps, but I stay rooted in place.

"I don't think we're supposed to go up there."

He chuckles. "If they didn't want us exploring, don't you think they'd put up a rope or a sign?"

"Even so, Amelia mentioned something about a tour of the space after dinner," I remind him. "We should wait until then."

Joey frowns. "But then we'll be stuck in a big crowd. Who knows what we'll be able to see? Wouldn't you rather take a peek now?"

Before I can turn and head back, Joey grabs both Etta and me by the hand.

"Come on, let's go check it out!"

I let myself be dragged up the stairs. When we reach the landing, we circle to the left and all stop in our tracks.

"Wow," Etta murmurs, speechless for the first time.

Wow, indeed. It's clear the second floor is an indoor/outdoor space meant for hosting private parties. The front half of the floor has a similar design to the dining rooms downstairs, with the decorative wooden lanterns hung above our heads and shoji screens all around. However, instead of the tatami floor, the cherrywood from below covers the space. In the center is a bar with counter seating, surrounding what looks like a minikitchen. More of the horigotatsu are spread through the whole space.

The highlight, though, is the outside patio, which is currently protected by a set of clear plastic awnings. We cross the room and peer through the large panes of glass. Similar to the small Japanese Zen garden in the front foyer downstairs, the outdoor space is filled with gorgeous plants, a koi pond, and even a little red step bridge. Hanging on wires extended from wooden poles are paper lanterns of various shapes and colors, casting a rainbow onto the foliage below.

Joey follows the wall over to the far corner of the room, while Etta and I continue peering through the glass. We're so absorbed with taking in all the details that we don't hear the voices until they're practically on top of us.

"This has to be the private party space. It'll be perfect for my birth—"

Etta and I twirl around and come face-to-face with Summer and Tyler. The minute she recognizes us, Summer moves to put distance between them. Even so, it's obvious they came together.

"T-Tyler? What are you doing here?" Etta asks.

"I . . . I didn't know you'd be here," Tyler says after clearing his throat. "I thought you were gonna stay home and catch up on *Bleach*."

I turn to Etta with a question in my eyes. Hers fills with panic as her cheeks turn beet red.

"Gigi invited me at the last minute," she mumbles without looking at him. "But obviously you changed your mind too."

"What does she mean, you changed your mind?" Summer asks, smacking Tyler on the arm. "And how did you know what she was planning on doing tonight?"

"I—"

Before he can answer, Joey walks up. He glances at each of us and raises an eyebrow.

"What did I miss?"

It takes exactly one second for Summer to shove Tyler out of the way—and out of her mind. He scowls at her, but shakes his head and walks back to the landing at the top of the staircase. Etta's eyes follow him, but she stays rooted in place near the glass panels. I start to move toward her, but I'm also worried about Joey. Singapore might have given him good looks and newfound confidence, but I doubt it's prepared him for the force of nature heading his way.

Before I can intercept her, Summer tucks herself next to Joey and flutters her lashes at him.

"Hi. I'm Summer. Summer Benson."

If he's thrown off by her directness, Joey keeps it under wraps. Instead, he brandishes a charming smile.

"Joey Kwan. It's nice to s—" He clears his throat. "Nice to meet you."

Summer gasps. "You're the one everyone's been talking about at Superbia."

"What? They are?" he asks.

Only I notice the flash of panic in Joey's eyes, much like how he used to react when there were only unkind words to be had.

"Of course, silly," Summer answers, moving another inch closer and touching him on the shoulder. "It's not every day a K-pop idol shows up at our door."

My mouth drops open.

You've got to be kidding me.

He's the Korean guy Kyle mentioned? I glance at Joey, but he is strangely unperturbed. In fact, he seems . . . amused.

"But he's not a K-pop idol," I start to clarify. "He's not even K—"

"What Gigi means is that I'm not much of a singer," Joey interrupts rather loudly. "I'm more of a . . . thespian."

"Oh, even better," Summer croons. "I'm going into acting too. We should run lines together sometime."

"Um, sure, I guess," he replies.

She giggles and gestures for him to lean down, whispering something in his ear that sends his eyebrows to the ceiling.

I clear my throat. "Joey. I think it's time for us to go back. They're probably serving the next course now."

His eyes stay pinned on the petite girl latched on to his every word—and now his arm.

"Joey," I repeat more firmly.

"Why don't you go? I'll take good care of Joey," Summer says, smirking at me.

I expect Joey to tell her he's with us, but he just shrugs.

"You can go ahead, Gigi. I'll be right there."

"Fine."

Shoving aside my annoyance, I turn toward Etta. She's gone. *Great.*

She probably got upset and left. With our next course likely chilling at our empty table, I head back in search of my friend.

About halfway down the steps, I hear the hushed tones of a conversation. Once my feet hit the floor, I find Tyler and Etta in a heated conversation in the alcove behind the stairs. I can't make out what they're saying, but it's not hard to guess she's upset based on the way she's jabbing her finger at him.

I scoot closer, hoping she'll notice I'm nearby, but she's absorbed in whatever they're talking about. As color rises into Etta's cheeks, I cough loudly into my hand. That gets both their attention, and Etta walks off. Tyler starts to follow her, but a warning glare from me sends him skittering in the opposite direction.

I catch up with Etta outside our dining room, staring unseeingly at the embroidery on the silk-covered wall. I loop my arm through hers and tug her gently inside. Our table is empty.

That's weird.

Where's Anna?

"She said she wasn't feeling well and needed to leave," Mrs. Kwan pipes up from the next table. "Anna. I'm assuming that's who you're looking for."

"Yes," I confirm. "Thank you for telling me."

"I do hope she'll be all right," Mrs. Kwan adds. "She was rather pale."

I don't remember her looking sick before we took our break, but she did run to the bathroom awfully quick. Maybe something upset her stomach.

"I'll check in with her a little later," I promise.

"Where's Joey?" Mr. Kwan asks.

"Oh, um . . . he ran into one of the other students from our school. They were still talking when we came back," I hedge. "I'm sure he'll be here soon."

Mr. Kwan appears satisfied with this answer, but his wife frowns. Seconds after we sit, our waitress appears with the next course—miso-and-soy-glazed sea bass with steamed pumpkin and butternut squash. The aroma fills my nostrils, clearing my mind of all but the thought of putting a bite into my mouth. It's a minute before I realize Etta hasn't touched her plate.

I nudge her elbow. "Are you okay?"

She shrugs. "I'm sorry."

"Why are you apologizing?" I ask. "I wanted to know if you're okay."

"Yeah, but I know you're upset because I've been talking to Tyler."

I stay silent. I told her she had a right to be friends with whoever she wanted, and I meant it . . . even if I think she's making a huge mistake. Etta's eyes meet mine before she drops her head again.

"Well, don't worry. I'm not going to do it anymore. You were right. He's not a good guy."

"Etta, did he say something to you?" When she doesn't answer, my heart sinks. "Did he . . . do something?"

"No! Nothing like that. In fact, he didn't do or say anything." Etta picks up her fork and pokes at the sea bass. "That's the point. The only time he talks to me is in DMs, or when no one's around."

Something about what she says nags at me. It almost sounds like Etta . . . No, it can't be. She wouldn't. Not after I warned her.

I touch her arm. "Etta, tell me the truth. Do you like Tyler?"

"It . . . it doesn't matter. He's still got feelings for Summer. He practically told me so."

"Etta . . ."

The screen to the dining room slides open, and Joey walks in. Mrs. Kwan scowls as he passes them.

"You're late, son. You kept Gigi and Etta waiting."

He bows his head slightly, first to his mom, and then to us. "I'm sorry."

Joey moves toward our table, but he pauses at the sight of two empty chairs.

"Wh—" He swallows and tries again. "Would you mind if I still sit at the table?"

Considering the way his eyes went to Anna's now-empty seat, I suspect that wasn't his original question. Nonetheless, I turn to Etta.

"What do you think? Should we let him back in, or leave him out in the cold?"

She doesn't seem to hear me, staring intently at the food still neatly arranged on her plate. With Mrs. Kwan watching like a vulture nearby, I force a smile and nod at Joey. He slides back down into the horigotatsu.

"Thank you."

Joey wisely keeps quiet, aware the mood has shifted around us. The waitress brings his plate while I pick up my fork and sink it into the buttery sea bass. It flakes apart easily, and I place it in my mouth. It's utterly delicious, just like the other courses we've had, but I no longer enjoy it as much. I put the utensil down and heave a sigh.

"Would you like to leave, Etta?"

She stiffens. "I—"

"Please don't go," Joey interrupts softly. "I'm having a really good time with you guys."

I narrow my eyes at him. "Really? Because a little while ago you were too busy talking to Summer to notice we were leaving."

"I . . . I didn't want to be rude," he answers weakly. "She was holding on to me really tightly, and I didn't know how to tell her I needed to go."

"I didn't realize Summer was so terrifying."

Joey lowers his voice so only I can hear. "Look, the truth is . . . I had a huge crush on Summer back in middle school, but she never knew I existed. So when we were up there and she started talking to me, I got carried away. I'm really sorry."

"Well, I'm not the one you should apologize to," I tell him. "Etta was really excited to finally meet you in person."

That's mostly true. While I never told her Joey was coming—because I had no idea he would be there—she was clearly enjoying herself before. Plus, even if she's admitted to liking Tyler, there's no denying she has a crush on Joey. I mean, the girl literally fell for him earlier.

Joey takes in our despondent dinner companion. "Oh . . . I didn't realize."

"Now you do. So if you want us to stay, you're going to have to convince her, not me."

He nods resolutely. "I can do that."

Joey climbs partially out of the horigotatsu and shifts to sit next to Etta. Planting one hand on the edge of the table, he leans over to whisper something in her ear. When she doesn't respond, he says something else. This time, her mouth drops open.

"You take that back! How dare you even consider that abomination the best adaptation of such a beloved manga?"

"I knew that would get you," he says, flashing the easygoing smile he perfected during his time in Singapore.

"What are we talking about?" I ask.

"*Ghost in the Shell*," Etta answers. "This imposter said he loved the 2017 movie."

It's my turn to be shocked. "The one with Scarlett Johansson? Even I know that movie was blasphemy."

Joey throws his head back and laughs. "I don't really believe that. I only said it so you would talk to me."

"How do I know you're telling the truth now?" Etta scowls, crossing her arms. "It would be just like a guy to enjoy a movie because of a hot girl in a skintight suit."

"Hey! For your information, I watched it for the plot," he refutes. "And it had a hole so big you could have driven a truck through it."

He waits a beat for his words to set in, then we all burst into laughter. Joey's joke breaks the tension that had settled over us. True to his word, for the remainder of our meal, he makes sure to keep Etta smiling.

When it comes time for us to leave, Joey walks us to the front of the restaurant. He even helps Etta with her coat, a gesture that fills her cheeks with color. With Fernando pulling up, and his parents waiting for him to rejoin them, Joey raises his eyebrows at me.

"So . . . am I forgiven?"

I look over at Etta, who is grinning from ear to ear. "For now."

"Oh, it's going to be like that, huh?"

"Yep."

"Good. I like a challenge," he says, turning to Etta before I can ask him what he means. "I'll catch you later in the chat?"

"Yes, I'd love that," she answers.

"Well, then, good night, ladies."

He returns to his parents' side while I usher Etta into the car. As Fernando shuts the door and comes around to the driver's side, I turn to her.

"That was a nice dinner, don't you think?"

"It was," she answers with stars in her eyes. "Everything was so nice."

"Don't you mean Joey was so nice?" I tease. "You were so busy talking you barely ate anything."

"Oh, he is really nice . . . and handsome, and so funny too." She presses her hands against her cheeks. "I mean, he was all those things before we met in person—except the part about being handsome because I didn't know what he looked like. It's like we've been talking forever and we like all the same things and . . ."

I put a hand on her arm. "Breathe, Etta."

She sucks in a comically deep breath and lets it out. "Okay. Sorry."

"It's okay. I'm glad you like him."

"Is that weird?" Etta asks. "You know, for me to like him and someone else too?"

"I'm guessing Tyler is the 'someone else' you're talking about, so I'd say it's a great thing," I tell her. "Because it shows you there are better guys out there, and you deserve the best."

"Do you really think I have a chance with Joey?"

I shrug casually. "I'm not one to jump to conclusions, but he did spend the better part of the night talking to you, so . . ."

As if right on cue, Etta's phone goes off. She pulls it out of her pocket and gasps.

"It's Joey! He sent me a Quizlr message."

A Quizlr message. There's something so satisfying about hearing that said aloud. I watch as a smile spreads across her face.

"He said he wanted to tell me again how much he enjoyed meeting me tonight." She purses her lips as a new message comes through. "And he wants to know what my favorite color is. Why do you think he's asking me that?"

I have my suspicions, but I keep them to myself. After all, I'll find out if I'm right on Valentine's Day. After sending her reply, Etta clutches her phone to her chest and giggles. I laugh and lean back against the seat. I forgot how much I love it when a plan comes together. Turning my face toward the window, I shut my eyes.

This is only the beginning.

Chapter 17

The drama during our dinner at Shibui pales in comparison to the chaos that follows. On Sunday, Auntie Rose is rushed to the hospital with severe stomach pain. She's ultimately diagnosed with pancreatitis, and has to be admitted for treatment. That same evening, Mom suffers a fainting spell while visiting Auntie Rose, ironically landing her in the hospital for observation.

While Mom's discharged quickly, with Dad back in Japan until week's end, I'm forced to juggle schoolwork, caring for Mom, and checking in on Auntie Rose. Add to that some last-minute tweaks Quizlr 2.0 requires before I can turn it in for quality assurance, and it's a wonder *I* don't collapse by the time Friday rolls around five days later.

"Ugh! It's the third time this app has crashed," I groan. "And we're only on day one of testing."

Kyle tries to hold back a laugh, but ends up looking like he's tasted something foul. With *Worldly*'s February issue needing to be ready within the next two days, he's come over to do one last run-through of the print file. We made some final edits, and are now taking a quick break in my sitting room.

I toss the school-assigned Android phone onto the coffee table, barely missing a vase of blue and purple hydrangeas.

"These don't look like the flowers from school," Kyle comments.

I shake my head. "No. I put those in my room. My dad had these delivered to the house for Valentine's Day. They're my mom's favorite."

Yesterday, Etta texted me in all caps to say she'd gotten a flower from Joey. I didn't have the heart to tell her he sent one to me too. I'm guessing it was his way of continuing to apologize for dinner. Etta then revealed that Summer received the most flowers until minutes before they closed up shop . . . when Kyle stopped by and bought two dozen. He gave six to Etta and six to Anna right on the spot, and sent the remaining twelve to me. I'll admit, seeing Summer's eyes bulge out of her head when they were brought to me during computer science class made my year.

Kyle scoots forward on the couch and points at the discarded phone.

"So what kind of app is it, anyway?"

"It's *supposed* to suggest recipes based on the ingredients in my fridge," I explain, waving a hand in its direction. "But I've tried submitting my list five times, and it keeps crashing."

"So break it two more times. Maybe it'll give that student good luck," he jokes.

I make a face. "I'm not the reason it's not working, Kyle. Something's not right with their source code. And this isn't the first app I tested. That one didn't even open when I tapped on the icon."

"I know it's shocking, but not everyone has your programming skills," Kyle quips, reaching for his Coke. "The rest of us commoners have to pay IT to tell us what we did wrong."

I take a sip of my iced mango green tea. "That's the other thing.

I'm so tempted to see how the chat feature is working on Quizlr, but I can't look at it until quality assurance is officially complete."

He presses his back against the couch. "It works, G."

"How would you know?"

"I tested the app myself," he reminds me. "In fact, I'm still using it to chat with Etta."

His words settle my nerves for a couple of minutes. I gulp down more tea before setting the glass on a coaster.

"The two of you were only in one chat room, though," I think aloud. "What if something's gone wrong with the program? What if no one's receiving their invitations . . . or the computer's not matching them properly?"

I press my face into my hands and groan. "I don't know if I can make it a whole week without knowing."

Kyle drags a hand through his hair. "You're gonna have to, G. But honestly, there's nothing to worry about. Etta, Joey, and I all tested Quizlr before you turned it in. It functioned perfectly."

I lie back against the couch, and a soft sigh escapes my lips as I stare at the ceiling. A second later, his head pops into view.

"Okay, come on. Let's go."

I let him tug me to my feet, but resist when he tries to drag me to the staircase.

"Where are we going?"

"To my house," he tells me.

Originally, the plan was for me to meet him there and have dinner, but Dad's flight from Japan was delayed. He had to go straight from the airport to the office this morning after he landed at JFK, which means he won't be home for a few more hours.

"I already told your mom I wouldn't make it tonight," I remind him.

Kyle shrugs. "So? You know she always cooks too much food. Besides, she's missed you."

"And I miss her too, but I can't leave the house right now, Kyle. My mom's sick."

"And you've spent the entire week at home taking care of her. You have to take a break."

Rationally, he's right, but I can't bring myself to agree. The last time Mom landed in the hospital was two years ago. This isn't one of her usual episodes.

"You can go back if you want, Kyle, but I need to stay here in case Mom needs me."

"Your mom took her medicine half an hour ago and went to bed," he points out gently. "She's sound asleep upstairs."

"Still . . ."

"Okay, we don't have to go to my house, but you need to get out for a bit." Before I can protest further, he grabs me by both shoulders and walks me to the landing. "Go leave a note saying we're grabbing dinner and to call if she needs anything. There're plenty of restaurants close by, so we can come right back if she does."

I might be hesitant, but my stomach is not, grumbling its agreement in stereo.

I sigh. "I'll meet you downstairs."

We split up, with Kyle descending the stairs while I climb the steps. When I reach the master bedroom, I skip the knock and ease open the door. Padding my way down the narrow corridor toward the bedroom, I manage to avoid bumping into any furniture. When I reach her side of the bed, Mom's face is partially covered by her hair. I carefully brush it away, noticing how peaceful she looks in the moonlight. Using my phone as a flashlight,

I grab a pad from her bedside table and scribble a note for her. After placing it by her charging phone, I tiptoe out of the room.

Once I reach the foyer, Kyle helps me slip into my jacket. I set the security alarm, and we exit the house. Just outside our front gate, he tugs me toward the right side of the block.

"You seem to know where you're going," I comment.

"I'm in the mood for sushi, so we're going to Shoga."

I side-eye him. "And you didn't think to ask if that's what I wanted to eat?"

"Did you suddenly decide sushi's not one of your favorite foods?" he counters.

"That doesn't mean I want to eat it all the time," I retort.

"Fine, then." He stops and turns to face me. "Where do you want to eat?"

He raises an eyebrow, calling my bluff. I put my hands on my hips, and we stare each other down for a minute. When my stomach lets out another angry growl, I tip my chin in the direction we were headed.

"Keep walking."

Kyle smirks, his lips parting. I level a glare his way.

"Don't even think about it."

He wisely swallows his laughter, and we arrive at Shoga Sushi a few minutes later. The large glass and steel doors that are usually open during the spring and summer are closed, the light fog on the clear panes hinting at the warmth within. Since it's Friday night, I expected the small restaurant to be packed, but we arrived before the dinner rush and are seated fairly quickly. Sliding into one of the booths lining the wall across from the sushi bar, our waiter brings us the menu.

"Good evening. My name is Shane, and I'll be your waiter today."

He takes our drink orders and returns to check on us a few minutes later.

"Are you ready to order?"

"Yes," Kyle answers. "We'll start with an order of the yellowtail, salmon belly, tamago, and ebi, along with some edamame and seaweed salad."

"Oh, and also a futo maki, shrimp tempura roll, fantasy roll, and an 88 and 2nd roll," I add.

"Anything else?" he asks.

We shake our heads, and he reads our order back to us.

"Okay, so we have one order of yellowtail, salmon belly, tamago, and ebi sushi, plus edamame . . ."

"No, not sushi," Kyle corrects. "The yellowtail and salmon belly should be sashimi."

"Are you sure?"

He frowns. "Yes, I'm sure."

"You know sashimi is only the fish, right?" Shane points out.

Kyle answers him with stony silence. Our waiter clears his throat.

"Um, right. So one order of yellowtail and salmon belly *sashimi*," he repeats aloud, editing our order on his notepad as he repeats it again.

"Yes, that's correct," I confirm.

Kyle waits until Shane walks off before scowling. "I hate it when waiters assume I don't want sashimi."

"We're high school students," I answer gamely. "Sashimi isn't exactly something we eat on the regular."

"That's not why and you know it," he grumbles. "It's because they think I'm white."

"Kyle . . ."

"It's true! How many times have we eaten in Chinatown and the staff insists on bringing me a fork?" He rubs his chin. "They never offer you one."

My reply is put on hold when our waiter brings the edamame and seaweed salad. I glance across the table at Kyle.

"Okay, but you have to admit that being white passing has its advantages." I pick up a pod and suck the soybeans out of it before dumping the shell into the empty bowl. "Remember what happened when COVID first hit? Wong Consulting lost a ton of clients because people were afraid my dad would infect them. He had to go through ridiculous lengths to convince the others to stay. It's only been in the last year that the firm has recovered."

"He wouldn't let you out of the house for weeks," Kyle recalls.

"Exactly. Plus, we both know I would have faced down more than just dirty looks at school if you weren't always with me."

I neglect to mention one particular queen bee's monthlong campaign to convince the school to ban all the Asian students from attending "to protect the health of the general public" when the news reported COVID had reached the United States. I would've been more offended, but it was comical to see her marching into the principal's office with a petition only to belatedly recall the head of our school was also . . . Asian.

Somehow word still got out that she had done this, and rumors started to spread that she was racist. Within hours, Summer posted something on her Instagram story apologizing and insisting she had been misled by some article she read online. The very next day at school, she announced to anyone who would listen that her newest bestie May was teaching her how to be a better ally.

"It shouldn't have been necessary," Kyle answers, bringing me back to the present. "But I'd do it again in a heartbeat."

Our eyes meet across the table, and I'm caught off guard by the intensity in Kyle's gaze. The moment is interrupted when Shane presents our sashimi and sushi orders. I pluck a piece of shrimp tempura roll and dip it daintily into the soy sauce.

"Did I tell you Etta thought I was white when we first met?" he reveals.

I giggle. "Okay, but to be fair, your name is Kyle Miller. That's like . . . super white."

"I suppose that's true, but on the other hand, that's part of why I like her. She understands how I feel."

"What do you mean? There's no way anyone would think Etta is white."

"No, but a lot of times people think she's Hispanic even though she's Filipina. We both know how it feels to be mistaken for something we're not."

There's an unfamiliar twinge in my chest when he says this. It's not like I assume Kyle doesn't have other friends, but knowing he and Etta share something that we don't bothers me more than I want to admit.

"I know the feeling too," I can't help but say.

Kyle shakes his head. "I don't think you do. No one questions what you are. I'm half Chinese and was born in Taiwan, but I've been accused of lying about not being white."

I'm taken aback by his admission. I had no idea people could be so insensitive. Kyle's right. I can relate to the frustration of not living up to someone's expectations, but I'll never experience what it's like to constantly justify being Asian.

"Maybe you should start talking to people in Mandarin," I suggest, wanting to lighten the mood. "They'll definitely believe you then."

He chuckles. "I do speak better Mandarin than you."

"Thanks for rubbing it in."

"Anytime," he answers, grinning.

I pluck some seaweed salad from the plate. Kyle eats all of his sashimi—because ew, texture—before helping me finish the rolls. He then asks for the check and pays for our meal, despite my protests to split the bill. Once the waiter comes back with his card, we leave Shoga and head back to my house.

While he grabs his stuff from the living room, I check in with Mom. She's still asleep and doesn't look like she's budged from her spot. I carefully tear off the note I left her and take it with me. I crumple it once I'm out of the room, tossing it in the trash can in my room before going to say goodbye to Kyle.

"Don't stress out about Quizlr," he repeats after giving me a hug. "Everyone's going to love it, and Ms. Harris will nominate you for the contest."

"And then the world will finally learn of my brilliance?" I add cheekily.

"I wouldn't go *that* far."

I shove him, and he laughs. "Okay, and then the world will learn of the brilliance that is Gigi Wong."

"Much better."

The smile I give him is mirrored back at me, but brighter. My heart abruptly skips a beat. Kyle takes a step forward.

"Are you okay, G?"

I nod. "Um . . . yeah, I think so. I'm probably just tired. Maybe I'll take a quick nap."

"You do that. And text me later so I know you're okay," he instructs.

"I will."

He pulls me into his embrace again, and this time, he holds

on for much longer than usual. I don't really mind, though. I've missed being hugged by someone who feels like home. With James gone and Dad traveling all the time, I'm glad I still have Kyle.

"I'll go so you can get some rest," he says, finally pulling away. "Don't forget to text me."

"I won't. I promise."

Once he leaves, I lock the door and head upstairs. I change into my pajamas and climb into bed, setting my alarm before closing my eyes.

"Just one hour. Then I'll get up and work on homework."

I jolt awake some time later, temporarily disoriented by the complete darkness around me. I barely hear Dad calling my name over the pounding of my heart before I remember where I am.

"Gigi?"

I glance at my phone and let out a curse. I accidentally set my alarm to a.m. instead of p.m. If Dad finds out I took a nap this late at night, I'll never hear the end of it. He hates it when I throw off my sleep schedule. I slide off the bed and flip on the light. After ducking into the bathroom to fix my hair, I rush out of my room and descend the stairs. About halfway down, I run into Dad. He's carrying one piece of luggage in each hand.

"Careful! You shouldn't run down the stairs like that," he chides. "Especially wearing socks. You know we just got the wood waxed. You could have slipped and cracked your head open."

Fernando must have just dropped him off. One look at the dark circles under his eyes and his slightly sunken cheekbones, and I know he's been overdoing it again.

"Sorry, Dad," I mumble. "I'll be more careful next time."

His face softens, and he puts the luggage down to drop a kiss on the top of my head.

"How's your mom doing?"

"She's fine. She took her medicine and went to bed a few hours ago," I answer while relieving him of one suitcase. "How was work today?"

"Hectic." He sighs heavily. "Our patent lawyer almost got sniped by one of our competitors while I was gone. He put in his two-week notice today. It took me almost the entire afternoon to negotiate a new contract and convince him to stay."

Dad instructs me to follow him to the guest suite, which is currently doubling as his temporary bedroom. It's located on the same floor as mine, but on the opposite end of the house. He's been pulling super-long hours at the office to get this expansion done, including taking last-minute red-eye flights out to meet with his partners in Asia. With Mom being a light sleeper, Dad didn't want to disturb her while coming and going at odd hours. There's little I can do to help, but I make sure there's always clean clothes in the closet and fresh sheets on the bed.

I lean against the dresser as he proceeds to unpack. "Does that mean you didn't eat lunch again?"

He frowns. "Hmm, I guess not. Kim made me a plate of something they ordered, but I may have left it in the break room."

I silently thank his personal assistant and make a mental note to tell Mom later. She'll want to thank Kim herself for watching out for him.

"Then why don't you get changed, and I'll heat up something for you?" I suggest. "I'm pretty sure I saw some flank steak and Mom's homemade chimichurri left over from the other night. Or

I can order your favorite pad kee mao from THEP and have it delivered."

I can tell by the look on his face that neither option sounds appetizing. So I change tactics.

"What about a smoothie instead? I can make you one," I coax. "We have strawberries, bananas, mango, papaya . . ."

He shakes his head. "I'm not really hungry, Gigi."

"Dad, you have to eat something," I implore. "It's not good for you to skip so many meals. You wouldn't like it if I did that."

That does the trick, and he concedes. "Fine. I'll take a . . . papaya smoothie."

"Great! I'll be right back."

"Be careful!" He shouts before my foot hits the landing. "Take it slow."

"Maybe I should take the elevator," I half joke.

"That's a great idea," he answers, oblivious. "Use it to come back up too since you'll be carrying something."

I groan. "I'll be careful going down the stairs, I promise."

To demonstrate my point, I keep one hand on the banister as I descend . . . at least until I'm out of sight. Once in the kitchen, I pull the bag of frozen papaya and ice cubes from the freezer, along with almond milk and his favorite vanilla-flavored vegan protein powder. After blending it all together, I pour it into the tallest glass I can find. I also decide to heat up the flank steak, hoping to entice Dad into eating more food.

With everything balanced carefully on a tray, I take the elevator as asked. Even if I were willing to tempt fate by walking up freshly waxed stairs with his dinner in my hands, Dad would kill me on the spot. In the bedroom, I find him propped up against the headboard with the TV on. His attention, however, is on the laptop in front of him.

"You're supposed to be relaxing!"

"I was!" he insists, though guilt riddles his features. "I had to take care of one last urgent email."

I narrow my eyes. "Dad."

He closes the laptop and puts it to the side. "See? All done."

I bring the tray to the side of the bed and hand it to him. He eyes the extra food I prepared.

"Didn't I say I wasn't hungry?"

"I haven't had a chance to eat dinner either," I lie with a winning smile. "So I figured we could eat together."

"In that case, pull up a seat," he jokes, patting the spot next to him.

I climb onto the bed, and he positions the tray between the two of us. I pick up a piece of flank steak and dip it into the chimichurri, popping it into my mouth. Dad takes a couple sips of the smoothie and purses his lips.

"What else did you put in here?"

"Some protein powder," I say after swallowing. "You need the extra calories if you're not going to eat."

He makes a noncommittal noise and continues to drink. Meanwhile, I have another slice of the steak with a happy moan. When I stab a third piece with my fork, his eyes follow the movement. I hold it out to him.

"Maybe I was hungrier than I thought," he begrudgingly admits once he finishes chewing.

I suppress a grin. "Here, eat the rest of it. I'll get more."

I hop off the bed before he can protest. When I return, there's nothing left on the tray except an empty plate. Dad's leaning back with his eyes closed, his fingers wrapped around the half-finished papaya smoothie. I leave my plate on the writing desk nearby and touch him gently on the forearm.

"Dad?"

He stirs, but doesn't wake. I wiggle the glass out of his hand and place it on the nightstand. I've turned off the TV and am almost out of the room when I hear my name.

"Where are you going?"

I turn back to him. "You fell asleep, so I was going to eat downstairs."

"No, no, I wasn't asleep. I was resting my eyes," he answers. "Come sit down and catch me up on what's been going on with you."

Dutifully, I scoot back onto the bed while he holds my food. He hands it back to me, waiting until I've taken a couple of bites before speaking.

"So how's school? It's been, what, two weeks since you started back?"

I laugh. "Dad, it's been a month."

"Ah. Time really flies." He cocks his head to the side. "And?"

"And . . . I kinda wish it was summer already."

He laughs. "That bad, huh?"

"We're not even to spring break and my teachers are already talking about finals," I vent. "Not to mention I've got at least two major projects due within the next two weeks, and my next round of tests at the end of the month."

"You'll ace everything. I have complete confidence in you." Dad pats me on the hand. "But remember not to overwhelm yourself. If that means your grades aren't the highest in some subjects, then so be it. Focus on what you're good at."

"That's not what you tell James," I blurt out.

He stiffens. "That's different, Gigi. James is—"

"A boy?"

"I was going to say the oldest, but I suppose there's a little bit of that too," Dad admits. "One day, James will be the head of this family. That comes with a lot of responsibility. Our future depends on his success. That's why we're so hard on him."

This has always been a sore point between us. Dad is forever emphasizing how important it is to be the best, but he also has very different expectations for his two children.

"I want to make you guys proud," I say in a low voice.

He frowns. "What makes you think we're not proud of you?"

"James graduated a semester early *and* was valedictorian of his class."

"That doesn't mean you have to follow in his footsteps."

That only makes me feel worse. Dad might be quick to boast about my accomplishments, but he's also the first to discourage me from pursuing anything he thinks is too hard.

He rubs his temples. "Aren't you one of the top students in your class?"

"One of . . . but not *the* top," I mumble.

Dad reaches over and strokes my hair. "Sweetheart, even if those other students have better grades, you're more well rounded. That'll get you further in life. Besides, your mom and I are worried you'll burn out with all this stress."

I lapse into silence, wringing my hands. Dad reaches out and cups my cheek.

"Sweetheart," he says again, "your mom and I are extremely proud of you. Not everyone can juggle all the activities you have and still get good grades. Not to mention, you take wonderful care of Mom. That's why I never worry about her when I'm on my business trips, or if I'm working late. I know you're here to make sure she's okay."

"I take good care of you too," I add.

"Of course you do." He tucks my hair behind my ear. "You're the best daughter we could ever ask for."

I smile. He leans over the tray and presses a kiss to my temple.

"That's my girl. Now, finish eating, and I'll let you decide what movie we watch tonight."

Not even thirty minutes later, I sneak out with the dinner tray, leaving Dad snoring lightly in bed. After rinsing the dishes and arranging them in the dishwasher, I head back to my room. Restless, I send James a text, but after waiting twenty minutes with no reply, I turn my laptop on instead. My fingers itch to log in to Superbia's server and sneak a peek at what's happening, but Kyle's words echo in my mind.

With a sigh, I log on to Netflix and cue up the next episode of *Rookie Historian*. It's a far cry from my usual choices—*Alice in Borderland* or *#Alive*—but I was drawn to Goo Hae-Ryung's struggle to prove she's more than what society believes she can be. I suppose that hits close to home. Of course, the fact Cha Eun-woo is in it doesn't hurt either. He's the perfect Prince Dowon. Now there's a guy worth giving up a few grade points for.

I pause the episode as my phone pings. It's a message from Kyle.

You okay? You never texted me.

I squeeze my eyes shut for a second. I completely forgot.

Sorry. Fell asleep right after and then ate dinner and watched a movie with Dad.

Better not have been Peninsula, he sends back. **That's our thing.**
I grin. **I would never. Besides, Dad's not the zombie type.**

We exchange a few more messages before bidding each other good night. I press play again, but a few seconds in, I yawn. Turns out I'm more tired than I thought. I climb out of bed and put my laptop on my desk before heading into the bathroom to get ready for bed. When I come back, there's a missed call and a new text from James waiting for me.

Didn't mean to call so late. Had to charge my phone. I know things have been rough, but if anyone can handle it, it's you. You're stronger than you know.

I can hear his voice as I read it to myself, and the ache returns to my chest. I really needed James here this week. He's so good at calming me down. As if by magic, another message appears.

Read it until you believe it.

By the time sleep comes for me, I very nearly do.

Chapter 18

"There's something I need to talk to you about, Gigi."

I'm walking into Ms. Harris's class the following Wednesday when she waves me over to her desk. Out of habit, my gaze drops down to her feet, and I'm surprised to find a rather subdued pair of black combat boots. That is, until I notice the skulls and roses embroidered over them in iridescent black thread.

I look back up at her face, trying to decipher if what she wants to tell me is good or bad news. She waits an agonizing ten seconds before leaning in and whispering conspiratorially.

"Congratulations. You're now an official contestant in the first annual SJW Tech Junior Coding Contest."

The words take a second to sink in, and then my heart starts to race.

"Thank you so, so much, Ms. Harris!"

I throw my arms around her impulsively before stepping back and apologizing profusely. She laughs.

"It's okay, Gigi. I'm excited for you too." She takes a breath. "I have to be honest, though. You're not the only one I nominated."

"Huh?"

Ms. Harris clasps her hands in front of her. "After looking at all the apps that were submitted, I found yours and someone else's to be equally fantastic. Since I couldn't choose between them, I reached out to the firm and explained the situation. They graciously offered for me to nominate both for the contest. So, you and—"

My heart sinks.

Oh no. Don't say it.

"—Anna Tam will represent Superbia in the contest."

Damn it.

I freeze, worried I've said it aloud again, but Ms. Harris continues to smile at me.

"I love what you did with Quizlr, and I'm sure their judges will too."

With other students streaming into the room, we leave things there. Ms. Harris does grab Anna to give her the same news as she enters class. Oddly, she says little and nods before going to her desk.

I try to catch Anna's eyes, but she keeps them steadfastly forward. After she left Shibui early, I asked Etta for her number and texted Anna to find out what happened. The only reply I got was that she wasn't feeling well and had to leave. My gut tells me there's more going on, but I haven't been sure how to approach her.

Ms. Harris clears her throat. "All right, class, today you'll be turning in all your quality assurance evaluation forms for the apps you reviewed. Please pass everything forward to the front of your row."

I pull my evaluations out of my binder and arrange them neatly before handing them to the student in front of me. After she collects all the papers and puts them on her desk, Ms. Harris grabs a cardboard box.

"Now, please take out the phones you were lent for class and put them in this box."

She walks up and the down the aisles, collecting the devices one by one. When Ms. Harris reaches me, I gently place mine on top of the others. She winks before moving on. With everything collected for the project, she puts the box on the floor behind her desk and grabs her slide remote.

"I will collate all the review feedback for your apps and send them to you by next Monday. You'll have two more weeks to work on your apps before you'll turn them in for your final project grade."

"But that's right before spring break!" Tyler whines. "I thought you weren't going to do that to us."

"I'm sorry, Tyler, it's that or have it hanging over your head during vacation, and I think that's worse," Ms. Harris tells him. "But honestly, there shouldn't be much to do."

"What if your app doesn't work?" someone blurts out.

"If it's not working after a whole semester, I'd say it's unlikely you'll get it working in the next two weeks. But don't worry, I'm looking at the progress you made, not the final product. Do the best you can. As long as I can see the work you put in, you'll still get full credit."

She waits to see if anyone else has questions, and then proceeds to start the lecture for the day. I open my laptop to take notes, and immediately see a ton of notifications from my Twitter app. Keeping one eye on Ms. Harris, I open it and suppress a gasp at the number of message requests waiting for me. None of them are from my mutuals, or even people I follow.

I check the first one, then the second, then the third, fourth, and fifth. All of them are variations of the same questions.

> Is your app available for iPhones? Why can't I find Quizlr in the app store? Can you send me a link to download?

I glance around the room, but everyone's paying attention to Ms. Harris or napping. A couple of students are staring at the phones in their laps, but no one is looking at me. I turn my attention back to Twitter and continue going through my DMs. I count a total of twenty requests, all within the last few days. This is four times as many messages as I'm used to, especially since I've been totally inactive on Twitter lately.

To be honest, I'm not sure how I missed them, but then I remember muting my notifications because of everything that was going on the last week or two. I quickly accept all the requests and send each a similar reply. To my surprise, some of them answer back almost immediately. One of them is a name I recognize from biology class, though I haven't spoken to the guy before.

> How did you find out about my app? I ask.

> Denny had it on his phone and showed it to me.

I frown. Is Denny in AP Computer Science?

> No, but I think he got your app from someone in that class.

My heart picks up pace. When another person DMs me back, I ask the same question. I get the same reply. Someone from one of Ms. Harris's classes shared Quizlr with them. This happens again, and again, and again, until another name pops up that I don't expect.

Joey Kwan sent it to me, a girl named Mellie messages. He said that I should download it because it was a lot of fun.

Joey shared Quizlr with her? But why? I sneak my phone out of my bag and shoot off a quick text to him. Ms. Harris turns around a second after I slide it out of sight. Only after she glances away do I let go of the breath I was holding. I feel the phone vibrate against my leg.

Yeah, I shared it. You said you needed more people to test it out, right? She saw me chatting with Etta and asked what it was, so I gave her the link. Is that okay?

I start to reply, but delete it before sending. I'm not sure what to do about the situation. I never intended for Quizlr to go any further than computer science class or the contest, but as I stare at the new messages still popping up in my DMs, I wonder—is there any harm to letting other people download the app? Joey's right. The more users on the app, the better chance I have of figuring out if there're any bugs in my code.

Something I remember from the SJW contest page prompts me to go back and read it again. As I skim down the long paragraph, one line catches my eye.

Our panel of esteemed industry judges will select the top three semifinalists, and their apps will be posted on our website for public voting.

Public voting. That means if I'm chosen as a semifinalist, I'll need people to vote on Quizlr 2.0 to win. Maybe letting the other students at Superbia download it isn't such a bad idea.

I send Joey a reply before checking the latest message requests on my account. I send anyone who asks a link to my shared drive, but let them know it'll only work on Android. There's no way I could get anything unofficial into the app store, much less something written by a high school student.

By the end of class, I'm getting DMs from people saying they can't download the file because the drive quota has been reached. I lean back in my chair. I had no idea there would be that many people trying to access it. I download the file to another drive and share that link. Within minutes, that one caps out too. I end up telling the rest to wait for the counter to reset in twenty-four hours.

"That's it for today, everyone," Ms. Harris announces, startling me. "We'll pick this up again tomorrow."

Wait. That's it? I missed the whole lecture!

I glance around in a panic, but most of the class has already packed up and left. Then I notice Anna still in her seat. Taking a deep breath, I shove my things into my bag and walk over to her.

"Hey, Anna."

She jumps, looking as though she's contemplating a run for the door. Ultimately, she settles for a small smile.

"Hi, Gigi."

"Congrats on being nominated for the contest," I offer.

"Thanks. You too."

"Um, I know this is kind of out of the blue, but would you mind sharing your notes from today with me?" I ask with an imploring smile. "I . . . forgot to charge my computer and it died halfway through class."

"Oh . . . sure," Anna replies. "Just text me your email."

"Thanks. I really appreciate it."

She grabs her bag and stands. I should be going too, but my feet remain rooted to the spot. As she starts to walk past me, words tumble out of my mouth.

"I hope you're feeling better, by the way."

She blinks. "What?"

"I hope you're feeling better. You know, after Shibui."

Her eyes go wide. "Right, right! Yes, I am . . . Thank you for asking."

"O-okay, then. Thanks. I'll text you my email."

I start to leave, but pause after a few steps. "Actually, there's one more thing."

You can do this, Gigi. Say it like you practiced.

Unable to meet her eye, I aim for a spot just past her right ear.

"What you said before at Kusina Pinoy Bistro . . . you know, about being different. I'm sorry if I wasn't there for you. I know I can't change the past, but I wanted to tell you that."

I don't know what I was expecting from her, but it's not blotched cheeks and a quivering lower lip.

"A-Anna?" I stammer.

She sprints past me and out the door. At first, I don't go after her, but then I remember I've already left her behind once. Thankfully, it's the end of the school day, so it isn't long before I discover her sitting in the *Worldly* room. Her back is to me, shoulders bowed and shaking ever so slightly.

She's crying.

My hands fist at my sides, but I force my feet forward, making sure she catches the sound of my footsteps.

"Anna?"

"Please leave me alone, Gigi," she whispers as I reach her.

Every inch of me wants to do exactly that, walk out the door and pretend none of this ever happened, but I sink into the chair next to her. I clutch my hands in my lap.

"Anna . . . I don't know why we stopped being friends. Maybe I did something wrong, or said something to hurt you. And I'm probably the last person you want to talk to right now, but I'm trying to—"

"It wasn't you."

Anna utters the words so softly I nearly miss them. I wait for her to continue.

"You didn't do anything. It was me." She shifts in her chair, raising her reddened eyes to mine. "Did . . . did you know Joey was my only friend before you?"

I shake my head. Her gaze drops to the floor.

"Well, he was. We did everything together. He was the only one who understood what it was like not to fit in, even though I know it bothered him more than me. Then you came along. Everybody wanted to be friends with you, including Joey."

I open my mouth, but close it when she keeps talking.

"At first, I was okay with it. You seemed so nice, and because we were friends, people who didn't know I existed before started talking to me. But after a while, things changed. Joey started saying he was too busy to meet up, and later I'd find out he was with you. It really hurt to see him choose you over me. That's why I stopped talking to you." Anna takes a steadying breath. "I was jealous."

By this point, my head's ready to explode. Anna was jealous . . . of me?

"The worst part is that I can't blame Joey." She heaves a sigh. "You're perfect. You're pretty and fun and super smart. You make friends so easily, and all the teachers love you. Not to mention all the volunteering you do outside of school. I can't compete with that."

Laughter bubbles into my throat, but I manage to keep it inside. I rub my cheek.

"If anyone can't compete, Anna, it's me with you, not the other way around. My mom's always talking about how great you are, and honestly, your grades are better."

"I would still trade places with you in a heartbeat," Anna whispers.

My mind is reeling, but something she mentioned comes back to me.

"I had no idea Joey was lying to you about being too busy. I swear," I tell her. "I never wanted to exclude you. He told me you were the one who kept canceling on us."

Anna's head snaps up. A mix of emotions plays across her face as she processes what I said. Before either of us can say anything else, my phone pings. It's Kyle.

Where are you?

I check the time and gasp. School's been out for thirty minutes.

"I'm sorry. I have to go!" I exclaim, jumping up from my seat.

She stands as well, but with neither of us sure what to say next, we stare awkwardly at each other. With seconds ticking by, I say the first thing that comes into my head.

"For what it's worth, Anna, I would have picked you over Joey."

A wobbly smile spreads across Anna's lips. She starts to speak, but then my phone rings. I tap on the automatic **I'm on my way** reply before shooting her a helpless look.

"Anna, I—"

"Go," she says. "And thank you for listening . . . for everything."

I return her smile. "Anytime."

I jog out of the room and down the stairs to the front of the building. When Kyle spots me, he relaxes, though a scowl creeps onto his face.

"Where were you? I was worried."

"I'm sorry."

He throws my book bag over his shoulder, and I thread my arm through his free one.

"Something happened and I lost track of time."

"What do you mean?" Kyle asks as I pull him toward the street. "What happened?"

"Well, for starters . . ."

Chapter 19

For the next week and a half after Quizlr 2.0 gets out, I'm at the center of a storm of attention. Walking down the corridors between class, random students keep coming up to me, asking me to change this or add that.

"Are you planning to add more quizzes? Can I make a request?"

"When will you do an update so I can send GIFs?"

"Can you change it so you don't have to answer all the quizzes to get into the chat?"

"Is there a way for you to add other languages?"

People start tagging me on Twitter and Instagram, to the point where notifications come in so frequently they play a melody. Even in class, I can't escape. The number of notes I'm passed while a teacher isn't looking could be bound into a book.

I discover early on that the part everyone loves most about Quizlr isn't the quizzes. It's the chat. Though it's a simple feature, people spend more time sharing what room they were sorted into than their Hogwarts house.

Of course, not everyone's happy.

Take May, for example.

Three days ago, she stomped down the hallway to my locker

as I was switching textbooks between classes. I nearly ascended when I closed the door to find her glaring at me.

"Why am I not in the same chat as Summer?"

I reared back. "What?"

"Your app. I took the quizzes, but it only put September in there with her."

"Well, Quizlr puts you in chats based on compatibility," I explained.

"What the hell does that mean?"

I took a deep breath. "It means that you have to share enough of the same answers on the quizzes to get invited into the same chat."

"Then you need to switch me into Summer's chat."

"I can't. The app sends out the invitations automatically. There's nothing I can do."

May scowled. "You're lying. You don't want me to be in her chat because you're jealous."

"Jealous? Of what?"

"You used to be one of her best friends, and then she dumped you," she sneered. "You want to get back in with her, so you're trying to drive us apart."

I took a step toward her, making the most of the four-inch height difference between us.

"Okay, first of all, I don't want anything to do with Summer. I'm very happy we're no longer friends. And second of all, if you think she cares about you, think again. The only person Summer loves is herself. If she's friends with you right now, it's because you make her look good."

"How dare—" May sputtered. "Summer . . ."

"I'm sorry, but it's the truth. You'll see it sooner or later, but

I hope it's before she hurts you," I told her as nicely as I could manage before walking off.

She's not the only one who hasn't been happy with the compatibility results. Just last period, I came around the corner and found myself smack in the middle of a fight between two guys.

"It's not my fault I ended up in the chat with Daniel!" the shorter one with dirty-blond hair was shouting. "The app put us together!"

"That doesn't mean you had to talk to your ex! You didn't have to click on the invitation!" the taller redhead shouted back.

"That doesn't make sense, Russell! How would I know who was in the chat before I clicked on it in the first place?!"

"You could have left the chat . . . or deleted the app once you knew, Cal!"

Cal scoffed. "Maybe I don't want to. Maybe I'd rather talk to someone who actually listens to what I have to say!"

"Excuse me if I don't want to listen to you complain about your life for hours!" Russell yelled back.

I ducked around the corner before they caught sight of me. I didn't want to risk being recognized, and I definitely didn't want to get in the middle of that fight.

Apparently, there've been more than a few arguments like this after Quizlr unintentionally separated couples into different chats. I don't get why they don't text each other instead, but it's enough to make my shoulders tense and my steps quicken at school.

Despite this, there's no denying how it makes my day every time someone tells me how much they love Quizlr. Above all, I'm most proud of how much it's helped Etta. When I turned in the app for quality assurance, I kept her answers—along with

Kyle's and Joey's—and their original chats before adding them to the rest of the database. At last count, she's made a dozen new friends.

In fact, we're having lunch off campus today to catch up. As soon as the bell rings, I rush out to meet her. I nearly careen into a couple of girls who are trying to flag me down.

"I'm sorry, I'm in a hurry!" I yell back before continuing on.

I burst out onto the front steps of the school. Etta spins around with a yelp.

"Oh my gosh, Gigi! You scared me to death."

I grab her by the elbow and drag her down the street. She does her best to keep up until we round the corner at the next light. Then I slow down and let go of her.

"What was all that about?" she asks, huffing.

"Sorry. It's been a little stressful since people started download-ing Quizlr. I didn't expect it to be this popular," I tell her.

She grins. "Are you kidding? I love it, and so does everybody else! I know it's not an official app, but it's one of my favorites."

"Really?"

"Yeah! I mean, Kimmie and Denise were telling me about how it's so hard for them to talk to people because they're introverts, and now we hang out at least once a week and we check out mu-seum exhibits and go to the movies and—oh! I took them to the thrift shops you introduced me to and they love them . . ."

For once, I don't interrupt Etta's chatter, happy to listen to the rise and fall of her voice as we walk to Mighty Bowl. Though I do my best to pay attention, after about three blocks, my mind wan-ders to which new quizzes to add to the app.

". . . so I don't know what to do, Gigi."

I start. "What to do about what?"

"Joey," she says, looking at me expectantly.

"I . . . got kind of confused toward the end," I fudge. "Can you explain it to me again?"

She sighs. "I was saying that we've been talking almost every day since we met at Shibui, but in the last couple of days, he's left me on read for hours at a time. I asked him what was going on, but he just said he was busy."

That sets off alarm bells in my brain. This is exactly what Anna said he did with her. I turn to Etta.

"Have you two met up since Shibui? Like, in person?"

"Um, we went to Plug and Play a few times. It's a gaming café," she explains. "And that was a lot of fun."

"Did he . . . you know, do something other than play games with you?"

She turns bright red. "We did . . . kiss once. It was really nice."

"And that was it? He didn't ask you out after?"

"No," Etta answers, her face falling. "I thought maybe he would after the kiss, but that's when he stopped talking to me."

I frown. If Anna hadn't revealed what happened between the two of them, I would've told Etta Joey wasn't that kind of guy. Now I have a sneaking suspicion about where his attention has gone, and it makes my stomach churn.

I put an arm around her shoulder. "Don't worry. I'll talk to him."

"Actually, Gigi, I'm not sure I want you to," she admits. "I've . . . heard some things about him."

We finally get in line at Mighty Bowl, and I pull her against the wall with me.

"What kind of things?"

"Well, Anna said this isn't the first time he's ghosted someone. They—I mean, he was dating one of her friends for a while, but broke up with her after he moved to Singapore. He said he was too busy with school, but then he posted pictures of himself with this other girl."

If there's one thing I know about Etta, it's that she can't tell a lie to save her life. Her face is turning the color of ripe tomatoes as she speaks. I'm starting to think Anna left a few things out during our conversation.

I want to ask her more about what Anna said, but the line moves again. Trying to save time, I place a mobile order while we're waiting. Since we're already here, I choose the option to pay when we reach the register. I'm about to put my phone away when my notifications blow up. Curious, I tap on Twitter. A few seconds into checking my DMs, I gasp.

"What? What's wrong?" Etta asks.

I groan. "Quizlr crashed. I don't know why, but it's not working."

"Are you sure?"

"Give me your phone."

She takes out her phone and unlocks it, handing it to me. I find Quizlr and tap on the icon. The minute I try to do anything on the app, it crashes.

"Oh no. This is bad. This is really bad." I put a hand on her elbow. "Can you grab the food for us? I need to get back and fix this."

"Um . . . sure?"

"Thank you!"

I race back to school, sprinting most of the way. Once I reach my locker, I grab my laptop and head to the *Worldly* office. I know it'll be empty, so it's the best place to work. It isn't until I've sat down and started typing that something occurs to me.

I didn't give Etta any money.

My heart sinks, but another DM pops up on my phone.

I'm sure it'll be fine.

I'll pay her back later.

♡

Etta never shows up with the food. I expect her to text once she's back on campus, but I don't hear from her. With my mind full of code, and desperate to troubleshoot whatever is going on with Quizlr while pretending to pay attention in class, I completely forget about her. It isn't until I walk out school at the end of the day that I'm unexpectedly reminded.

"I need to talk to you," Kyle states the minute I appear.

I'm so wrapped up in my calculations I don't hear him right away. In fact, I'm inches from walking out onto the road when he drags me back onto the sidewalk.

"Hey! What was that for?" I say.

"Did you *want* to get run over?" he growls. "Because you almost became roadkill."

I duck my head. "Sorry . . . I wasn't paying attention."

"No, you weren't. What is going on with you today?"

"I've got a lot going on right now. Quizlr crashed at lunch, and I haven't been able to figure out what's wrong with it."

His eyes soften. "That explains a lot."

"Explains what?"

"Etta."

I squint at him for a second as my mind tries to decipher what he means. I slap a hand over my mouth when it finally clicks.

"Etta! I left her at Mighty Bowl earlier." I grimace and turn back toward school. "I have to look for her—"

Kyle's arm wraps around my waist, and he twists me around to face him.

"Etta's fine . . . now. But when she called me, she was in a panic."

I frown. "Etta called you? Why?"

"Because you left her holding the check, and she didn't have enough money to pay for everything. She said she tried texting and calling you, but you never answered. She didn't know what else to do."

I fish my phone out of my pocket to check my calls and messages. Sure enough, I missed multiple of both from her. That's when I remember I'd set my phone to Do Not Disturb while I was trying to figure out what was wrong with Quizlr.

I groan. "Did you go help her?"

"Of course I did. I couldn't very well leave her there by herself," Kyle replies. "I took care of the bill and walked her back to school."

I sag against him. "Thank you for doing that."

"You're welcome."

Since I have my phone in hand, I quickly shoot Etta an apology. We continue on our way, but when we reach the next intersection, she still hasn't texted me back.

"Why hasn't she replied?" I ask, half to myself. "She read the message."

"Think about it, G. How would you feel if Etta ran off and didn't answer your phone calls or texts when you didn't have enough money to pay for the food?" Kyle asks gently.

"I'd be pretty upset," I admit, shoulders slumping. "What am I going to do?"

"You should probably give her some space, and then try to apologize again."

I nod. "You're right. This is totally my fault, and I need to own that. I'll find her tomorrow."

"Good, because she's too nice a friend to lose."

"Sounds like you might like her," I tease.

"Of course I do. She's a really nice girl. Last weekend she found out Forbidden Planet was bringing in some of the newest manga from Japan, so we went and spent most of Saturday there," he tells me.

"Oh. That's . . . great."

It doesn't feel great at all. Neither him nor Etta told me they were hanging out so much.

This must be how Anna felt.

My chest tightens as the thought pops into my head, and I do my best to brush it aside.

He wouldn't do that. Kyle's not like Joey.

Nonetheless, by the time we reach my front walk, I'm spiraling. Desperate to prove I'm worrying for nothing, I lean toward Kyle, anticipating the hug that usually accompanies our goodbyes. He only nods.

"Don't forget to call Etta and apologize."

My heart drops. "I won't."

"All right. I'll see you later."

Kyle spins on his heel and walks up to his house, unlocking the door and stepping inside.

He never looks back.

Chapter 20

Needing a distraction, I spend all of Friday night and half of Saturday hunched over my laptop, trying this way and that to sort out what caused Quizlr to crash. I go back into the IDE and look over the source code line by line. I find nothing out of the ordinary, so I check the logs.

That's when I notice a large group of people answered the quizzes in very similar—no, identical—fashion. This makes no sense. There's no way that could happen unless they were sitting in the same room or sharing the answers with each other. I'm puzzled, but too tired to chase down what happened. It's probably a group of friends trying to get into the same chat.

Just to be safe, however, I delete their data and reset their profiles. I also switch out some of the quizzes in the app, both to keep people interested and to prevent this from repeating. Once everything is done, I change the setting of my shared drive to private so no one else can download the app for the time being. Satisfied, I lie down for a nap.

I wake up in a daze a couple hours later when my alarm goes off, and drag myself to the kitchen to make myself some dinner. It's only then that I remember I never ate dinner last night, or breakfast today.

No wonder my brain feels like it's gone through a meat grinder.

I head to the refrigerator and grab the handle. That's when I see the note Mom left on the door.

Auntie Rose is getting discharged today. She'll be staying with us for a few days. Please get the guest bedroom ready for her.

I groan aloud. The last thing I need is to take care of another person right now. I grab some leftovers from the refrigerator and stick them into the microwave. I sit down to eat, though I taste very little of it. After putting my dirty dishes into the dishwasher, I head to our house's second guest suite in the basement.

It's been quite a while since anyone's stayed down here, so I strip the mattress and put on fresh sheets and pillowcases. Once the comforter is back in place, I carry the old set to the laundry room. Figuring I have maybe a couple hours before my parents come home with Auntie Rose, I head back upstairs and open up my laptop. After more thought, I pick the quizzes that are easiest to replace and change some of the questions as well. I've barely put the finishing touches on the update when Mom calls my name from downstairs.

"Coming!"

A few minutes later, I find Mom easing Auntie Rose into bed. I quickly jump in to help. It's only been a couple of weeks since she went into the hospital, but my great-aunt looks like she's aged ten years. Her skin has taken on a sickly pallor, and her hair is dull and lifeless. She's easily lost ten pounds from her already-thin frame, making her look frail.

"Can you get her some water, please?" Mom asks.

"Of course."

I run up the flight of stairs to pour a glass of cold water. Mom's propped her up against the headboard with pillows when I return, and I give her the cup. Auntie Rose wraps both hands around it and takes a single sip before handing the glass back. I place it on the nightstand and perch myself on the edge of the bed.

"How are you feeling, Auntie?"

"Like I've been fed nothing but ice chips for days," she grumbles. "I want some real food."

"I'll make you something to eat, but we have to stick to the diet the doctor gave us," Mom answers. "You don't want to end up back in the hospital, do you?"

Auntie Rose grumbles in response. Mom gives me a helpless look before leaving to start dinner.

"I'm glad you're here," I say.

Auntie Rose slips her hand into mine. "I'm glad too. I bet you were pretty worried about me."

To be honest, I've been so busy with Quizlr I'd nearly forgotten about her. In fact, I haven't visited her in the hospital since the first week she was admitted. The thought makes me sick to my stomach. I hide it with a bright smile.

"I missed you a lot, Auntie. Saturdays haven't been the same without you."

"Well, no need to worry. As soon as I get my strength back, we'll be back in business. In fact, I got a call from Miss Wu while I was in the hospital, and . . ."

She pauses, looking at me expectantly.

"Oh! And what?" I exclaim a little too loudly.

Auntie cocks an eyebrow at my delayed reaction, but continues anyway.

"*And* she decided to go on a date with one of your picks, Mr. Lu."

"She did? How did it go? Does she like him?"

"Mmmhmm. They've already been on two dates, and have a third planned this weekend."

I can't believe it. I did it! Well, technically, Matchmaker 3000 did it . . . but I wrote the app, so I'm counting it.

"I did it," I whisper in disbelief. "I made a match."

"You did," she agrees, patting the back of my hand. "And I'm very proud of you."

I lean over and envelop her in a hug, careful not to squeeze her too tightly. She chuckles as I sit back.

"At this rate, you'll be matching clients on your own by the time you graduate. Looks like I'll be handing over the reins to you sooner than I expected."

Her words hit me like a punch to the gut. I don't understand. I should be thrilled. This match is the culmination of all the work I've put in for the last year training with her.

So why does it feel like my life is ending?

"Don't say that, Auntie. You have lots of matches in you yet."

The words have a hint of desperation, even to my ears. Auntie Rose's fingers tighten around mine as she pins me with her gaze.

"If you're worried I'll expect you to take over right away, don't be. I want you to go to college and get a degree. Any modern woman should be able to stand on her own two feet. Then you can come back and we'll take the matchmaking world by storm."

Her words don't have the effect she was probably hoping for. Turning college into a delay tactic for the inevitable has me feeling worse about my future. Nonetheless, I take a deep breath and plaster a smile onto my face.

"That sounds great, Auntie."

Great-Aunt Rose tilts her head to the side, but she opts not to share whatever she's thinking with me. As the minutes tick by, I grow more restless, so I pull my hand away and stand up.

"You should get some rest, Auntie. I'll go see if Mom needs any help with dinner."

As I reach the doorway, she calls out.

"Gigi?"

I glance back over my shoulder at her. "Yes?"

"Are you sure you're okay?"

"Yes, Auntie. I'm fine," I lie. "I'll be back to check on you in a bit, okay?"

I'm halfway up the stairs before she has a chance to respond.

The next forty-eight hours go by in a whirlwind of putting down code, tending to Auntie Rose, and sneaking catnaps. When the updates I made to Quizlr 2.0 finally come together, I celebrate by passing out on the couch. In fact, Dad snaps a picture of me with drool dripping out of my mouth and sends it into our family group chat.

Gigi said namaste in bed, he captions it.

James replies with an eye-roll emoji while I leave Dad on read. It's better if he doesn't think he's funny. As always, however, Mom supports his dad-joke agenda by sending a GIF of someone rolling on the floor, dying of laughter.

By Monday night, the only thing fueling my homework session is caffeine and adrenaline. That's clearly not enough, because about halfway through my precalculus homework, my brain just . . . stops. All the numbers start looking the same. I add when I should subtract, and label a graph logarithmic when it should be exponential. I'm almost positive half the answers I come up with are incorrect, but I'm running out of brain cells.

I decide it's time to take a break from the books—which means opening Twitter to read my messages. Most of them are people telling me Quizlr is working again. I pause to send a silent thanks to the universe for that. After scrolling through my timeline to like and retweet some posts, I'm about to log out when a new DM comes through. It's from Joey.

> Hey, Gigi. Haven't talked to you in a while.

I think back to my conversation with Etta the other day . . . which reminds me I haven't reached out to apologize again. I check her account and see she was active a couple minutes ago, so I send her a quick message.

> I'm really sorry about what happened on Friday, Etta. I didn't mean to leave you there like that.

I switch back to reply to Joey.

> I've been busy, Joey. I hear you've been too.

> What do you mean?

> Etta says you haven't been chatting with her lately.

I notice she's sent me a reply, and I click on our chat to see what she wrote.

I was really scared, Gigi. The cashier was so annoyed, and the customers behind me were cussing at me because I was taking too long.

I'm so sorry, Etta. I never meant to put you in that situation.

I don't know how to make it up to you, but I swear I will.

Please forgive me.

I get three blinking dots, so I go back to Joey.

I knew she would say something about that. I can explain.

Okay, then talk.

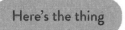

I wait a minute, but nothing comes through. Whatever he's writing, it's taking a while. A notification pops up for Etta, and I flip back to our chat.

Why didn't you answer your phone?

Honestly, I had my phone on Do Not Disturb so I could work on Quizlr.

I didn't realize I had missed your calls and texts until it was too late.

Oh. I didn't know.

It doesn't matter. It's not an excuse for not checking on you.

I should have done that no matter what.

It's okay. I know you've been stressed out.

I growl when Joey's DM pops up in the middle of my reply to Etta. I'm about to switch back when I see the paragraph he sent me.

Etta's really cool.

I told you before that I've never met a girl who knew her stuff the way she does.

I totally get why you wanted to introduce us. She's the kind of girl I'd usually go for.

Then what's the problem?

It's not really a problem. I don't know how to explain it.

Try.

I really missed talking to you.

Aww. I missed talking to you too.

> And sorry if I'm not replying right away.
>
> Joey's messaging me too.

Joey?

At this point, the messages start coming back-to-back. If Joey is midreply, Etta's sending me something. I tap back and forth on the chat boxes, trying to keep up.

It's not that I don't like her. I like her a lot.

But she doesn't really fit what I want to be right now.

> What is that supposed to mean?

Why is Joey messaging you? Is he saying something about me?

> I'm asking him why he's been ghosting you.

Look, Gigi, you remember what I was like before. I wasn't popular.

I didn't have any friends. But ever since I got back, things have been different.

Everyone wants to talk to me, including lots of girls.

So what? You're saying Etta isn't good enough for you?

Has he told you anything yet?

Hold on, he's still writing.

That's not what I mean. Actually, maybe it is.

I think I should keep my options open, you know?

I mean, I'm on a different level now. I need someone who can match that.

Someone like who?

Summer?

Gigi?

What's going on?

Gimme a minute.

Brb.

Yeah. I told you I had a crush on her.

I thought I was over it, but then we ran into her at Shibui and

And what?

OMG. I can't believe he's saying this!

Saying what? Gigi, what?!

Every guy I know wants to be with Summer, okay?

And she says she really likes me, so I'm going to take my shot.

Are you kidding me?! You're dumping Etta for her?

Oh come on, Gigi. You can't seriously think Etta's better than Summer.

Yeah, okay, I get that Etta's super loud sometimes

and awkward and has more fashion cents than sense

and really doesn't know when to stop talking,

but she's still a genuinely nice person and you should give her a chance.

Is that really how you feel about me, Gigi?

I'm shocked to see Etta's reply under my message to Joey.
Oh my god. Did I just—

I scroll up through the earlier DMs and realize I've accidentally sent my message to the wrong person. My heart starts racing.

Etta, I

I thought we were friends.

We are friends! I didn't mean to send that to you. It was a mistake.

Obviously.

Etta, I'm sorry. I didn't mean it how it sounds.

Joey said something about why he was ghosting you and I was upset with him.

Of course you're my friend.

I love you.

Etta, please answer me.

Etta?

I give up typing and dial her number. The phone rings . . . and rings . . . and rings. Her voicemail comes on. I try calling again, and she sends me to voicemail a second time. The third time, I go straight to voicemail.

"Etta, it's Gigi. Please call me back. I didn't mean to write that. I was trying to tell Joey he needed to give you a chance. Oh god. Please call me back."

I hang up and check our chat. She still hasn't read any of my apology messages. I send a few more, hoping she'll look at them eventually. I'm so angry with Joey that I log off without getting back to him.

After pacing around my room for several minutes, I try calling Etta again. She still doesn't pick up. I stare at my phone, trying to figure out what to do. There's only one other person I can call, and I'm already dreading the conversation. Nonetheless, I hit my speed dial.

"Come on, pick up. Pick up."

When the phone clicks, I start talking, but I'm interrupted by his voicemail greeting.

"Hey, you've reached Kyle. Sorry, I can't come to the phone right now. Leave me a message."

I hang up and toss my phone onto my bed. I sink down onto the edge of my mattress and put my head into my hands. All I wanted to do was apologize to Etta. How did it go so wrong?

Even worse . . . what am I going to do now?

Chapter 21

First thing Tuesday morning, I drag myself out of bed and do my best to look presentable despite my raccoon eyes. After slapping on some makeup, I throw my hair into a ponytail and put on a black sweater and skinny jeans. I don't notice the hole in one sleeve until Fernando pulls up to Superbia, so I hold that arm against me to keep it out of sight.

I spend first period on pins and needles, counting the minutes until the bell rings. I notice a couple people whispering and glancing in my direction, but it's probably because I look like I've spent all winter in a cave. Things only get worse when I discover that in my haste, I left my homework binder at home. I won't be able to turn anything in today. It throws me off so much I spend the entire hour not hearing a word my teacher says.

Once we're dismissed, I race to the second floor, hoping to intercept Etta outside her classroom. As the minutes pass, students stroll in through the doorway a few at a time, but there's no sign of Etta. I wait as long as I can before running to my own class, sinking into my chair as the bell rings. People around me stare openly, but I ignore them. During class, I try to take notes, but the fifth time I catch myself staring into space with my cursor blinking on a blank page, I give up.

For the rest of the morning, I repeat the process—the bell rings, I make my way to Etta's next class, and I wait for as long as I can before leaving. Maybe she's out sick. Etta wouldn't miss school otherwise. Then I catch a break at lunch. I arrive outside of her classroom, which happens to be across the hall from mine. Within seconds of the bell going off, students start streaming out. My heart pounds when I spot Etta walking in my direction. Taking a deep breath, I call out to her.

"Hey, Etta, can I talk to you?"

She jumps at the sound of my voice. Her brown eyes are rimmed in red, and a mixture of anger and pain flashes within them.

"Etta, please. I—"

She shakes her head and bolts down the hall before I can finish my sentence. I want to go after her, but the corridor is brimming with people hungry for gossip. I keep my head low as I walk in the opposite direction, hiding in a library cubby to wait out lunch. It's not like I have much of an appetite anyway.

The afternoon goes by in a blur, and soon my feet are carrying me out of school. When I spy Kyle waiting in his usual spot under the awning, a weary smile tugs at my lips. It freezes when I see the storm brewing in his eyes.

"What the hell were you thinking?" he growls. "Etta's never done anything to you."

My jaw drops. "She told you?"

"Yes, she did. She even showed me the screenshot of what you wrote. Why would you send her something like that?"

"I didn't mean to," I insist. "It was an accident. I was talking to Joey and I mixed up the chats."

He glowers at me. "Oh, you *meant* to say those things. You just didn't mean to get caught."

"No, that's not—" I release an exasperated sound. "Okay,

maybe I do believe those things about Etta, but it doesn't mean I don't like her. Why else would I still be her friend?"

"I can't believe what I'm hearing, Gigi," Kyle answers. "Of all the people in the world, you were the last person I would have expected to act like this."

Each word slices through me, causing pain with every heartbeat.

"You can't tell me you don't agree with me! You even told me about how she sends you paragraphs in the chat."

"Yes, but that was an *observation*. What you gave was an *opinion*, and a terrible one at that. There's nothing wrong with Etta. She's fine the way she is."

"I've never tried to change who she is."

"Then why did you take her shopping?" he asks. "She told me you were the one who insisted on changing how she dressed, even though she was happy with her clothes."

"I was trying to help her fit in so she could make friends!"

"That's my point, Gigi. Most people at Superbia are a bunch of snobs who only care about what you look like, who you're wearing, and what neighborhood you live in. Etta wasn't going to fit in— not because she dresses differently than everyone else, or doesn't wear makeup or go to fancy events, but because her family isn't rich," Kyle asserts. "I thought you understood that, and saw beyond that to the person Etta is inside, but I was wrong."

"I do understand! I do see her," I insist. "I wrote a whole app to help her meet new friends!"

"That wasn't you helping Etta, Gigi. That was you helping yourself."

"How can you say that?" I ask, fighting back tears.

"You left her at Mighty Bowl because you wanted to fix Quizlr,

Gigi," Kyle reminds me, his voice rising. "That should have told me exactly who you thought was most important, but I gave you the benefit of the doubt. I thought you would apologize—"

"I did! Multiple times!"

"—but then you go and send her *that* message? I'm sorry, Gigi, but that's unforgivable."

I stare at him in utter shock. In all the time we've known each other, Kyle has never spoken to me like this. He squares his shoulders and gestures toward the street.

"Come on. I'll walk you home today, but you should probably get Fernando to pick you up from now on."

I shake my head. "You know what? Don't bother. I can get home on my own."

Shifting my book bag more securely onto my shoulder, I start down the street, resolutely keeping my eyes forward the whole way home. When I climb the steps to my house, I check to see where he is behind me.

Instead I find myself utterly alone.

♥

The next day, I leave school after my last class, expecting to see Kyle there with a lopsided smile. All that greets me is an empty doorway. After waiting fifteen minutes for him to appear, I walk home by myself. I don't tell Mom and Dad what happened, because they'll insist on hearing every painful detail, and I'm not ready to face more judgment.

Instead I lie and tell them Kyle can't walk me home anymore because he has to start staying after school to work on a project. On Wednesday afternoon, Fernando is waiting for me when I leave class.

For the next week, my life becomes a revolving door of boring—school, home, sleep, and repeat. Then, on day eight, something happens that makes me wish I had appreciated the mundane.

Mrs. Emerson is ten minutes into her AP English lecture when she's interrupted by a knock on the classroom door. She excuses herself to step out into the hall. A minute later, she comes back inside and looks directly at me.

"Gigi, Principal Gee needs to see you in her office."

My heart skitters. "R-right now?"

"Yes. Right now."

I collect my things amid a room full of whispers and curious looks before stepping out into the hallway. I come face-to-face with Miss Nelson, one of our school counselors.

"Is . . . is something wrong?" I ask her.

She smiles, but it doesn't quite reach her eyes. "Please come with me."

I follow her down the corridor and out of the building, walking across the open courtyard that separates the upper and lower school buildings. With every step, I consider and dismiss a reason for being called to see Principal Gee. We enter a third administrative building, one I have rarely stepped foot in. She guides me into the main office before pointing at the door with Principal Gee's name etched on a gold nameplate.

I take a deep breath, trying to calm the butterflies in my stomach as I raise my hand and knock on the door.

"Come in."

I step inside and am shocked to find Ms. Harris seated at an antique cherry writing desk across from Principal Gee. There are two additional chairs in the room, and Principal Gee gestures at the one next to my teacher.

"Gigi, please sit down."

I lower myself into the chair and clasp my hands in my lap. Principal Gee looks at me with a pair of piercing black eyes.

"Do you know why I called you here today, Gigi?"

I shake my head. "No, ma'am."

"Did you create an app called Quizlr?"

"Yes," I confirm, my heart beating faster than a rabbit's. "It's my computer science project."

"I see. Were you aware that many upper-class students have it downloaded on their personal phones?"

"Um," I clear my throat. "I—I did have some students ask to download it, yes. I don't know how many actually did."

"So you sent them this app?" Principal Gee asks in a tone that makes me wince.

"I shared the link, yes. But the app is only for taking fun quizzes," I try to explain. "You take them, and afterward you can share your results with your friends on social media."

"But it also includes the ability to message other users, correct?"

I glance at Ms. Harris, but she avoids my gaze. Today she's dressed in a white blouse and black slacks with a pair of simple black pumps. It's a far cry from her usual colorful style. I turn back to Principal Gee and nod.

"Yes. It has a basic chat add-on."

She props both forearms on her desk and leans forward. "Tell me again how it works. In simple terms, please."

"Well, Quizlr puts people who give similar answers on the quizzes into a group chat."

"Are these chat rooms private?"

"In a way, yes. Each group chat includes only the users who gave a certain percentage of the same answers from the quizzes," I explain. "The idea is to introduce you to people you might not know but have a lot in common with."

"Is it possible for someone to hack the app?"

"In theory, I suppose." I frown. "But why would someone do that? And for what reason?"

Principal Gee glances at Ms. Harris, who finally speaks.

"Gigi, do you remember where all the apps for our class are stored?"

"Yes, on the school server," I answer.

Ms. Harris nods. "That's right. And that means that all the data from every app a student creates is also stored on the server."

"Right."

"Including usernames, profiles, and *any* and *all* chat messages that are sent."

"Yes, Ms. Harris," I confirm.

Principal Gee takes a deep breath and pins me with a steady gaze. "So is there anything you want to tell us?"

This is obviously why I'm sitting in the principal's office for the first time in my life, but I don't have the slightest clue what they mean. I shake my head and remain quiet, waiting for one of them to enlighten me.

"Why did you let students outside of computer science class download your program, Gigi?" Ms. Harris asks.

My heart sinks. The disappointment in her eyes is unbearable.

"I—" I swallow hard. "I never planned to share it. I only gave the link to a couple of friends to test before I turned it in for quality assurance. It was one of them who shared it. Plus, I found out some of the other students who tested Quizlr sent it to their friends too."

"Do you know which students did that from class?" Principal Gee asks.

I shake my head. "No. I didn't ask for any names."

"I see. And is there anything else we should know?"

"No, ma'am. That's it."

Minutes pass in complete silence. I sneak a peek at Ms. Harris, but she's taken a keen interest in the books lining a shelf on the back wall. Principal Gee presses her forearms against her desk.

"Very well. Perhaps someone else can offer more perspective."

She picks up the phone and dials an extension. "Please bring him in."

We wait for what feels like an eternity before the door swings open. Miss Nelson gestures for the person with her to enter. I have no idea who I expected, but I'm nonetheless stunned when Joey reluctantly settles into the remaining chair. It takes a second for me to notice my mouth is hanging open, and I snap it shut. Principal Gee glances between us.

"I presume you two know each other."

My head bobs up and down, while Joey murmurs his agreement. I have little time to wonder what he's also doing here as Principal Gee trains her steely gaze on me.

"Let's cut to the chase," she says. "Gigi, I received a report that several students were planning to use Quizlr to sell exam questions. Do you know anything about that?"

My body goes cold. No, it couldn't be. They can't think I'm . . .

"No, I don't know anything about that. I swear," I deny. "And I'm not sure how they would use Quizlr to do that."

"Someone gamed your system. They figured out if you answer the quizzes in an identical fashion, you'd end up in the same chat," Ms. Harris states.

"A group of Superbia students used one of the chat rooms to share exams with each other," Principal Gee adds. "Apparently, some of them created a catalog of test answers with the intent of selling them."

Her gaze slides to Joey, whose head is bowed as he picks at his fingernails. Right then, my mind flashes back to the day I discovered Quizlr had gained a following.

Joey Kwan sent it to me. He said that I should download it . . .

Yeah, I shared it. You said you needed more people to test it out, right?

The memory sends blood roaring past my ears and twists my stomach into knots. I stare at Joey, desperately wanting him to look up so I can read the truth in his eyes. He keeps his eyes steadfastly forward.

"Principal Gee, Ms. Harris, I had no idea this was happening," I reiterate, clutching my shaking hands in my lap. "I would never encourage something like that."

Principal Gee turns to Joey. "Is Gigi telling the truth? Was she part of this in any way?"

He looks up for the first time, vehemently shaking his head.

"No, ma'am. Gigi didn't know anything about it. She wasn't involved."

"Did you really do this?" I whisper, my voice cracking. "Did you use Quizlr to help people cheat?"

Perhaps sensing the weight of three pairs of eyes, Joey takes a deep breath and speaks.

"I guess in a way I did. But I only shared answers." He pauses before continuing. "It was one person at first . . . this girl I met through the chat. We were talking on the phone about the chemistry test we had that week, and she mentioned how scared she was of what her parents would do if she didn't get a good grade. She begged me to copy down the answers for her, and of course I said no, but then she started crying, and I . . ."

Joey meets my gaze for a split second before he resumes examining his hands.

"I didn't think it was a big deal, that I did her this one favor. But a few days later, she invited me to join a chat room with her and some of her friends. I had no idea what they were using it for until after."

I have a sneaking suspicion who this girl is, but I keep it to myself.

"I know I shouldn't have done it," Joey says, eyes flitting between us. "But I thought I was helping . . ."

Ms. Harris smiles gently. "You did the right thing in the end."

"Joey is the reason we found out about the cheating ring," Principal Gee reveals. "He came to me as soon as he found out others were planning on selling the answers using Quizlr."

This does little to take away the sting of betrayal. I thought Joey genuinely wanted to help me with Quizlr, or at the very least use it to get to know Etta better. Between this and how he treated Anna, I'm wondering if I misjudged him all along.

"All right. I have more questions for you, Joey, but for now, please return to Miss Nelson's office while I finish up here," Principal Gee instructs.

He stands to leave. "Gigi, I—"

I break eye contact. He exhales loudly, but doesn't attempt to finish what he's saying. When he's gone, and the door is firmly shut once more, Principal Gee leans back in her chair and rubs her temple.

"Unfortunately, though Joey told us what was happening, he's refused to give up the names of the other students in the ring. As such, I've asked Ms. Harris to look into this matter further. Once she has the list of students we suspect are involved, I'll be speaking with them and their parents over the next few days. That part is straightforward."

She reaches up and rubs her left temple. "The hard part—and

where I foresee a problem—is that in order to make sure this doesn't happen again, we will need to email all the parents of the upper-school students asking them to delete the app off their children's phones. That means we'll have to explain how it ended up there in the first place, and where the app came from. The parents will demand someone be held accountable."

A chill runs up my back. How are Mom and Dad going to take the news that I'm suspended . . . or worse yet, expelled?

"I've told Principal Gee that I will take full responsibility for what happened," Ms. Harris states in a quiet voice. "After all, it was my job to monitor what was happening with the apps during the development process."

I glance from one woman to the other. "I don't understand."

"Ms. Harris will be suspended pending an investigation by the board. If she is found liable, she'll be fired," Principal Gee answers, her voice tinged with regret.

"No! Please don't do that! She didn't know anything about this," I protest, twisting to address Ms. Harris. "You didn't do anything wrong."

"Unfortunately, that's not up to you or me to decide," Principal Gee answers. "I'm sorry. It's out of my hands."

I glance from one woman to the other. "What . . . what if you suspended me? It's my app. Plus, I was the one who shared it with students outside of class."

"You weren't the only one who did," she points out. "As Joey made clear."

"That's true . . . but I didn't stop it when I found out people downloaded it onto their personal phones. I could have told Ms. Harris and had her take it offline, but I didn't. This is my fault, not hers!"

Ms. Harris reaches out and touches me on the shoulder. "It's all right, Gigi. I appreciate what you're trying to do, but as a teacher, it was my job to know what was happening with my students. If I had checked the server more often, it would have never reached this point. Principal Gee has generously offered to provide half pay during my suspension, and she'll advocate for me when the board meeting occurs."

"But . . ."

"The decision's been made. I've already informed the board, and the email will go out tonight," Principal Gee states. "You should be grateful I'm not suspending you. Ms. Harris insisted it would be too harsh a punishment given the situation, especially with your exemplary record up until this point."

This only twists the knife deeper. If I had never created Quizlr, never shared it, Ms. Harris wouldn't be paying with her job.

"I will still need to speak with your parents about this," Principal Gee informs me.

"Of course," I answer in a small voice. "I understand."

"All right, then. We're done here for now."

"There is actually one more thing, Gigi," Ms. Harris adds softly. "I will have to withdraw you from SJW's app contest."

The blow strikes me square in the chest, but I'm too numb to feel it. They stand, and I follow suit.

"We can't change what's happened. All we can do is move forward," Ms. Harris tells me.

"I'm so sorry," I whisper. "I never meant for this to happen."

Tears stream down my face before I can stop them. Ms. Harris puts an arm around me, stroking my back as I cry. I manage to pull myself together a few minutes later, the heat in my cheeks as much from sadness as from embarrassment.

"If you want, you can sit in the waiting area until you feel ready to go back to class," Principal Gee offers.

"No, it's okay. I'll go back now."

I take a deep breath and walk slowly out of her office.

"Hold it together, Gigi," I tell myself. "You can cry when you get home."

I keep the promise I make to myself, for the most part, outside of a couple quick trips to the bathroom to keep from completely falling apart. If Fernando notices the puffiness around my eyes when he drives me home, he doesn't mention it.

Mom's waiting in the foyer when I walk in the door. One look at her face and I know she's already talked to Principal Gee.

"Mom, I can exp—"

"I don't know what kind of trouble you've gotten yourself into, Gigi Wong, but we're not talking about anything until your dad and I meet with Principal Gee. Now go to your room."

A couple of hours later, I hear Dad come up the stairs after returning from the office. He pauses outside my door and knocks. Before I can answer it, I hear Mom saying something to him in a hushed tone. Then they move down the hall. I wait until their voices fade before letting slumber take me away.

Chapter 22

My parents take the news of my near suspension—and the reason for it—about as well as expected. Since Dad had to fly out at dawn for business, Mom accompanies me to Principal Gee's office the next day before school. Though she stays quiet the entire meeting, I can tell by the vein pulsing in her temple that she's furious. She refuses to speak a single word to me after, climbing into the car without looking back. Only Fernando waves goodbye before pulling onto the street.

By the time I head to my first class, the news of the cheating ring has reached everyone in the upper school. Though Principal Gee kept her promise and never mentioned any names, it's the worst-kept secret at Superbia. From the minute I step into the building, I walk a gauntlet of dirty looks, snickers, and gossip. Even students I've never met point at me as I pass by, whispering to their friends about how I caused the biggest scandal the school has seen in decades. No one bothers to ask if I was actually involved; everyone assumes the whole scheme was my idea.

I manage to make it through the morning without breaking down, but I get absolutely nothing out of class. It's impossible to concentrate when every pair of eyes in the room aims the heat of a thousand suns at you. When it's time to break for lunch, I sprint out the door of my classroom and climb the steps to the second floor. I make my way to the *Worldly* office, finding it empty. I walk to the back and sink into one of the chairs before putting my head down on the table.

Not long after, I hear footsteps coming into the room. I raise my head slightly to find Tyler frozen by the doorway.

"Oh . . . sorry, Gigi," he says, dragging a hand through his hair. "I thought no one was going to be in here today. I'll come back."

I stand. "No, it's okay. I was . . . taking a break. I'll leave."

Throwing my book bag over my shoulder, I trudge across the room.

Tyler clears his throat. "Are you . . . are you okay? You look upset."

For a second, I can only stare. Why is he being so nice to me? Maybe I'm too exhausted to care about the reason, or maybe it's the openness of his gaze, but I answer honestly.

"'Upset' is an understatement. I feel like I've been hit with every car of a subway train . . . twice."

He grimaces. "Ouch."

"Yeah," I say. "Anyway, I'll get out of your way."

I have one foot out the door when he waves at me to come back.

"It's okay, really. Gigi, you don't have to go. We could always . . . sit together and not say anything."

"Are you sure you can manage that?" I joke weakly.

He laughs. "I guess I deserve that. I'm not good at being quiet."

The fact that Tyler readily admits this is a kick to the stomach. I drop my eyes to the floor.

"I'm sorry. That was wrong of me to say. You were only trying to be nice."

"It's okay. Everybody says I talk a lot. It's one of my many charms," he answers, smiling.

With forty-five minutes left before lunch ends, I plant myself back in the chair I just vacated. Tyler sits down next to me and pulls out what look like two packs of gourmet Lunchables from his bag.

"That's what you're eating?" I ask.

He shrugs. "My mom's not the greatest cook. In fact, I'm pretty sure she's trying to kill me with her home-cooked food. The other night, she grilled hamburgers. I dropped one and it nearly broke my foot."

The ridiculousness of that image cracks me up, and he grins along with me. He pushes one of the packs toward me.

"You don't look like you brought anything."

"Oh, I don't want to take your lunch from you, especially since it sounds like you're being starved at home," I quip.

"Nah. My dad's always working, so we order out whenever Mom burns something—which is most days. In fact, she accuses him of sabotaging meals so he can get his favorite foods delivered."

He gestures at me to take a container, so I accept. As I pop open the plastic lid, I glance at him.

"Is this one of his faves?"

"Kind of," Tyler answers. "He likes going into Zabar's and browsing their meat and cheese counters. He'll usually bring home whatever their staff recommends, and we pack them into these boxes for lunch."

We dig in without preamble. After the first couple bites, I realize how hungry I am. It takes me less than fifteen minutes to scarf down the rest of what's inside the box.

"That was really good, thank you," I say.

"You're welcome," he answers, giving me a peek at what's still inside his mouth. "If it's not enough, you can have some of mine."

My gaze falls on a cabinet along the side of the room.

"Actually, I can do you one better."

I pop out of my chair and twist the dial on the combination lock until I hear a satisfying click. I open the cabinet door and pull out the basket of snacks we usually reserve for *Worldly* meetings.

Tyler's mouth falls open when I place it on the table. "Hold up. Summer never told me you guys get snacks if you're on the *Worldly* committee."

"Only the best for our writers."

By the end of the hour, Tyler's proven himself to be quite the nice lunch companion. He never once asks me what happened with Quizlr, or why Ms. Harris is no longer teaching our class. Granted, he's probably already heard the story from someone else, but I appreciate the discretion nonetheless.

"Thank you again for sharing your lunch," I tell him as we head to our next classes. "And for keeping me company."

"You're welcome," he answers. "In fact, I usually have lunch there every day. I kinda like how quiet it is. If you want to come back up tomorrow, I'll be there."

I turn to him and smile. "I'd love that."

Days later, Mom remains as silent as a Buddhist monk. The only time she opened her mouth was to tell me I'm grounded until further notice. To be honest, it's not like I have anywhere to go. Now that I'm the social pariah of Superbia Prep, nearly everyone is avoiding me like the plague.

Meanwhile, Dad's stopped posting in our family group chat,

something we all joked would only happen when hell froze over. Looking back at this past week, I'd say it's an apt description. The only thing worse than the cold shoulder is the lecture I'm sure to get once he's home again.

At least one good thing comes out of all this mess. Since Auntie Rose has been recuperating at our house, we've had more time to talk. She knows about everything, from the scandal with Quizlr to my falling-out with Kyle and Etta. I even own up to Matchmaker 3000. She takes the news far better than I expected, and definitely more so than Mom and Dad. In fact, on Friday, Auntie Rose insists we grab dim sum from Nom Wah Tea Parlor to start the weekend off right.

"You can't be sad if your stomach is full," she says after placing our order for takeout. "Good food can heal the deepest of wounds."

I'm not convinced sticky rice and turnip cakes have that kind of power, but I'm not turning down a meal from one of my favorite restaurants. Since Fernando is coming by to pick Mom up for a charity dinner downtown, he offers to get our food. When I hear this, I ask Auntie Rose to order a little extra.

"I don't mind, but why?" she asks. "I thought your parents paid him overtime after five o'clock."

"They do, but when Fernando works late, he misses dinner with his family," I explain.

Auntie Rose hums approvingly. "That's very thoughtful of you, xiǎojī."

I wish I could take credit, but it was Etta who first brought this to my attention. If it weren't for her, I would have never known what he was giving up to drive us around. The ache that hasn't left my chest for days sharpens at the reminder she's not talking to me. The one thing that makes it better is the brilliant smile on Fernando's face when I tell him to keep one of the bags from Nom Wah.

I bring the rest into the kitchen, laying it out on the island before grabbing plates and utensils for us both. Auntie Rose is on the road to recovery, but she's still pale and gets tired quickly. The last thing I want is for her to end up back in the hospital. Once I've filled her plate with some of everything we ordered, I pile my own and sit beside her at the table.

"Are things any better at school?" she asks, popping a shrimp dumpling into her mouth.

"If by better, you mean I'm not at the top of everyone's shit list, then yes."

"Language, Gigi," she chides.

"Sorry, Auntie."

"On second thought, I'll allow it this time." Auntie Rose puts down her chopsticks. "I know it's not easy to hear, but these things take time to resolve."

"I just want life to go back to normal," I lament. "People are acting like I did all of this on purpose. There was a rumor the other day that Quizlr was some elaborate plan to spread fake test answers so I could be valedictorian."

"But you know that's not true."

"Yeah, but what if people believe it? I've worked so hard, Auntie. I don't want anyone thinking I cheated to get to where I am."

"You can't control what people think about you, xiǎojī," Auntie Rose states. "What matters is how the people you love see you."

"I'm pretty sure they think I'm a horrible person too."

She reaches over and clasps my hand in hers. "I may not know this Etta girl, but I do know Kyle, and he would never think that."

"Then why won't he talk to me?" I whisper.

She sighs. "Matters of the heart are always the most complicated."

I don't understand what she means by that, and she doesn't explain. Instead, Auntie Rose changes the subject.

"Why didn't you show me this matchmaking app before?"

I bite my lip. "You've always talked about how computers can't do what humans can. I wanted to prove it worked so you would give it a chance."

"But why did you decide to make it in the first place?"

"I'm not sure," I answer, carefully biting a small hole in my soup dumpling. "I guess I thought it would save you a lot of time. That way, you'd be able to see more clients with less work."

"Hmm."

Auntie Rose polishes off a piece of siu mai, a piece of scallion pancake, and a fried shrimp ball before speaking again.

"One of the things I enjoy most about matchmaking is getting to know my clients, xiǎojī. Sometimes they're flowers, and other times they're onions, but peeling back their layers is part of the fun."

Kyle is going to die laughing when he hears this one.

I reach for my phone before remembering we're not on speaking terms, and I wince at the pain that shoots through me.

"Yes, my matchmaking takes time and a lot more work," Auntie Rose continues, unaware. "But it's also what sets us apart. We use our intuition, not some formula, to make matches. Do you understand?"

"I mean, I do, but I still think it would save time to use an app."

Auntie Rose sits back in her chair. She says nothing for a long time, and I squirm beneath her intense scrutiny.

"Is this what you want, xiǎojī? To be a matchmaker?"

"Of course, Auntie," I answer automatically.

She raises her eyebrow. "Don't tell me what you think I want to hear. Be honest. Do you really *want* to be a matchmaker?"

"I . . . I don't know. I think so."

She straightens. "What if I told you that you could only become a matchmaker if you didn't use the app? Would you still want to?"

The answer hits me like a ton of bricks. Though I can't bring myself to say the words, Auntie Rose reads them in my eyes. She heaves a sigh.

"I thought so. I was hoping you'd come to me on your own, but you never did. Then when you jumped at the chance to match Miss Wu, I figured you had decided this was for you."

"I did! Or at least I thought I did," I admit. "Maybe I was so focused on proving I could be a great matchmaker I forgot to ask myself if I wanted to be one."

But James did. And Kyle did. Even Liza, and we've only chatted on video call.

Why didn't I listen to them before?

Why did it take me so long to figure it out for myself?

"What now?" I ask quietly. "Are you going to talk to Mom and Dad?"

Auntie Rose shakes her head. "I think you need to tell them that yourself."

I was hoping she wouldn't say that. After Quizlrgate, they've lost all trust in me. I have no idea how they'll react if I tell them I'm quitting matchmaking too. I cover my face with my hands, but Auntie Rose tugs one away so I'll look at her.

"Your parents love you, xiǎojī. They want you to be happy. If that doesn't include being a matchmaker, then so be it."

Whatever else Auntie Rose might have wanted to say is forgotten when she's hit with a headache. I bring her a glass of water and a dose of her pain medication before helping her back to bed. I'm about to turn out her light when the doorbell rings.

"Who could that be?" she asks.

"I'm not sure," I reply, "but don't worry. I'll go check. You rest."

On my way to the foyer, I pull out my phone and check our doorbell app. I skid to a stop when the visitor turns to face the camera.

You've got to be kidding me.

I consider pretending I'm not home, but force myself to keep walking when two more people pop into view. Taking a deep breath, I plaster a smile on my face and open the door.

Chapter 23

"Good evening, Gigi," Mr. Kwan greets me politely. "Are your parents home tonight?"

Though his heather-gray overcoat is impeccably tailored, it practically swallows him whole. His face is as pallid as Dad's when he pulls too many all-nighters, and dark circles rim his eyes, which don't quite meet mine. Mrs. Kwan hasn't fared much better. Her usually bright smile barely holds a flicker. While I don't know exactly what went down in their meeting with Principal Gee, Joey hasn't been back at school. Mom's daily calls with Mrs. Kwan have dropped off too, though one night they were on the phone for hours. I shake my head. "I'm afraid not, Mr. Kwan. Dad's plane hasn't landed yet, and Mom's having dinner with a friend. It's just me and Auntie Rose tonight."

"Too bad. Maybe we should come back on another day," Joey pipes up, turning to leave.

Mrs. Kwan reaches up and grabs him by the ear. "Oh, no you don't. You don't get off that easily."

"Okay, okay, Mom." Joey grumbles, rubbing his earlobe. "May we come in?"

Considering what he did, I should slam the door in his face. But his parents are with him, and they've done nothing wrong.

Between that and my deeply ingrained politeness, I step aside so they can enter.

"Would you like to go up to the living room?" I ask, gesturing toward the stairs.

"No, we won't be staying long. We're actually on our way to dinner as well, but we wanted to stop by because Joey has something to say," Mr. Kwan tells me. "Don't you, son?"

Mrs. Kwan prods him in the shoulder. "Go on. Tell her."

"I'm sorry," Joey murmurs under his breath, his gaze pinned on the ground.

His mom pokes him in the side. "Say it louder. She can't hear you."

I heard him the first time, but I'm not going to contradict her. Instead, I clasp my hands in front of me and wait. Joey drags a hand through his hair and rubs the back of his neck before raising his eyes to mine.

"I'm really sorry, Gigi. I shouldn't have shared your app without your permission."

"*And?*" Mrs. Kwan prods.

"And I should have told you what the others were doing before it got out of hand," he adds, staring back down at the floor.

"Then why didn't you? If you had, none of this would have happened."

"I . . ." Joey glances back at his parents. "Could I talk to Gigi in private?"

Mrs. Kwan looks at me. "It's up to you, Gigi."

I open my mouth to refuse, but he takes a step forward and drops his voice to a near whisper.

"*Please*, Gigi. I promise I'll answer any question you have. But not in front of my parents."

Part of me wants to say no, to give him a taste of the scrutiny

I've had to deal with because of him, but I ultimately give in. I turn my attention back to his parents.

"Please excuse us. We'll be right back."

I lead him down the hall into the kitchen, perching myself on a stool and nodding for him to sit as well. He sinks into one opposite me while I wait expectantly.

"Well?"

Joey squeezes his eyes shut before starting. "You knew me from before. I had terrible skin, a mouthful of braces . . . and the outfits." He grimaces. "No one wanted to be my friend. I had nothing going for me."

"You were smart," I interject.

"Yeah, like that kept people from laughing at me in the hallway, or talking about me behind my back." Pain flashes in his brown eyes. "All I wanted was to have more friends. To know what it's like to be popular. I thought coming back would be my chance to start over and be someone different. That if I looked better, wore nicer clothes, people would finally accept me."

His words echo back to the conversation I had with Etta the weekend before I took her shopping. Now I would give anything to tell past me how wrong I was. Joey lapses into silence, his jaw working as he tries to gather himself. He clears his throat once, then twice, before wiping roughly at his eyes and squaring his shoulders.

"Anyway, none of that makes up for what I did, and I know it probably doesn't mean much, but I am really sorry," Joey states, his voice cracking. "For everything."

It would be easy to refuse forgiveness, to blame him for making my life miserable. But Joey's not the only one who's made mistakes. If I want a chance at redemption, then he deserves one too. Since he's doling out apologies, he should make a couple more.

"I'll forgive you . . . under one condition."

A small smile touches his lips. "Name it."

"There's someone else you should apologize to."

Joey ducks his head. "Ah . . . right. Etta."

"And don't forget Anna."

"Anna?" I can almost see the gears turning in his head. "She . . . she told you about us?"

The way he says *us* confirms what I've suspected all along. The "friend" Anna told Etta was dating Joey? The one he broke up with after moving to Singapore because he secretly started seeing another girl?

It was her.

"What you did was wrong, and you know it," I say. "She deserves to hear you admit that."

"I know. And I've been trying." His shoulders slump. "But she won't talk to me."

"Then ask her to listen."

We're interrupted when Mr. Kwan ducks his head into the kitchen.

"My apologies, Gigi, but it's time for us to go."

The two of us stand, and I walk with father and son back to the foyer. Mrs. Kwan rises from the bench nearby, and she presses a smile to her face.

"Thank you for letting Joey apologize for his behavior. I hope you enjoy the rest of your evening."

I move to open the door for them, but Mom walks in. She stiffens at the sight of the Kwans, but quickly composes herself. Despite this, the smile on her face is strained.

"Susan, Peter, I didn't realize you were stopping by tonight."

"I apologize for the intrusion," Mr. Kwan informs her quietly. "But Joey insisted on speaking to Gigi in person since he won't be seeing much of her after he starts at Chawton next week."

Mom looks at Joey, and he withers beneath her gaze. Satisfied her message was received, she turns back to the Kwans.

"You must have plans tonight."

"We do. In fact, we need to get going," Mr. Kwan comments. "We have reservations downtown."

"Let's get together soon," Mrs. Kwan adds a little too brightly. "We'd love to have you over to the house. Just let us know when you're free."

"I'll do that, Susan."

I know Mom well enough to recognize that tone, and I suspect Mrs. Kwan does too. Her cheeks flush pink, and she ushers her family out of the house with a hurried farewell.

After locking the door, Mom turns to me. I assume she'll demand an explanation, maybe interrogate me about what Joey said while he was here, but she says nothing.

"There's leftover dim sum from Nom Wah," I say before belatedly recalling she was out for dinner.

"Let me know when your dad comes home," she says after what feels like an eternity. "And then we're going to sit down as a family and talk."

I wince at the anger in her voice. Still, there's no avoiding the conversation, so I nod. Without another word, she sweeps up the stairs.

Dad arrives an hour later, but I'm forced to wait another fifteen tense minutes while he finishes dinner. Seated at the circular breakfast table, I focus on the darkness of our back patio as I await my fate.

"Dad and I are very disappointed in you."

I fidget with the hem of my shirt. "I'm sorry, Mom."

"What were you thinking?" Dad asks. "Why would you do something so . . ."

"Stupid?" I whisper.

Mom sighs. "No, bǎobǎo, something so reckless. Do you have any idea how many things could have gone wrong?"

"I never meant for any of this to happen," I say, glancing at the both of them. "Quizlr didn't originally have a chat option. It was supposed to be a fun quiz-taking app. I didn't think people would use it to cheat."

"That doesn't explain why you shared it with people outside of class," Dad replies. "You knew the rules."

"Technically, I didn't share it . . . at least, not at first. Other students sent the link to their friends. I didn't even know that had happened until people started messaging me." I slouch against the back of my chair. "I thought they were sharing the app because they thought Quizlr was cool."

Mom frowns. "So you did all this to be more popular?"

"No!" I shake my head. "That's not it at all."

"Then explain it to me," Dad demands, taking a sip of his water. "Because I don't understand why you would risk your future for some silly app."

"I . . . I really wanted to win the contest. Once you get to the final round, the public votes on the app they want to win. I thought if I could get enough people at school using it, they'd vote for me when the time came."

Mom rubs her temples. "Why are you stuck on winning a contest? We talked about this, bǎobǎo. You make good grades, have lots of extracurricular activities, and Dad and I can easily round up any letters of recommendation you need. So why? Why is this contest so important to you?"

"Because I want to prove I'm more than what people think I am!"

They both rear back at my outburst. Dad says nothing for several minutes before leaning his forearms on the table.

"What exactly do you mean by that?"

"It's hard to explain," I mumble, bowing my head.

"Try."

"Everyone around me has this idea of who I am and how I should act," I begin slowly. "If I don't match up, then I'm not perfect, even if I am the best."

"That doesn't make any sense, bǎobǎo. How can someone be the best, but also not perfect?" Mom asks.

I pause, trying to make sense of my thoughts so I can explain it better.

"Dad, you know how you told me you expect James to make good grades and go to the best school so he can be successful and help the family?" I wait for him to nod and then continue. "Well, you do the same with me, except you want me to be perfect at *not* doing those things."

He stares at me like I'm speaking in a foreign language. Despite this, I press on.

"Like Columbia. I mentioned I was thinking about applying to other colleges—some of them out of state—and that I would need to make better grades and bulk up my application to get accepted."

"And we told you that's not necessary."

I groan. "That's the thing! If I want to get into someplace like . . . MIT . . . it *is* necessary, and I'm willing to put in the work to be the best. But you have your heart set on me going to Columbia, so you expect me to be good enough to get into that college, but not any others. Do you understand?"

I turn to Mom. "And you're always telling me that I shouldn't worry about being the best student or figuring out a career because you and Auntie Rose expect me to take over the matchmaking business."

"But you love matchmaking," she says. "You've said that since you were little."

"That's just it. I don't—I don't love matchmaking. I love being good at it. But I'm also good at other things, like math, and biology . . . and programming." I lean my forearms on the table. "In fact, I'm great at it. Even better than I am at matchmaking. And before what happened with Quizlr? I was having fun learning how to write code so the app would work. That's why I got so excited when people started asking to download it."

I pause to take a deep breath. "Maybe that's the real reason I wanted to win the contest. I wanted to prove to myself that I could do it, that I could be the best at something *I* decided to do, not what someone told me I should."

Mom and Dad exchange a long look before she turns to me.

"None of this was what *we* wanted, bǎobǎo. We were trying to support what we thought *you* wanted. You always insisted on staying home whenever I was sick, or volunteered to take care of Dad for me when I'm out. Even Auntie Rose told me you asked to turn her questionnaire into an online form."

"That's why I suggested Columbia, so you could stay at home," Dad agrees. "And why I came home to eat instead of staying at the office and ordering takeout."

My head starts to pound as I try to wrap my mind around what I've heard. Could all of this really be a big misunderstanding?

"But then why do you guys act like you don't believe I can be the best? That I can't be as successful as James"—I glance from Dad to Mom—"or become a valedictorian instead of Anna?"

"Of course we believe in you, bǎobǎo," Mom tells me, reaching across the table and squeezing my hand. "But we see how much pressure you're putting on yourself. We don't want you to burn out or get sick from all that stress."

Silence settles between us, but one nagging question won't leave me alone.

"Does that mean you'll let me consider going out of state for college?" I ask in a small voice.

Dad closes his eyes and sighs. "I don't know. Your mom and I have to talk about all of this."

"Okay. I understand."

I grab my bag off the floor and stand up slowly. As I turn to leave, Mom stands and pulls me into her arms.

"It's been a rough few weeks for all of us, bǎobǎo, but don't forget that we love you no matter what, okay?"

Dad comes around the table and presses a kiss to the top of my head. "Mom's right. We'll always be here for you."

I smile at them. "Thanks. I love you too."

He pats me on the back and points toward the stairs. "Now, how about I make my famous bananas Foster for dessert?"

Mom and I look at each other.

"I'll get the fire extinguisher," I say.

"I'll pull up the takeout menus," she adds.

"Hey!"

Chapter 24

Though the conversation with Mom and Dad smoothed things over at home, school is another matter. First thing Monday morning, Mrs. Brown calls me into her office. The last time we spoke was when I stopped by to apologize for not being part of Flowers for Dollars, so my stomach is already in knots when I sit down across from her.

"I'm sorry to tell you this, Gigi," she says, "but the senior mentors have expressed concern about your continued participation in the peer-mentoring program. They feel that under the circumstances, it would be best if you stepped down for the rest of the year."

To be honest, I had been expecting this to happen. When I showed up for the monthly Peer Squad meeting last week, the students I was mentoring were stunned. Apparently, they'd been told I had quit. One of the freshmen, Sofia, came up afterward and asked me to stay. I gave her my phone number and told her we could always meet up outside of Peer Squad.

"It's okay, Mrs. Brown. I completely understand. Will the students assigned to me be transferred to someone else?"

A small crease appears between her brows as she nods.

"As a matter of fact, we had someone volunteer to take your place. One of your own mentees, in fact."

"Really? Who?"

"Etta Santos."

My breath hitches at the mention of her name.

"Are you all right, Gigi?" Mrs. Brown asks.

I nod. "Yes, I'm fine."

"I am truly sorry this happened," she continues gently. "You're a wonderful mentor. I would love for you to reapply next year. By then, this should have blown over."

"Thank you, Mrs. Brown. I'll definitely keep that in mind."

As I leave her office, I careen headlong into Etta. I grab her by the arm as she stumbles backward, and hold on until she rights herself.

"I'm sorry," I say.

She nods, not quite looking at me. "S'okay."

"I mean it, Etta. I'm sorry. About everything," I reiterate, figuring this is my only chance to do so. "And good luck with the mentees. They're very lucky to have you."

I don't wait for her reply before walking to my first class. At least I'm no longer the sole subject of gossip now that spring break is nearly here. Most of the students are too busy comparing glamorous vacation plans to keep torturing me.

That is, minus one incredibly glaring exception.

"I still can't believe you got Ms. Harris fired," Summer sneers at me as I change books at my locker. "You couldn't stand the fact that Anna's app was better than yours, could you?"

She's flanked, as usual, by her two faux besties. As I predicted, though, May is no longer among them. Instead, a sophomore girl named Tina Hsu has taken her place.

I slam my locker closed. "First of all, Ms. Harris isn't fired. She's suspended, and only until the school board clears her to come back. Second of all, Anna's app *is* better than mine, and I honestly hope she wins."

Anna's app, Timely, was just announced as one of the three finalists earlier this week. In all the chaos, Mr. Reynolds, the substitute computer science teacher, forgot to tell her. The only reason we all found out was because Tyler looked it up on the website.

I twirl on my heel and walk off in the opposite direction. Summer, however, decides she isn't done and chases after me.

"You're right. This isn't about Anna. It's about Joey."

I come to an abrupt stop and turn to face her. "Excuse me?"

"You heard me," she snarls. "Joey told me all about how both you and Etta were trying to get with him, but he wanted me all along."

"I know those were all English words, but none of that made sense."

"Yeah, it does."

I laugh harshly. "No, it really doesn't."

"That's the whole reason why you convinced him to download your stupid app. Admit it. You were jealous Joey wanted me, so you decided to break us up by getting him into trouble so he'd have to transfer."

That's news to me. I had no idea Joey broke things off with her. Maybe he is turning over a new leaf. Then again, he clearly didn't tell Summer the whole truth either, because I heard the rest of the story from Mom last night. Principal Gee gave Joey two options: suspension or voluntary withdrawal. She only offered the choice because he had come forward on his own and was proven not to be involved in the actual test selling. The Kwans wanted to keep it quiet, so they ultimately chose the withdrawal to avoid the mark on his record.

Summer's shrill voice has drawn a crowd around us. Like an audience watching a bullfight, they're secretly hoping to see some blood spilled. Too bad I'm not interested in bull of any kind.

"Okay, you got me," I tell Summer. "Everything you said was true. Now, if you'll excuse me, I have a lunch to eat."

I push past a few people and make for the stairs. I've climbed two steps when I hear her cackle.

"See, Tina? You picked the right person to be friends with . . . not like Etta. That's why people don't like her. She reached too high. Stick with me, and you'll be one of the most popular girls soon."

Now I'm seeing red. I stomp back to Summer. "Let me make something very clear, Summer. Etta has more class in her little finger than you have in your entire body. She's one of the sweetest, kindest, most considerate people I've ever met. She didn't reach too high. The rest of you are too busy climbing over each other to notice she's already at the top."

"Whatever," Summer scoffs. "She could never."

"I wouldn't laugh if I were you. You're the one who got dumped."

The corridor erupts into a cacophony of noise. Summer opens her mouth to retort, but I don't give her a chance. Instead, I leave her gaping after me like a goldfish and turn my back to her a third time.

"Hey!" Tyler calls out when I walk into the *Worldly* room. "I didn't know if you were coming."

Lunch with him has become part of my new routine, one of the few things that doesn't suck post-Quizlrgate. I cross the room in a few steps and sit down at the table beside him.

"Sorry. Thanks for waiting."

Tyler slides another lunch box in front of me. I shake my head and push it back.

"You didn't have to bring me anything! I brought lunch today."

He shrugs. "Eh, my mom always packs me two just in case I get hungry. Besides, Dad says today's picks are the best yet."

Considering I know absolutely nothing about deli meats or cheeses—hello, lactose intolerance—I take his word for it. It is pretty fun to build little towers from the ingredients, though.

"Well, since you're sharing, I think it's only fair that I do the same," I tell him, pulling out the container of Vietnamese vermicelli from my bag. Separating the pieces of charbroiled pork onto the lid, I put a napkin over it and bring it to the microwave we have in the corner of the room. Fifteen seconds later, it's just hot enough to place on top of the bed of vermicelli, lettuce, carrots, and cucumbers.

"That smells so good," he murmurs.

"Have some, then. Just make sure you grab a little bit of everything. Oh, and pour some fish sauce over it first."

We each have a little bit of the food we both brought. I eat the dishes separately, but Tyler practically shoves everything into his mouth at once.

"It's East meets West," he jokes.

Pieces of vermicelli escape his lips, with one narrowly missing my cheek as it flies past my ear. He claps a hand over his mouth.

"Sorry," he mumbles from behind his fingers.

"It's okay," I say with a smile before brushing my cheek with a napkin just in case.

He takes time to finish chewing and swallowing before saying anything further. "So why were you late today?"

"I ran into Queen B herself," I tell him.

He winces. "I didn't realize how miserable I was when I was with her. All I ever did was try to make her happy. She never once asked me what I wanted."

"That sounds horrible."

He glances around the empty room before leaning in. "One time, she dragged me to the spa . . . to watch her get her upper lip waxed."

"No!"

"Yes," he says, smirking. "And those diamond earrings she's always showing off? They're fake. She lost the real ones when we went to the Hamptons last summer, but she was afraid to tell her parents."

He builds another meat, cheese, and cracker sandwich and crams it into his mouth. I take a sip of the orange oolong tea Mom brewed a couple nights ago.

"Well, it's her loss. You're a really nice guy," I say earnestly. "I'm sorry I didn't see that before."

"Don't be. I didn't exactly try to change your mind . . . or anyone's, for that matter. I was too busy telling myself I was lucky to be with Summer."

Etta pops into my head. I peer over at him.

"I know one person who knew you were nice from the very beginning."

"You're talking about Etta, aren't you?" Tyler asks.

I nod, and he sighs. Leaning back in his chair, he balances precariously on its two hind legs.

"I really messed that up. I was so focused on what everybody else was going to think that I didn't stop to consider how she would feel."

"I totally get it," I admit. "I never thought about how much time I spent doing things so other people would think I was perfect. Now, after all this, none of it seems to matter."

"Don't say that, Gigi. You're an awesome person," Tyler comments. "You're always pointing out nice things about other people, and you see the good in everybody."

I roll my eyes. "And you got all this from having lunch with me?"

"No. I got it all from Etta. She talked about you all the time. At least, she did before . . ."

He lets his chair fall back to the floor. I take a deep breath.

"I think that's my fault. When I saw you guys at Shibui, I told her to stop talking to you."

"What? Why?" he asks.

"You and Summer have been so on-and-off, and I saw how you treated Etta when you were in public. I . . . I thought you were just going to break her heart." My shoulders droop. "I'm sorry."

He shakes his head. "No, you're right. If she had kept talking to me then, I probably would have done something dumb like that. I didn't deserve her."

"You do now," I offer quietly.

Tyler shrugs. "Yeah, well, I think I lost my chance."

I'm not sure what to say to that, so I don't say anything at all. Instead, I glance at the clock hanging on the wall and gasp.

"Oh! We should finish eating. We only have fifteen minutes."

The two of us polish off the remainder of the food, packing up the empty containers and wiping down the table. Then we head out the door together. As we round the landing between the first and second floors, I catch sight of Etta and Kyle at the base of the stairs. They're standing close, and her book bag is in the crook of his arm. She glances up at him when he speaks, and a smile blooms across her face. Out of the blue, his words come back to haunt me.

Etta seems nice.

. . . she understands how I feel.

There's nothing wrong with Etta. She's fine the way she is.

With every one, my heart drops a little more, until it feels as though it's been swallowed into the depths of the earth. My mind struggles to make sense of how I'm feeling. Kyle's dated dozens of girls in the time we've known each other, and it's never bothered me before.

Why now?

Why Etta?

I sneak another look at the two of them, regretting the decision immediately. As Etta tells him something, Kyle grins and bumps his shoulder against hers. My stomach twists into knots. Unable to stand it any longer, I spin around and smack right into Tyler.

"Whoa!"

I step away quickly, but out of the corner of my eye, I spy Kyle and Etta turning our way.

"Where are you going, Gigi? Did you forget something?" Tyler asks, not yet aware we have an audience.

"No, sorry, I . . . never mind."

With no choice but to head down the stairs, I descend with him close behind. Tyler finally spots the two of them.

"Oh . . . hi, Etta," he mumbles.

"Hi, Tyler," she answers. "Gigi."

"Hey."

Though she tries to hide it, I notice how Etta's face turns slightly pink when Tyler smiles at her. For a heartbeat, I think of telling him, but then there'd be two broken hearts sitting at our lunch table.

"Nice to meet you," he says to Kyle, extending a hand. "I'm Tyler."

"Kyle," he answers, giving it a shake.

We haven't spoken since the day he called me out. It's the longest we've ever gone without talking, and I didn't expect it to hurt this much. I never paid attention to how much I looked forward to our afternoon walks, or how he randomly showed up whenever he knew I was home alone and needed some company.

The five-minute warning bell goes off then, effectively ending any chance at further conversation.

"I have to go," I tell Tyler. "I'll see you tomorrow."

"Yeah, sounds good," he answers, though he continues to stare at Etta.

I can't bring myself to look at Kyle, not prepared for what I might find in his eyes. Instead, I turn to Etta.

"Bye, Etta."

Not waiting for a reply, I escape down the hall to my next class.

Chapter 25

On Saturday, I'm sitting in the back room at Rose and Jade, keeping an eye on Auntie Rose during her first official day back on the job. Despite promising to take it easy, she's on her third client of the day, and we haven't stopped for lunch yet.

After I admitted I wasn't sure about matchmaking, we talked a lot about what I do love—programming. While I've shelved Quizlr because of the bad memories, I've continued tinkering with Matchmaker 3000. At some point, Great-Aunt Rose became curious enough she gave me a chance to show her what it can do.

"That doesn't mean I'll use it down the line, xiǎojī," she was quick to remind me. "One successful match does not perfection make. You have to prove it's worth the risk."

To do that, I needed to continue observing her matchmaking sessions, but that hasn't been easy today. Since Auntie Rose decided to open the shop last minute, Amy wasn't available to work, so I've had to man the front for most of the morning. To be honest, I wasn't in the mood to take notes anyway. When her first client arrived before we opened the shop, I perched myself on my usual chair behind the screen, but found myself only half listening to the conversation and scribbling only the criteria I'd need to input into Matchmaker later.

The sound of the front door chime startles me out of my thoughts. I put down the stack of paper fan kits I was counting and check the aisles for the customer who walked in. I spot a girl standing by the small Korean skin-care kiosk Auntie Rose installed a few weeks back and greet her with a practiced smile.

"Welcome to Rose and Jade. How may I—"

"Hi, Gigi."

For a moment, I forget how to talk. Etta is standing in front of me with a grin I haven't seen in weeks—even if it's a little wobbly. I would have recognized her sooner, but her trademark jacket was hidden behind the kiosk. Without thinking, I scan the rest of the store, searching for someone whose head I could easily spot over the aisles, but we are alone. Not sure what to make of her visit, I repeat the only thing that comes to mind.

"Hi, Etta. Welcome to Rose and Jade. How may I help you?"

She freezes, not expecting to be spoken to so formally.

"Uh, I'm . . . looking for . . . a gift."

"A gift."

"Yes, a gift," she repeats. "For a friend."

Kyle's face pops into my mind unbidden. I force a smile. "Okay. What kind of gift are you looking for?"

"A figurine," Etta answers. "Wait, no, a scarf. Maybe both?"

"So . . . a figurine and a scarf," I repeat, pointing at the two sections sitting on opposite walls of the shop as if blood isn't rushing in my ears. "We have lots of different figurines on those shelves, and the scarves are hanging on racks against the window here."

"Oh, okay. Thanks."

We stare at each other for a long second before I clear my throat.

"Well, if you need anything else, let me know. I'll be by the register."

I wait for another moment, but Etta is uncharacteristically silent.

Not knowing what else to say, I turn to leave, but then she reaches out and grabs me lightly by the elbow.

"Wait!" She lets out a sigh. "Okay . . . the truth is, I'm not here to get a gift for a friend."

"I kind of suspected that," I say, doing my best not to smile.

"Gigi—"

She's interrupted by the chime of the doorbell. For the second time today, someone familiar walks through the door.

"Are you almost done, Etta? I'm starv . . ." Anna's eyes widen when she sees me. "Oh . . . Gigi. Hi."

"What are you doing here?"

In hindsight, that wasn't the nicest way to greet her, but she's the last person I would've predicted would walk through that door. We haven't spoken since she told me her story in the *Worldly* office, and after what happened with Etta, I assumed we wouldn't be talking anytime soon. I take a deep breath and force myself to relax.

"I'm sorry. I didn't mean for it to come out like that." I glance at Etta. "It's been happening a lot to me lately."

"It's okay. I'm sure you weren't expecting to see me."

"I . . . wasn't expecting to see either of you. Not that it's a bad thing. I'm glad you're here," I answer truthfully. "But why *are* you here?"

Anna and Etta glance at each other. Judging by their dancing eyebrows and tipping chins, they're trying to decide which one of them will answer. Etta ultimately loses. She turns back to me with a small smile.

"Do you think you could take a break and come have a sponge cake with us?"

"I don't—"

"Yes, she can," Auntie Rose says loudly from behind.

I turn to see her walking her latest client to the front of the shop. After confirming the man's next appointment, she sends him out and glances at the three of us.

"You must be Gigi's friends."

"Yes," Etta answers with a firmness I don't expect. "I'm Etta, and this is Anna."

"I've heard so much about both of you," Auntie Rose replies with a smile. "All good things, of course."

She ignores the look I shoot her. As of a second ago, their names were the only things she knew about either of them.

"Gigi, go. It's not like we're busy right now." She walks over to the cash register and pulls out a twenty-dollar bill. "Here. Have a round of sponge cakes on me. Just make sure you bring me—"

"A coconut one. Of course, Auntie," I tell her as she presses the money into my hand. "I'll be right back."

"Take your time," she says, emphasizing each word. "I'm not going anywhere."

Auntie Rose practically shoves me toward the door, but I remind her it's cold and I need to grab my jacket. I hurry to the back room and grab it off the rack, shoving my arms through the sleeves before returning. Etta and Anna murmur their goodbyes, and the three of us walk out the door.

Our stroll to Kam Hing is painfully quiet. I spy Anna jabbing Etta in the ribs as we walk, pointing and tossing her head in my direction. In the end, I'm the one who breaks the ice as we're standing in line, inhaling the sweet aroma of the airy pastries.

"Congratulations on being chosen as a finalist, Anna."

"Thank you," she answers with a faint smile. "I'm honestly still in shock."

"You shouldn't be. I meant what I said before . . . your app is amazing. The way Timely combines all the things we want in a clock app and puts it into a super-cute widget? I had a lot of fun customizing mine."

Her eyes widen. "You were one of the testers?"

"Yours was the only one of the three I was assigned that worked," I tell her. "I hope you win."

"That's awfully nice of you to say."

"It's the truth."

We lapse into silence again, moving two spots before Anna pipes up.

"I'm sorry about what happened with Quizlr. It was an amazing idea."

"It's okay. To be honest, it's for the best." I look over at Etta. "I got so carried away with all the attention it was getting that I forgot what was actually important to me."

For a moment, it looks like Etta might burst into tears. Then a sunny smile erupts onto her face. She throws her arms around me.

"You're important to me too."

Etta's arms dig into my back as she hugs me with surprising strength, and it's a struggle to catch my breath.

"Thank you, Etta, but please let go," I gasp. "I'm not an orange. I don't want to be freshly squeezed."

She loosens her grip. I smile down at her.

"Does this mean I'm forgiven?"

Etta rolls her eyes. "You think I would be here if you weren't?"

"Touché."

We move up again in line, and I decide to address the elephant in the room.

"Would one of you please tell me why you're here? I know the sponge cake alone is worth the trek, but you don't need me to enjoy it."

"It's . . . it's Kyle. Etta has something to tell you about him," Anna blurts out.

My mind flashes back to earlier this week, when I saw him holding Etta's bag at school. Of course she wouldn't let me find out that they've started dating from someone else. Unlike me, she would never hurt a friend. As for why we're here at Kam Hing . . . well, she's probably hoping the sponge cake will soften the blow.

"Go on, Etta," Anna prompts. "Don't be shy."

Normally, I would be tickled by the irony of that statement, but today I'm too busy trying to keep the smile plastered on my face. Despite Anna's encouragement, though, Etta never quite gets any sound to come out of her lips.

"You don't have to tell me," I force out. "I know."

Etta's jaw hits the floor. "You . . . you do?"

"Yes, and as long as you're both happy, then I'm happy for you," I grind out, every syllable cutting me like a piece of broken glass.

"Wait . . ." Etta frowns. "What are you talking about?"

"You and Kyle," I say, convinced the whole bakery can hear the churning of my stomach. "Together. Dating."

She and Anna look at each other, then burst out laughing.

"No! That's not it at all!" Etta chokes out between giggles. "We're not dating!"

The tension that had taken hold of my chest snaps, and I can breathe again. Seconds later, though, I deflate.

"Then what do you want to tell me about Kyle?"

"We need you to talk to him. Please. We can't take it anymore," Etta tells me.

"Huh?" I scrunch my nose. "I don't understand. What's going on?"

"Kyle won't leave us alone. Well, technically, he won't leave Etta alone, but the two of us have been hanging out a lot, and he keeps inviting himself along," Anna adds.

"At first I thought it was because he felt bad for me and was being nice. But then he kept asking to hang out," Etta says to me. "And I know you're dating Tyler . . . but Kyle really likes you. In fact, I think it's more than that. Give him a chance."

When she mentions Tyler's name, her voice hitches. I throw my hands up in front of me.

"Okay, full stop. I'm not dating Tyler. We're friends. We started hanging out after everything happened with Quizlr." I meet Etta's eye. "And you were right. He's a super-sweet guy. I was wrong about him."

"Really?" she whispers.

"Yes, and although I'm done telling you what to do, if you decide to give him another chance, I have it on good authority that he likes you back."

Etta's cheeks tinge pink. "That goes for you too, you know. I told you that you and Kyle would make a cute couple."

"And *I* told *you* it's not like that between us. We're friends," I repeat, the words sounding hollow.

"Right . . . because my guy friend carries my bag and walks me home from school every day, shows up to my house with food, hangs out with my friends, and talks about me all the time," she points out.

"If a guy did that for me, I'd probably tattoo his name on my forehead," Anna jokes. "In invisible ink, of course. I can't have people thinking I'm not . . ."

"Perfect?"

I say it without thinking, but she nods. I'm reminded again

we're more alike than I originally thought. Our conversation is put on hold while we order the sponge cakes, but a tiny bud of hope blossoms in my heart. Nonetheless, I'm reluctant to give it space.

Once we pay for the pastries and find a corner of the shop to stand and eat them, Etta continues.

"Seriously, though, admit it. You like Kyle. You should have seen your face when you thought I was going to tell you I was dating him."

"You looked like she had told you Quizlr sucked," Anna agrees. "Or that it had crashed again."

"And Kyle looked like someone crashed into *him* when we ran into you and Tyler this week," Etta informs me. "He didn't say it, but it was obvious he was upset."

Anna nods. "He sulked the whole rest of the week."

"Our point is you like him, and he likes you. And you're already best friends." Etta asks, "So what are you waiting for?"

She makes the situation sound far easier than it actually is, but I can't help the smile that attaches itself to my lips.

"Does that mean you'll talk to him?" Anna asks.

"Maybe."

"Gigi!" Etta pokes me in the side.

"Ow, okay! I'll talk to him," I say, dodging her second attempt.

"Thank heavens!" Anna exclaims. "Now, can we get out of here? I saw something in your great-aunt's shop I am dying to buy!"

Chapter 26

He's on his way.

"Wait, what?"

I read Etta's message again.

After we left Kam Hing earlier, we came back to Rose and Jade so Anna could buy the silk scarf she spotted on the rack. It was black with pink cherry blossoms on it, and she said it reminded her of Japan. While Etta was browsing in a different part of the store, Anna pulled me aside.

"Could I ask you something, Gigi?"

I nodded. "Of course."

"Did you . . ." She checked to make sure we were completely alone. "Did you talk to Joey?"

"He came to my house last weekend to apologize for getting me into trouble," I replied carefully. "Why?"

"He's been blowing up my phone all week. He even sent me this super-long text message."

"What did he say?"

"That he wanted to say sorry for treating me so badly before, and that he wouldn't blame me if I never spoke to him again."

"Deserved," I commented.

Anna hesitated. "I didn't tell you before . . . but we were . . . more than friends."

I widened my eyes, acting as though it was the first time I had heard this. "I had no idea."

"Yeah . . . I guess when you spend so much time with someone, things happen." She smiled faintly. "Anyway, he also said his biggest mistake was breaking up with me. That he knows he doesn't deserve another chance, but he hopes I'll consider forgiving him."

"What are you going to do?" I asked after a beat.

She shrugged, and before she could say anything else, Etta came back.

After Anna paid for her scarf, we all said goodbye, and the two of them left to meet Kyle at Kinokuniya for their weekly anime-reading session. Etta promised she would figure out how to get him to come by my house, since I told her my parents were out for the night.

Now, within seconds of reading her text, I hear the doorbell ring, followed by someone's frantic pounding on the door.

"Gigi? Gigi, it's Kyle! Open up!"

I clench and unclench my fists, though it does little to calm my shaking hands. I take a deep breath and count to ten before finally opening the door. Though Etta's message warned me he was coming, my heart leaps into my throat at the sight of him.

"Kyle? What are you doing here?"

He strides into the house without asking to come in. Using his foot to shut the door behind him, his eyes run down my form, examining me from head to toe.

"Etta said you were sick, so I came right over."

My eyebrows shoot up. "She did?"

"Yeah. She said you told her you passed out earlier."

"She did," I repeat. "I mean, I did. In the . . . kitchen."

I grab the back of my head for effect, and he pulls me closer to inspect it. I hold as still as possible while he runs the pads of his fingers over my scalp, feeling for any bumps or bruises.

"I don't feel anything," he murmurs.

I, on the other hand, am feeling too many things. Between the way my heart is racing from his breath tickling my forehead to the tingles he leaves everywhere his hand wanders, it's taking everything I have to stay upright.

"Uh . . . actually, now that I think about it, I didn't really pass out on the floor," I fudge. "I . . . hit my head. Because I tripped . . . on the area rug. The one by the kitchen. Not the one upstairs."

Thankfully, he assumes my rambling is related to my imaginary head injury and doesn't question me about it. I resist the urge to lean into him, instead pressing my suddenly sweaty hands against my thighs. All my efforts to stay calm nearly evaporate when he cups my cheeks and tilts my face.

"Does your head hurt now? Are you having any dizziness? Blurriness? Do you feel weak?"

"Um . . . maybe a little weak?" I answer.

It's not exactly a lie. My knees are on the verge of buckling.

"You should sit down, then! No, wait, you should lie down," he states, putting one arm around my waist and leading me toward the elevator. "Let's go up to your bedroom."

He calls the car, holding me against him as we wait for it to arrive. We step in and he closes the door and presses the button for the fourth floor. The idea of talking to him in my room makes my heart pound twice as hard, and I push the button for the third as well.

"Why did you do that?" Kyle asks. "You should be in bed."

"I—I think I left my phone in the living room. I need to get it," I stammer.

He shakes his head. "I'll grab it for you after we get you into bed."

"Please stop saying that."

"Saying what?"

I cringe. I didn't mean to say that out loud.

"Uh . . . I . . . I don't want you to keep telling me what to do, Kyle. I can take care of myself," I tell him, faking a scowl.

"Okay . . ."

I risk a glance at him. "Just help me to the couch, okay? Please."

He nods. The seconds it takes for us to reach the third floor feel more like an eternity. When the car pulls to a stop and he opens the door, I have to keep myself from tumbling out ahead of him. He walks me to the couch as promised, and I sink onto it, putting my legs up while he piles cushions behind my back.

"Where do you think you put your phone?" he asks once I'm settled.

Considering it's currently wedged in my back pocket, I scramble to come up with a distraction. As luck would have it, I'm struck with a coughing spell. He moves toward the minibar tucked into the far corner of the room.

"Does that faucet work?" he asks, pointing at the sink tucked into it.

"I think so? I've never used it."

"I'll go check."

I wait until his back is to me before reaching into my pocket and pulling out my phone. Thankfully, he's so focused on filling a glass with water he doesn't see me tucking the phone under a couple of magazines. When he returns, I point at the coffee table.

"I think I left it somewhere over there."

He finds it almost immediately and holds it out to me. I ignore the heat that shoots up my arm when our hands touch. As I take the phone from him, a notification pops up. It's a text from Etta, asking me if Kyle has shown up. I unlock it and quickly send off a reply, then set it next to me on the couch. Kyle perches himself on the edge of the couch, staring at me with a strange expression.

"What?"

He shakes his head. "I'm sorry. I shouldn't have barged in like that, especially since . . ."

"Since what?"

"Well, you know."

I frown. "No . . . I don't."

"Especially since . . ." He straightens his shoulders. "Since you're with Tyler now. That's who you texted a second ago, right?"

"I—"

Before I can get any more out, Kyle pushes onto his feet. I watch him rub the back of his neck as he circles the room, murmuring to himself. Eventually, he nods and turns to face me.

"I should leave. In fact, I'll leave right now, before he gets here. I don't want him to get the wrong idea."

He starts toward the staircase. I push off the couch and grab him by the hand.

"Wait! Don't go."

Kyle stares down at my fingers wrapped around his. I pull away but glance up at him.

"Please stay."

"But I don't want Tyler—"

"He's not coming. He has no reason to," I explain. "Plus, I didn't text him."

"Don't you think you should? I mean he is your . . ."

Kyle blinks several times, his face scrunched as if he's tasted something bitter.

"He's not my boyfriend," I say despite the flush in my cheeks. "That's . . . what you were going to say, right?"

He clears his throat. "Uh, yeah."

We stand opposite each other, separated by only a few physical inches, but far more in thought.

"So he's . . . not . . . your boyfriend," Kyle repeats.

"No, he's not," I confirm.

"Oh."

I gesture at the armchair next to him, and he sinks onto it. I return to the couch and perch myself on the end closest to him. Unable to tolerate the unending silence, I plunge forward.

"Etta came by Rose and Jade today."

He meets my eye with more than a little relief. "She did?"

"Yeah. We talked things out, and I apologized, so we're friends again."

The moment the words leave my lips, I want to smack myself on the head. Of course he'd know we made up. She texted him to say I wasn't feeling well.

"That's really good to hear."

Ugh. This is not going at all how I wanted it to. Then again, I don't have the slightest idea what I expected to happen. I promised Etta and Anna I would admit how I felt, but thinking about it makes me so nervous I want to run away. What if they're wrong about him? I can't risk our friendship like that. In the end, I settle for clearing the air.

"I'm sorry, Kyle. You were right about me." I stare down at my hands. "I was judging Etta as much as everyone else, even if I wasn't willing to admit it."

He comes over to sit beside me.

"I'm sorry too. I shouldn't have yelled at you. Even if you were judging Etta, that wasn't the way to help you understand that." He turns to look me in the eye. "Forgive me?"

I smile. "You're my best friend, Kyle. I could never stay mad at you. Will you forgive me?"

Something flashes across his face, though I'm not entirely sure what it is.

"Always."

The conversation lapses again. My phone goes off, and Kyle starts beside me. He shifts and pulls it out from under him. As I go to grab it, he glances at the text Etta just sent me.

Have you told him yet?

He cocks an eyebrow. "Told me what?"

Tell him you like him, an annoying little voice inside my head demands. *That you think you might even love him.*

"Oh, um . . . funny story. When Etta came by to talk to me, I—" I swallow hard. "I thought she was going to tell me that you guys were dating."

Kyle's mouth falls open. "What?"

"Well, I saw you with her the other day at school. You were holding her bag, and she was standing really close to you. Plus, you guys have been talking a lot and spending time together. I figured that you liked her."

"Yeah, as a friend," he stresses. "Not as a potential girlfriend. I can't believe you would think that."

"Why wouldn't I? You said so yourself. You two have a lot in common, and she's really nice."

"Gigi . . ." He groans. "That doesn't mean I want to date her."

"It was a fair assumption," I point out. "Look at all the girls you've dated. None of them have anything in common except for the fact that you always break up with them before it gets serious. Like, what is so bad about not wanting to eat salad with dressing? Or wearing shoes that are too small for you?"

My next words slip out automatically. "If you're going to be that picky, I might as well use your Quizlr data and—"

"I don't want you to set me up, Gigi!"

I fall silent. Why did I even bring it up? I don't want that either. Kyle stands and runs a hand through his hair. I rise as well, refusing to let him tower over me.

Don't ask, Gigi. Don't ask a question unless you really want to know the answer.

"Why not?"

For a second, it looks like he's going to explode, his eyes flashing and his face red. Then, abruptly, his shoulders droop, and he lowers his eyes to the ground.

"Because you're the only one I ever wanted."

Kyle says it so softly it takes me a moment to register his words. When they sink in, the warmth I had kept bound in my heart breaks free. Unfortunately, Kyle seems to mistake my silence for rejection, because he spins on his heel to leave. I cross the room and grab his hand once more, this time holding on tight.

"Kyle, look at me."

He stands resolutely, giving me his back. I move to stand in front of him, stepping as close as I possibly dare to keep him from leaving. I tip my head back and look into his face.

"Ask me."

Kyle frowns, his eyes searching for clues as to what to say. I hold my breath, hoping our connection is as strong as I think it is.

"Ask me," I repeat.

I recognize the moment it dawns on him what he should do. The lines on his face soften, and the corner of his mouth twitches, hinting at the smile to come.

"Gigi Wong . . . will you be mine?"

Not trusting my voice, I nod my reply. Kyle breaks into a giant grin before his gaze drops to my mouth. As he leans down toward me, I rise up on my toes to meet him halfway. My eyes flutter closed as our lips touch. At first, the pressure is so light it almost feels like I imagined it, but then his arms come around me. As he tugs me against him, my hands snake up to cup the back of his neck. He tilts his head to deepen the kiss, and I'm soon lost in a flood of sensations.

When we pull apart, I slide a hand over his heart. The pounding I feel beneath my fingertips matches that of my own.

"Did that really happen?" he asks, pressing his forehead against mine. "Because I'm worried I'll wake up and find out it was all a dream."

"Then you better come back and ask me again."

He smirks. "Are you telling me what to do?"

"Yes, and you'd better listen this time, Kyle Miller, or else I'll never forgive you."

"In that case . . ."

He closes the distance between us, sealing his promise with a kiss I won't soon forget.

Chapter 27

"I'm sorry I wasn't there when you needed me."

James sighs, dragging a hand through his hair. Although his original plan was to come home for spring break, his professors hit him with an intense midterm schedule. As a result, not only did he not make it back, he spent the entire week in the library. It's why he surprised me with a video chat today.

"What are you apologizing for? You were super busy with school." I take a bite of my seafood pasta. "Besides, I've moved on to bigger and better things."

"I heard," he replies, grinning. "I was wondering how long it was going to take Kyle to admit how he feels."

I don't have to touch my cheeks to know they're burning. James and I have always talked about everything, but dating? It's all new territory.

"So you knew this whole time?"

"It might come as a shock to you, dear sister, but I do know a thing or two about love."

"Says the guy whose idea of flirting was to insult me," Liza interrupts, plopping down on the couch beside him and handing him a char siu bun. "Hey, Gigi."

I wave. "Hi, Liza. Thanks for taking care of my brother."

"Don't mention it. He's easy to please. As long as I keep feeding him, he's a happy boy," she says, ruffling his hair.

"Hey!" James protests, though it's quickly muffled by the giant bite he takes.

Liza's expression softens. "But seriously, Gigi, how are you doing? James told me what happened. That had to be so stressful."

"I'm fine. Really." I tug at my ear. "I won't lie . . . it was really rough there for a while, but I'm over it now."

It's the truth. Once everyone came back from spring break, they were too busy sharing vacation pics and cramming for exams to gossip about me. Now that I'm no longer under everyone's scrutiny—or grounded, thank heavens—my life has gotten back to normal.

The only thing that worries me is Ms. Harris's school board meeting. It's happening tonight, and try as I might, they wouldn't allow me to speak on her behalf. At least Principal Gee agreed to read the letter I wrote for the meeting before the board makes a final decision. As usual, James homes right in on my thoughts.

"You did everything you could, Gigi. It's up to the board now."

I pout. "I know, but if it wasn't for me, Ms. Harris wouldn't be in this situation. I feel terrible."

"It'll be fine," Liza tells me. "You've said how great of a teacher she is. I'm sure they'll see that too."

The two of them spend the rest of our video chat distracting me with stories from the baking contest where they met last summer. Since I was studying abroad for two weeks, I never got a chance to hear how everything went down. All I knew was that it was a junior baking contest Liza's mom hosts every year. From the contestant who threw a tantrum—and his cake—to the one who made a cookie portrait of Liza while trying to impress her, each story gets funnier than the last. By the time they're done, I'm laughing so hard I'm wiping tears from my eyes.

No sooner have I said goodbye and hung up than there is a knock at my bedroom door. Mom pokes her head in a second later.

"Are you still talking to James?"

I shake my head. "Nope. We're done."

"In that case, bǎobǎo, how would you like to come down and help me whip up some goodies for the bake sale?"

One of the unintended, but pleasant, consequences of Quizlr-gate is that Mom's stepped down from a couple of the boards she's on to spend more time at home. Though it started as a way to keep an eye on me and Auntie Rose during her stay, it's kept Mom healthier as well. She hasn't had a single fainting episode in nearly a month, and her energy is so high she's started baking again.

"Yeah, I'll be down in a minute."

I shut down my laptop and put it back on my desk before meeting Mom in the kitchen. She already has the ingredients set out for the recipes we're making tonight—matcha cookies, pandan muffins, and mango milk custard buns. They're all recipes she borrowed from Liza's baking book. Apparently, Mom's idea of deciding whether James was dating the right girl involved testing the quality of her pastries. Liza must have passed with flying colors, because Mom would never put her baking reputation on the line for anything less than perfection.

Since Dad's finishing up his last meeting and should be home soon, we split up the work. I start on the cookies, while Mom prepares the dough for the custard buns. She pauses periodically to check my work, making sure I mix the ingredients properly and that I'm rolling my dough to the right thickness before cutting. While I get the cookies into the oven, she sets her dough aside to proof and turns to her filling. Soon the aromas of matcha and mangoes perfume the air, a reminder of days past when we used to bake as a family.

I've pulled the cookies out of the oven and am transferring them onto a cooling rack when my phone pings on the counter. I finish what I'm doing before checking to see what I missed. I nearly drop my phone when I see it's an email from Ms. Harris.

"Is something wrong?" Mom asks, walking over to me.

I show her the notification with shaking hands. She takes the phone from me. "How about I read it?"

I hold my breath as she opens the email. My heart slams against my rib cage as her eyes scan the screen.

"What does it say?" I whisper.

"The board voted in her favor," Mom tells me with a brilliant smile. "She'll be reinstated immediately."

I sink into the nearest chair. She hands my phone back to me, and I read over the email myself, needing to see that it's real. Mom puts her arms around me and tucks me against her side.

"I told you the letter would help, bǎobǎo."

I lean my cheek against her stomach. "Thanks, Mom."

After sending Ms. Harris a quick reply to thank her for letting me know, I stay in Mom's embrace for a little while longer. I only raise my head when I feel a tap on my shoulder. Mom smiles down at me.

"Now that we've gotten the good news, how about we get back to baking?"

I grin and pop out of my chair.

"Ready when you are!"

♥

"When are they gonna get to the good stuff?" Tyler groans. "There've been three speakers, and all we've had are appetizers and salad."

Ms. Harris tsks. "Patience is a virtue, Tyler. Besides, there's only one more to go, according to the program, and then we'll find out who won."

Tonight is the big dinner SJW Tech is hosting to announce the winning app for their inaugural junior programming contest. As one of the three semifinalists, Anna was given the opportunity to invite guests to attend the event with her, along with Ms. Harris as her faculty advisor.

Sitting on either side of her are her parents, Mr. and Mrs. Tam, and it's clear which parent she took after. While Mr. Tam is dressed in a white shirt, a black tie with a silver diamond pattern, and a charcoal-gray suit, Mrs. Tam is wearing a burgundy sheath dress with a matching Chanel brooch. Anna is wearing a simple black pantsuit with floral embroidery.

Etta and Tyler and Kyle and I round out the rest of the table. Though we've been hanging out more, I wasn't expecting Anna to include me.

"If it weren't for what happened and you having to withdraw, Quizlr could have easily been a finalist tonight," she insisted when she invited me.

"She's right," Ms. Harris added. "Like I said before, both of your apps had an excellent chance of winning. The lead judge was quite surprised when I withdrew your entry. I suspect you were one of their top choices."

So here we are, sitting in a modern banquet hall downtown

with stone walls and exposed steel piping. Fifteen circular tables are spread around the room, each covered with a black tablecloth and a vase of brightly colored flowers. At the front, there's an elevated main stage, and a podium sits atop one end of it. The SJW Tech logo spins slowly on the wall behind it via a projector.

Etta is wearing the forest-green cocktail dress we snagged at one of the thrift stores last weekend. It was a little too long for her initially, but I had it tailored for her as a surprise. It's clearly a hit, because Tyler hasn't been able to take his eyes off her all night. He's also looking stylish in a white button-down shirt, black-and-white-striped tie, and black slacks, opting to pair them with a black leather jacket rather than something more formal.

Etta looks over at Anna. "Are you nervous? My heart is pounding, and I'm not even the one nominated."

"I am a little nervous," Anna admits. "But I'm grateful I got this far, so whatever happens, I'll be happy."

"I'd wanna win. What's the point of entering a contest if you don't?" Tyler comments.

Etta pokes him in the arm. "Babe!"

"What? It's true." He pouts at her scowl, but turns back to Anna. "I'm sure you'll win."

"Thanks," she answers.

Tyler's eyes meet mine, and then I exchange looks with Etta and Kyle. Though I learned my lesson with Quizlr, I couldn't resist getting involved in a little voting stacking. Technically, what we did wasn't against the rules. It said one vote per email or social media account, but they didn't specify they couldn't all belong to the same person. Besides, Etta found out one of the other finalists asked her followers to do the same thing on her Instagram story. So really, we're evening the playing field.

Among the four of us, we banked close to eighty points, but we also made sure to recruit everyone we knew to help, from parents to friends and teachers at Superbia. Auntie Rose even used the Instagram and Twitter accounts I created for her matchmaking business to vote—though I did have to pretty much do it for her. I have no idea if it's enough, but at least we gave Anna's app our best shot.

Kyle nudges me with his shoulder. "Have I mentioned you look beautiful tonight?"

We've been on a date every day since we became official, but tonight is the fanciest event we've attended together as a couple. That's why the blush-pink Valentino dress I paired with strappy red heels was the tenth one I tried on. I only settled on it minutes before Kyle arrived. He picked me up dressed in a perfectly tailored Tom Ford black silk suit. He opted to go without a tie, and the white button down shirt he has on underneath is unbuttoned at the neck. The Cartier cufflinks he's wearing were lent to him by his dad, and are designed to look like the wings of a plane when clipped on.

"You don't look so bad yourself," I reply.

He leans over to place a gentle kiss on my lips. I spy Etta and Tyler grinning in our direction and blush, pressing my face into Kyle's neck. His cologne is light but distinct, reminding me of fresh laundry. I inhale deeply before pulling back to look into his eyes.

"What?" he asks. "What did I do?"

I smile shyly. "Nothing. It's just this . . . us . . . I'm still getting used to everything."

"Do you want me to stop?"

Even if he wasn't giving me full puppy eyes, I wouldn't have the power to deny him.

"No." I lean over and kiss him on the cheek before making sure none of my lipstick transferred onto him. "Never."

The waiter interrupts our little moment, placing down our plates of roast beef, whole spring potatoes, and grilled asparagus. He also brings over a couple of gravy boats, and comes around with a breadbasket. With my stomach growling, I hear little of what the next speaker says as I take bites of the entree. While it's not the best thing I've ever eaten, like Tyler, I'm happy to be fed.

"It's happening, it's happening!" Etta suddenly squeals, barely managing to keep her voice to the table.

She's right. The three partners of SJW Tech are climbing onto the stage, and they quickly surround the podium. The blond man in the middle, dressed in a navy pinstripe suit, steps up first.

"Good evening, everyone. My name is Thomas Snyder, and these are my partners, Samuel Jing and Morgan Watson. We are very excited to welcome you to the first SJW Tech Junior Coding Contest dinner."

He steps aside so that Mr. Jing can come to the podium next.

"Tonight, we will be announcing the winning app for this year, but first I'd like to ask all three of our finalists to come to the stage."

"That's you," Ms. Harris says to Anna with a proud smile. "Go get 'em."

Anna stands, straightening her pantsuit before making her way to join the other two contestants. Mr. Jing clicks a remote for the projector, and brief descriptions of every app are shown on the wall. He reads off each one before changing the slide and turning things over to Mr. Watson.

"All right, everyone, it's the moment we've all been waiting for. The winner of the First Annual SJW Tech Junior Coding Contest is . . ."

He clicks the remote, and a bar graph appears. I hold my breath as bars appear over each name, rising to match the percentage of public votes tallied before the dinner.

Please be enough. Please be enough.

When the two bars not belonging to Anna stop and hers keeps rising, our table erupts. Tyler picks up his napkin and waves it over his head. Kyle puts his fingers between his lips and whistles. Etta and I clap and call out Anna's name, and her parents applaud enthusiastically.

"Congratulations to the winner of the first annual SJW Tech Junior Coding Contest, Anna Tam!" Mr. Watson announces. "Your app, Timely, received the most votes from the general public. Our panel of judges were also very impressed with the detail you put into it. We'll be looking forward to seeing you this summer."

He grabs the glass trophy etched with her name and walks it over to her. Anna and he hold it together, posing for a series of photos. Then Mr. Watson turns to the audience with a broad smile.

"Let's give another round of applause to our winner!"

After the clapping dies down, Mr. and Mrs. Tam are called up to take pictures with Anna, after which Ms. Harris joins them. The four of them eventually make their way back to the table. I'm surprised to see Mr. Snyder walk up behind them.

"Ms. Harris, it's lovely to meet you in person," he says as he offers his hand.

"And the same to you, Mr. Snyder," she replies, shaking it.

He turns to Etta and me. "Now, which one of you is Gigi Wong?"

"Oh, that's me."

I manage to hide my surprise as I stand and shake his hand as well. He smiles.

"The judges were quite intrigued with your use of a compatibility algorithm to sort users into private chat rooms," Mr. Snyder tells me. "In fact, one judge in particular was so impressed he wanted to meet you."

Mr. Snyder moves to one side. A tall, thin man who looks to be in his twenties with black hair and brown eyes partially hidden behind a pair of browline glasses steps forward. I immediately recognize him from his Apple Design Awards profile.

"You're . . . you're Austin Jang," I breathe as he stretches his hand out.

He smiles as I shake it. "I see my reputation precedes me. It's lovely to meet the mind behind one of our most creative entries."

"Oh, wow." My cheeks flush at the compliment. "Thank you so much."

"I know you didn't get a chance to reach the popular vote round because your entry was withdrawn. However, I suspect it would have been quite popular with our audience," Austin states. "Because of that, I'd like to offer you an internship position with me this summer. What do you say?"

It's a moment before I'm able to get any words out.

"See you in June?"

"Excellent. Looking forward to working with you both."

None of us react until both men are out of earshot. Then everyone at our table starts talking at once.

Tyler jumps up and down. "Yes! Yes, yes, yes!"

"Oh my god! Gigi!" Etta exclaims. "Congratulations!"

"I'm so happy for you," Anna says with a warm smile.

"Mr. Snyder actually called me a couple days ago to tell me the news," Ms. Harris admits. "That's part of the reason why I wanted to make sure you came tonight."

I go over to her and give her a big hug. "Thank you. For everything."

"You're welcome."

After thanking Mr. and Mrs. Tam for their congratulations, I hug each of my friends in succession, starting with Etta, then Tyler, and finally Anna. When I turn to face Kyle, he wraps his arms around my waist and leans down to press a kiss on my lips.

"I knew they'd love you. I already do."

I thread my arms up around his neck, tugging him down to answer his kiss with one of my own. This time, when we pull apart, the flush on his cheeks matches mine.

"I love you too," I whisper.

Kyle clears his throat. "So what next?"

I take a deep breath, considering his question. When the answer finally comes, I look up and smile.

"I'm not sure. Whatever it is, though, it's going to be perfect."

Acknowledgments

Guess what?

We've made it.

These past two years challenged us in ways no one ever expected. Yes, we faced down a global pandemic that threatened our health, but it was much more than that. This was the first time we ever had to spend most of our days . . . alone. Alone with our thoughts. Alone with all the nagging voices we usually push aside by staying busy. We were thrown into the storms of our minds without a life preserver, and it was either sink or swim.

But look. We're still here, fighting the good fight, waking up every morning and hoping for the best. Some days, we're disappointed. Maybe more than we'd like to admit. However, there have been good moments, and we hang on to those so we don't fall into the abyss.

As for me? I'll admit it. *Love, Decoded* was a fight from beginning to end. Every word, every scene—the pages did not come easily. Trying to write a lighthearted romance while struggling through anxiety and isolation took every ounce of determination I had. There were many long days and sleepless nights . . . and moments when I wasn't even sure I could finish the story.

Ultimately, though, writing this book taught me a valuable lesson. When you feel like quitting is the only option, take one more step before giving up. It doesn't matter how big the step is, or how long you wait to move. What's important is that by doing so, you get a little farther away from the negativity that's been holding you back.

Even so, I am blessed to be surrounded by amazing sources of support. Shetal and Joyce, thank you for the dinners to recharge, and the tough-love conversations when I got too deep into my insecurity. Pri and Eunice—despite the distance between us, your unwavering faith and encouragement helped push me through those writer's blocks. There are also my new friends—Mau, Alina, Em G., Christine, Mallory, and Kendra. Our late-night chats mean more to me than you'll ever know. The laughter and fun you've gifted me kept the tears at bay.

I am eternally grateful to my agent, cheerleader, and constant advocate—Jessica Watterson. You lent me your strength even when you had little to spare, and I am so fortunate to have you by my side. I couldn't imagine traveling this path with anyone else.

To the wonderful Annette Pollert, who stepped in as editor during a period of transition with such care and consideration. Thank you for your passion and enthusiasm in helping me mold *Love, Decoded* into the story it is today.

I also had an incredibly dedicated team working on this book. My sincerest gratitude goes to Simone Roberts-Payne, Marinda Valenti, Michelle Millet, Sola Akinlana, Madeleine Vasaly, Vanessa DeJesus, and Casey McIntyre for your valiant efforts during such a challenging time.

Last, but most definitely not least, I want to thank everyone who picked up *A Taste for Love* and gave it a chance. So much of what I was looking forward to in my debut year ended up not happening. Thankfully, every tweet, Instagram post, and video filled a little part of the hole that it left behind. I will always have a special place for your words, and for the love you've shared with me. I hope *A Taste for Love* brought you moments of laughter and comfort, and that *Love, Decoded* will do the same.

It's been quite a journey to get to this point. Not all of it has been smooth, but we've weathered it together. I don't know what the future will hold, but there is one thing I am sure of.

I will continue to step forward.

So, lovely readers . . . will you come with me?